T0107393

Angels' Keep

Angels' Keep

a novel by

MICHAEL HODJERA

ANGELS' KEEP

iUniverse books may be ordered through booksellers or by contacting:

iUniverse
1663 Liberty Drive
Bloomington, IN 47403
www.iuniverse.com
1-800-Authors (1-800-288-4677)

ISBN: 978-1-4917-8393-1 (sc)
ISBN: 978-1-4917-8394-8 (e)

Library of Congress Control Number: 2015919331

Print information available on the last page.

iUniverse rev. date: 12/03/2015

"The ocean is full of souls …" Gustav Gunnerson

"Everything dies, babe, and that's a fact,
But maybe everything that dies someday comes back …"
Bruce Springsteen

THE
OFF-SEASON

Chapter 1

It was one of those days when Angels' Keep was as close to heaven as you could get. The sky was a periwinkle blue after the spring rains. The ocean sparkled like zirconium crystals among the moored fishing boats and yachts in the harbor, while whales and dolphins frolicked on the vast Monterey Bay beyond.

But on this mild spring day, a Tuesday to be exact, there was someone who was ill-equipped to appreciate the dazzling seaside idyll.

Antiques dealer Willy "Wild Bill" Rasp lay bleeding in the vintage clothing section at the back of his store, Granny's Antiques, his chest stitched with bullet holes. It had never been clear who the "Granny" in the store's name referred to. There were skeptics in Angels' Keep who questioned whether there had ever been a granny of any stripe associated with the enterprise. But this didn't seem a sufficient explanation for Willy Rasp's current dire condition. Statistically speaking, false advertising claims rarely led to homicide.

Customers had been few and far between at Granny's of late. The town had ceased to be an antiques mecca long before Rasp had acquired the shop. It was common knowledge that most of the action in antiques had migrated south to Pacific Grove and Carmel-by-the-Sea by the late nineties. But that hadn't discouraged Willy Rasp from leasing the shop a few months before.

The shooting aside, it had been a particularly slow day at Granny's Antiques, so it came as somewhat of a surprise to the exsanguining proprietor when the bell at the front of the store tinkled amiably, signaling the arrival of a potential customer. It wasn't a customer, as it turned out. It was Doc, a German emigre who was Rasp's next door neighbor at the shop. Doc lived in a weatherbeaten tugboat that was dry-docked in the otherwise empty adjacent lot. The man's real name was Manfred St. Michel, and though he looked like a swarthy barroom brawler, he was in fact mild of manner and well respected in Angels' Keep as a blues guitar player and amplifier repairman. At 6 ft. 3 he had to duck to get in the front door to Granny's.

"Back here," Rasp rasped.

"Mein Gott! What has happened?" Doc ran over and kneeled at the man's side. He pulled a mostly clean rag out of his shirt pocket and dabbed the wounded man's forehead with it, all the while studying Rasp's injuries with dismay out of the corner of his eye. Even with an ER on the premises and a team of Swiss doctors prepped and standing by, it was unlikely Rasp could be saved, in Doc's opinion. There were too many holes, and there was too much blood spreading out across the yellowed linoleum at the back of the shop. It was a miracle the man was still breathing as it was.

"It's my own damn fault," declared Rasp. "They would have gotten me one way or the other."

"Who did this to you?"

"They was just doin' their job. I get that. But shit, I didn't think they'd go this far." He coughed into his palm and his hand came away with blood on it.

"I was pushing it, I'll be the first to admit," he went on. "But damn. This?" He nodded vaguely at his torso. "I don't know whether to be pissed or flattered." His convulsing laugh sent bloody spittle flying.

"It is best you save your breath, Willy," Doc said sternly, standing. "We must get you to a hospital immediately. Kindly bear with me for a moment." He pulled a cell phone out of jeans grown a tad too tight in the preceding year and punched in 911.

Willard Rasp raised his arm as if to pull the big man down to his level.

Doc obliged, crouching next to him on the floor, his cell phone pressed to his ear. "Verdammt," he said glancing disgustedly at the offending accessory. "They have me on hold. Would you believe it?"

"It's like I said," Willy said, a humorless grin on his blood-smeared face. "This is a done deal. There's nothin' you or anyone else can do. I knew my number was up. Damn shame, though, I was startin' to really like livin' here in The Keep."

"Angels' Keep is a fine place," said Doc awkwardly, trying to be supportive.

"Business was shit. But that was OK. I knew that goin' in. Turned out I had a real affinity for antiques. And livin' near the ocean. Never would have guessed. But hey, who am I kiddin'? I always knew this was comin'. I wasn't gonna be let off the hook that easy. Once you've signed on for the tour, you're on it come hell or high water. Ain't no wiggle room."

Doc didn't have any idea what the man was talking about. Delirious, he thought.

"Take a load off, Doc," Rasp said calmly, patting a dry spot on the floor next to him. "Make yourself comfortable." He attempted to move sideways to make room for the big man but proved too weak to overcome the frictional resistance of the aged and pockmarked flooring. "Ah, hell," he said and gave up.

Doc looked incredulously at his phone. The tinny strains of "Love Will Keep Us Together" wafted from the earpiece. "Gott steht mir bei," he said imploringly to the ceiling. "I cannot believe no one is picking up! The first real emergency we've had around here in years and here the line is busy!" He brought the phone back to his ear. "Scheiss Bullen," he said under his breath. He tended to revert to his native German when expletives seemed called for.

"You've been a good neighbor, Doc," Rasp said reassuringly. "Just wanted you to know. I never held you bein' a kraut against you."

"You must hang on, Willy," Doc said. "If I am unable to get a response from these idiots in the next ten seconds, I will get you to the hospital if I have to tie you to the back of my motorcycle and drive you there myself."

"Relax, Doc," said Willy Rasp reasonably. "No need to risk injury on my account."

Doc would have been the first to admit his glory days as a soccer star in his native Germany were far behind him. And his noodly leads as the guitarist in the Beluga Blues Band hardly qualified as exercise. Bandying about a vintage Telecaster on stage night after night, grimacing as he tugged relentlessly at his extra-light GHS guitar strings, while appearing to be life threatening, didn't in fact burn that many calories. Especially when punctuated by stints at the bar, hoisting pints. Despite that, he still thought of himself as in excellent shape as he closed in on the half-century mark. The challenge was not in getting Willy "Wild Bill" Rasp onto to his bike. It was that he couldn't see Rasp lasting until they reached the hospital in Monterey, bouncing along on the back of his Harley Fatboy.

"Listen Doc, I want you to promise me right now you won't make a fuss on my account," Rasp said. "There's no point. You'll just be making trouble for yourself. Take my word for it. They're holding all the cards. And it's like I told you. This is all on me, sure as sunrise. I left 'em no choice. They had to do something." He looked down at the bullet holes in his denim jacket. "Looks like this was it."

"Damn it, Willy," Doc pleaded, cutting the Captain and Tennille off as he pocketed the phone. "If you will not let me help you, at least give me a name."

Wilford Rasp seemed to relax as he stared at a point above the front door to the shop, a look of pure amazement on his face.

"Willy?"

Silence met Doc's query.

Willard Rasp was gone.

Chapter 2

"Your name, sir?"

"Manfred St. Michel."

"Nationality?" The detective looked like he had stepped out of a 40s noir movie. He had on a baggy, nondescript brown suit, scuffed wingtips, and a fedora to match.

"I have dual citizenship, American and German."

"What part of Germany?"

"The western part. A stone's throw from the border with France."

"St. Michel is your last name?"

"My father was French."

He made a notation on a small notepad. "OK Mr. St. Michel, so tell me what happened."

"I heard popping sounds coming from the antique shop. Five or six in rapid succession. It took me a moment to realize they might be gunshots."

"And what gave you that idea?"

"I was a marksman during my military service in Germany, before I emigrated to the States. I have some idea what small-arms fire sounds like."

"And where were you at the time?"

"I was in my shop, working. In the tugboat over there." He nodded toward his idiosyncratic dwelling.

The detective's eyes took in the weed-covered lot adjacent to the shop and the dilapidated boat in the center of the open space, held aloft on a wooden cradle. White paint was peeling off the weather-beaten hull, giving the impression of feathers molting. There was a doorway cut into the side of the vessel at ground level and a sign staked out front that advertised "Manfred's Expert Amp Repair." A rickety orchard ladder led up to the gunwale. At the rear of the tug, a winch system had been pressed into service as an elevator. A steel mesh cage dangled below a twenty-foot crane fastened to the aft deck, which could be raised and lowered with the push of a button. On the crabgrass in front of the boat a vintage 1950 Harley Fat Boy motorcycle was parked. It was sky blue in color and had a golden decal of a winged skull on the gas tank. Like the tug, it was an antique. But unlike the re-purposed vessel, it was in showroom condition.

"You ever take it out on the water? The boat?"

Doc shook his head emphatically. "Never," he said. "Since I converted it into a workshop, its days of seaworthiness are far behind it. It would most assuredly go straight to the bottom if I put it in the water."

The man nodded and scribbled something on the pad. "What sort of work do you do, Mr. St. Michel?" He looked and sounded like Richard Widmark. His expression never changed and his features gave nothing away.

"Like the sign says, I repair amplifiers. I specialize in tube gear."

"Guitar amps?"

"Also bass amps. And the occasional piece of stereo gear."

"I see." More scribbling. "So you heard what sounded like gunshots. And then what happened?"

"I ran over to the shop to see what the noise was about. My fears were confirmed when I found Willy."

"He was alive?"

"Yes."

"Did he say anything?"

"Nothing that made sense. I believe he was delirious."

"Did he say who shot him?"

"Unfortunately, no. He passed away within moments of my arrival."

"Did you see anyone leave the shop?"

"No. But I must say, it took me a few moments to get here. I was in the process of soldering some connections when I heard the shots, and I had to make certain my equipment would not start a fire in my absence. There is a small fortune in equipment in the shop. Not to mention that people become very attached to their musical instruments."

The detective took in the man's substantial size. He seemed to be studying Doc's face, looking for any sign of subterfuge. "So you're saying there was no one else around when you arrived at the shop."

"That is correct."

"Did you see any cars drive away?"

"No. Wait a minute. I did hear a car, come to think of it. It sounded like it was heading in the direction of the highway. It may just have been a marina patron."

"Do you remember anything about it?"

"It had a big-block V-8 from the way it sounded," Doc said. "I'm pretty sure about that. And a manual transmission. It made a slight clunking sound when it shifted. I remember thinking it had a transmission job in its future."

The detective paused to consider Manfred's bulging tattooed arms. Serpents coiled from his wrists to his biceps which strained a black unstenciled T-shirt.

"Did anyone else come by—anyone who might also have, uh, witnessed what happened?" asked the detective, clearing his throat. Under the emotionless facade, Doc detected a note of anxiety. The man's eyes were scanning the block as if he were expecting someone and didn't especially want to be around when they arrived.

"No. I did not see anyone else," Doc replied. Sea gulls wheeled overhead. And a mild breeze blew in from the southwest, a hint of warmer weather to come. There was the faint hiss of traffic passing on Highway 1 a couple of blocks inland from where they stood. And an approximately equal distance to the west came the similarly pitched cadence of the Pacific Ocean lapping against the seashore.

"You say the victim was alive when you entered the shop. Is that right?"

Doc nodded.

"Did he say anything you could make out?"

"It was quite strange. He was talking as if he blamed himself for his getting shot, if you can imagine. He seemed to believe it was his own fault."

"Do you have any idea why that might be?"

"I have not the faintest. To be honest, I didn't know Willy all that well. He was a relative newcomer to the neighborhood."

The detective glanced apprehensively down the vacant street once more and cleared his throat. "I think that'll be all for now …" He consulted his notes. "Mr. St Michel. We know where to find you, if we need anything else."

With that he dismissed the burly biker. The detective then strolled over to where the medics were transferring the covered body from a gurney into the back of the ambulance. He looked around nervously. "Let's get a move on here," he whispered urgently to the men taking Willy Rasp's remains away. "We need to wrap this up, pronto."

This struck Doc as odd. This was a murder investigation, after all. Surely it deserved a bit more gravitas than that, no matter how busy the police department might have been on that particular morning.

He turned and started to walk back toward the tug feeling let down. He'd expected to be hammered with questions, maybe searched for a murder weapon—he being a hulking tattooed biker, the only witness to the crime and certainly a potential suspect at this point. Wasn't that how it was done? Maybe he'd been watching too many police procedurals lately.

He hadn't so much as been asked for his ID.

Chapter 3

At 230 pounds and well over 6 feet, Manfred "Doc" St. Michel had managed to stay reasonably fit since his days as an athlete. It was only recently that his waist size had gone up a notch, necessitating a wardrobe upgrade. The weight gain was likely due to the complimentary drinks he nightly consumed as a performer, part of the payment he received. In the early days of his career as a musician, they had often been the only payment.

Not to say that he was making a bundle playing at The Fish Tank even now. But the modest amount he received there was compensated for by other factors. One was the fact that the popular Central Coast live music venue and bar was just 150 yards away from where he lived. The other (not necessarily in that order) was that he was enamored of the Tank's proprietress, a certain Lucy Tang.

Luckily, he didn't have to rely on the money he made there to make a living. If he had, he wouldn't be much better off right now than Eric the Red, the town derelict, who lived under the blue tarp in the empty lot across the street. But his repair business, if not exactly booming, kept the lights on and his fridge stocked.

He gazed absently down the street in the direction of the town's nightlife hot spot. One would have thought somebody would have noticed the commotion in front of Granny's Antiques. But the Keep could have been a ghost town at 10:30 that particular spring morning.

Doc shunned his makeshift elevator system and instead grabbed an old wooden ladder which was leaning against the bow of the boat. He climbed the fifteen or so feet to the gunwale, each of the worn rungs bending and bleating in protest during his ascent.

"Hey dude!"

The voice came from the doorway to the wheelhouse just as Doc was about to clear the railing, causing him to flail, arms akimbo, before he managed to regain his balance at the top of the ladder. Swearing prodigiously in German, he landed on the deck with a thud, grateful no one else was around to witness his distinctly ungraceful arrival.

"You mustn't startle people like that," he bellowed at the open door to the wheelhouse. He'd been so preoccupied on the way up that he'd forgotten his new house guest for a moment. She was a mocha-colored fifteen-year-old runaway, tall and skinny as a willow rod. She had been sporting a neon pink, mohawk-style haircut and horned-rimmed glasses when she had shown up the previous week at Doc's door, claiming to be his long lost daughter. Her name was Sticks, she had said. ("On account of I used to wear dreads with knitting needles stuck in them.") The recent rains had necessitated a style adjustment. She now sported a green fisherman's cap which hid her flaming hair. Doc Marten lace-up boots, dark kneesocks, a knee-length pink skirt over a tutu-like slip and a short faux leather jacket completed her look. She looked straight out of the eighties, Manfred observed, but chose not share this observation. He didn't know the girl well enough to know what might cause offense. Her intention with the outfit may have been something else entirely.

Doc had never been confronted with the prospect of paternity before, so he had asked the first thing that came to mind. "Where are you from?"

"Detroit," she said. "I'm hangin' with my aunt for a couple of weeks. Up in Pacifica."

"On the peninsula," Doc remarked, wondering what came next.

"My mom and stepdad are in France right now," the girl explained. "They're celebrating their tenth anniversary."

"I see," said Doc. "But are you not concerned that your people will be worried about you? Simply going off on your own like this."

"They're thinkin' I'm at a Girl Scout camp in Big Sur."

"You are a Girl Scout?" Doc said unable fully to conceal the incredulity in his voice.

"Got the Silver Award," she said proudly.

Doc had no idea what that meant exactly, but he said, "Very prestigious."

"So long as I check in with my aunt every couple of days, everything's copacetic," said the girl with complete self-assurance. "And from what I hear cell service is spotty in Big Sur, so I've got an excuse. I looked it up."

It had taken about three days, but he finally wheedled her real name out of her: Ophelia. "Now you know why I changed my name," she said sullenly.

"It is an exceptional name," Doc had remarked. At the same time he could understand how a modern young woman might take issue with it. It wasn't very "street."

"You know in Shakespeare she goes insane and drowns herself," she added.

"There is that." Hamlet. Another reason why she'd be averse to the name, Doc thought sympathetically. He'd simply been calling her Missy up until that point. He couldn't quite bring himself to call her by her preferred moniker, Sticks. Wasn't she aware of how unflattering that name was, especially in light of her gangly, boyish build? Now, after three days at Doc's, a decision concerning what to call her seemed called for. Not to mention what was to be done about her. He decided to try a different tack.

"Do you have a middle name?" he asked cautiously.

"Calista."

"Calista," Doc repeated with some relief. "I like it."

"You're welcome to it," said the girl. But then she softened. "It means "most beautiful" in Greek. Did you know that?"

"I did not," said Doc. "But that is entirely appropriate."

"Ophelia Calista Brown." She proclaimed the name defiantly.

"Very classy."

"It should belong to some old money society matron," she said. "Or be on a plaque on some granite monstrosity. 'The Ophelia Calista Brown Historical Society.' Or 'The Ophelia Calista Brown Museum of Art.'"

"It has a musical quality," said Doc ruefully.

"Well, it sure ain't the kind of music I listen to," said the girl peevishly.

"It is nothing to be ashamed about," Doc insisted.

13

She looked at him dubiously. Then she seemed to retreat into herself to consider her options. Convinced that he was her real father, she seemed willing to cut him some slack. She didn't want to hurt his feelings. Adults could be so … fragile.

"OK," she said magnanimously. "I'll let you call me Callie, if you want."

"Callie, yes. Callie it is, then," He was relieved that the problem had been resolved satisfactorily. "Admit it. You are somewhat enamored of it."

"Hardly," she said with a dismissive wave of a hand, just the way an old money society matron might.

Chapter 4

It was not inconceivable that he had met Callie's mom back in the bad old days. Nor was it hard to imagine they might have had a fling sixteen years before. Up until a dozen years ago he had played guitar in a rockabilly band—The Real Gone Cats—which had achieved a level of notoriety in the Bay Area. And if they never quite made the big-time, they were well loved by a ragtag army of misfits that favored motorcycle jackets, tattoos, piercings, and American Spirit cigarettes. The girl's mother might well have been among them before she turned "respectable."

But in spite of all this, Doc knew it was impossible he was the girl's father. The fact was that he was unable to conceive children. He'd known that since he was in his teens, when an extensive medical check up had brought the matter to light. The condition, it was speculated at the time, stemmed from his insistence on wearing gonad-squeezing Levi's from an early age. The pants, it was theorized, had throttled his unsuspecting spermatozoon into extinction.

Even so, he didn't have the heart to turn the girl away when she appeared at his door, drenched and looking like a punked out teenage Alicia Keyes, a military-style backpack slung over her shoulder. It was clear she wanted to think herself tough. But one look at her, the daughter of educated parents who worked for a Detroit school district he would later learn, told him she wouldn't have lasted a week on her own on the streets of a major urban center. Having grown to the age of five without a father, she was acutely aware that her current dad was not her real dad. And when she had questioned her mom about her real father, the latter had apparently invented some glorified story about how the girl was conceived, when the truth was perhaps too cliched and tawdry to confide to a child. In the embellished version, the story featured a brooding musician in the role of Prince Charming, a guitarist in a cool, marginally successful nineties band who she had followed once upon a time. Harmless enough, right? Up until the day the kid was old enough to look into the matter herself.

Doc had always been an easy touch. From a distance he looked scary, like someone who could crush rocks in his fists. But the eyes belied his true nature. They were kind eyes, intelligent, compassionate, curious. The German inflection in his speech also seemed to work against the biker stereotype he chose to cultivate. German was his native tongue, but his French wasn't bad either. Having grown up the son of a French pharmacist in the Alsatian region of Germany, he had picked up the language easily at a young age. English, which he had learned in school, had been the toughest of the three to master. And with his textbook delivery, he could hardly have passed for a native speaker even now, after some twenty-eight years in the States.

"So what was all the commotion about just now?" Callie wanted to know. The shaved sidewalls of her mohawk were just starting to stubble back in. Her eyes behind the glasses had been stenciled with kohl to the point where the girl resembled a skinny raccoon. He had found the incongruity of her look oddly touching the day she had first appeared. It could not be denied the girl had her own aesthetic. She was as anachronistic in her way as he was in his, he realized, with wry amusement.

"Somebody shot Willy."

"The old guy from the antiques shop?" Everybody in Angels' Keep was old in her eyes.

"Jawohl," Doc said, drawing in a breath as he sat down heavily on the bench outside the wheelhouse. "Plugged him in his own shop."

"Holy shit. Is he …?"

Doc nodded. He looked out over the houses and trees toward the calm waters of the Monterey Bay. "On this street. In this town!"

"He musta been into some bad shit, if he ended up like that," hypothesized the girl sagely.

"We weren't well acquainted, to be honest," Doc replied. "But even so, this is not Chicago in the thirties. There's no Al Capone here. No John Dillinger. Equally as disconcerting was the way the cops reacted. The detective I spoke with seemed distracted. It was if Willy's death were little more than an inconvenience to him. I, the sole witness, was interviewed for less than ten minutes, can you imagine? If you were a cop and found me at a murder scene,"--he indicated his hulking physique with the sweep of his hand,--"what would you do?"

"I'd lock you up and throw away the key."

"You'd be excused for wanting to question me at some length. At the very least."

"They'd skip the trial and go straight to sentencing," the girl quipped.

"It seemed to me the cop's main concern was to get the whole business concluded as expeditiously as possible, before someone else found out about it. I do not understand it. They seemed somewhat interested that I had heard a car drive away from the scene, though I hadn't actually seen it."

"Speak for yourself, Manfred." The girl found his name inexplicably comical and used it at every opportunity. "I saw a car tear up the street while you were on your way over to the shop."

Chapter 5

Doc looked at the girl in amazement. "What did it look like?"

"Old. Big."

"Do you remember anything else about it?"

She seemed to focus internally, trying to conjure up the memory of the vehicle in her mind. "It was a 1948 Packard," she said finally. "Straight eight probably, a four-door sedan. Midnight blue."

Doc gawked at her.

What are you lookin' at?" Callie said indignantly. "So my stepdad is into cars. What of it?"

"More than a little rubbed off, I would say. Your stepdad sounds like a rather cool fellow."

"He's not a musician," said the girl with finality.

Doc couldn't help but shake his head and grin before sobering again. "This Packard. Which way did it go?"

"It went … thataway!" She pointed dramatically toward the road at the end of the block that led from the marina to Highway 1.

"I'll be back," Doc said, sounding a lot like Arnold. "Stay on the boat. Pull up the ladder behind me."

"Can't I come along?" the girl whined.

"No, it is better if you stay here for now. I will not be long. I promise."

"Good luck finding the Packard," she said soberly. "It was going like a bat outta hell. And watch your six. I got a bad feeling about that car."

Manfred "Doc" St. Michel clambered back down the rickety ladder, hiked up his faded and fraying jeans, and threw a jackbooted leg over the Harley. It roared to life in an instant with a din that could have been audible in the next county. It was one of the peculiar charms of that particular variety of motorcycle. The heavy custom bike with the distinctive winged skull decal on the gas tank lumbered heavily streetward. Once there it accelerated as if fired out of a cannon. The throaty snarl of the big bore two-stroke engine echoed long after it had vanished from view.

Faced with the decision of which way to turn when he arrived at the main highway, he stopped and sniffed the air. For no particular reason, he elected to head south along the sweep of the southern end of the Monterey Bay. His chances of locating the Packard were fifty-fifty, he figured.

Meanwhile, Callie retreated into the cabin and started a pot of coffee. The old guy next door was dead. Offed gangsta-style. She couldn't get over it. She had assumed the worst thing that happened in this town was a sunburn.

Right now all was quiet in Angels' Keep. But who knew what evil lurked beneath the placid, picture postcard exterior? She imagined herself writing a magazine article, something for Slate or Rolling Stone, perhaps. It would be titled "Beach Town Confidential," she decided.

It was cozy in the wheelhouse, thanks to a tiny space heater that whirred on the floor at her feet. There was a galley kitchen next to the sofa that doubled as her bed. A small, boxy TV sporting rabbit ears rested atop an ancient VCR player next to the toaster. The view was amazing from here. You could see the entire sweep of the bay through the west-facing windows.

Doc's workshop and sleeping quarters were below decks. When the halogen track lights flickered on, the first impression from the top of the stairs was of complete chaos. The space below looked like an electronics bazaar, with bright flashes of color here and there—the lacquered bodies of electric guitars in all shapes and sizes, insulated wiring, knobs, transistors, resisters, mother boards, pick guards and vacuum tubes. It quickly became clear that there was a logic to the disorder. Everything was meticulously sorted and strategically placed.

"My inner sanctum," Doc called it. "This is my shrine to the history of American electric music."

It smelled like wiring, wood polish and solder. Workbenches along the walls supported guitars and amps in various states of disassembly, hand tools and coils of electrical wiring. On all the exposed sections of wall that lacked shelving, rare vintage instruments hung. Polished and shiny, they dazzled under the halogen lights. A doorway cut into the side of the tug's hull allowed customers direct access to the workshop from the street.

"You could almost, like, open up your own business," Callie had observed cheerfully.

"Ha, ha," Doc had replied.

The workshop was a bit intimidating once one knew that every object in it, large or small, was deliberately placed to insure that Doc could find it again when he needed it. So Callie tended to steer clear of it and confined her movements to the upstairs cabin and deck. A water hose ran onto the property from the rear and was the main water supply for the tug. Doc had a special arrangement with his neighbors, a trio of young country musicians who were renting the house behind his property, for the water hook-up. However, with no septic on site, it was necessary to use an outhouse in back of the tug for anything other than gray water applications.

By way of apology for the lack of indoor facilities, Doc had stated his intention to install real plumbing in the near future. "I began the renovation right here in the cabin," he had explained. "For those first months I was repairing amplifiers on the kitchen table. Not long afterward I began to clear out the area below decks and began the process of rebuilding and reinforcing the interior of the hull. It was a project that kept me occupied for a couple of years."

"And it's been how long since then?" Callie couldn't restrain herself from razzing him.

"Ten years give or take," Doc said sheepishly. "Mein gott, has it really been that long?"

Callie changed the subject. "Why do they call you 'Doc?'" she had inquired. "Is it because you live on one?"

"Very amusing," Doc had replied. "Have you ever considered a career as a comedian?"

Callie ignored this. "You're obviously not an MD," she said. "I don't see you doing brain surgery. Not with those hams." She indicated his hands.

She thought some more. "Steinbeck, then? Doc, the marine biologist. Cannery Row? Sweet Thursday?"

"I am impressed," Doc said with sincerity. "You have done some reading. To be quite honest, I don't know when people around here started calling me Doc. It was a bit of an embarrassment at first, but I suppose I have gotten used to it."

"Oh, come on, Manfred," the girl chided. "I can guess why they call you Doc."

"OK. What is your theory?"

"You're good at what you do. People respect you for that. Plus they probably like you, tattoos and all. It's a term of affection."

"I like it better already."

"Either that or they're trying to humor you because they think you're a psycho and figure they'd better try and stay on your good side."

"I like the first theory better," said Doc.

BEACH TOWN CONFIDENTIAL

Chapter 6

When Callie wasn't at the tug, she was in the tiny beach town exploring the shops around the harbor. Though a dyed-in-the-wool product of suburbia, she found she enjoyed hanging out on the beach. At her aunt's hillside house in Pacifica she saw the ocean from a distance, across a jagged range of rooftops, but it was different here. Everything was closer and quieter.

She found it liberating to walk on the beach between land and sea. She was often the only one on the sand at this time of year. She would hold her arms straight out and spin around until she fell in a heap, giggling. The only witnesses to her performance were the gulls overhead, the sandpipers scurrying diligently to stay ahead of the waves, and the occasional dolphin that surfaced near shore. It was funny how quickly she had become accustomed to the laid-back life of the sleepy seaside village.

The roar of Doc's Harley brought her out of her reverie. Laid-back until today, she amended.

Doc had company coming back. He was leading a small motorcade. Three Sheriff's cars, lights flashing but no sirens, were following close on Doc's heels as he pulled to a stop in front of Granny's. The police cars followed suit, angling into the sidewalk in the kind of haphazard fashion the police were known to employ when there was a matter of some urgency afoot. Doc waited patiently on the curb while the four cops occupying the three vehicles joined him. Two cops went around the back, guns drawn. One of the two cops Doc was with shouted, "Open up! Police!"

When there was no response from inside the shop, one detective put his shoulder to the door, but discovered in the nick of time the door was unlocked. Turning the knob, he and his partner plunged into the shop. They were soon joined by the other two cops who had found nothing out back. Doc followed the last of these through the doorway.

Nothing happened for what seemed like a long time. Then all four cops exited the premises, hopped into their respective cars and departed at a relaxed pace.

Doc arrived at the tug's "elevator" a short time later. His taking the elevator indicated he had some thinking to do.

"What was that all about?" Callie asked when Doc arrived on deck.

"I was unsuccessful in tracking the Packard," Doc said slowly. "So I stopped in at the Sheriff's office in Seaside to check on the status of the inquiry into Willy's death. I discovered that no such inquiry had been initiated. In fact, Willy's death was news to the authorities there."

"So the cops and the ambulance who came by earlier were, like what? Fake?"

"It would appear that way. I do not have an alternate explanation. So I told the police what I had seen, and they came along to have a look."

"And? What did they find?"

"Not a thing," said Doc wearily. "There was no evidence that a crime had been committed. No blood. No bullet holes. Nothing."

"Wow those killers were good," said Callie with unsettling admiration. "They must have been pros to clean up the crime scene like that. Did they run one of those luminol tests for blood like they do on CSI?"

"They sprayed the carpet and wall where I last saw Willy with a blue liquid," Doc said with a sigh. "But their test for blood traces yielded negative results. They explained to me that without a body, a corpus delicti, their hands were tied. They said the best they could do was have me file a missing persons report, which I did. Then they left."

"That's f—messed up, I mean. What are you going to do?"

Doc shrugged. "Unless I find some concrete evidence of Willy's murder, we are at an impasse. The cops have no compelling reason to investigate further. So it is up to me, as I see it, to find evidence. I intend to canvas the neighborhood for witnesses. Tomorrow I will stop at town hall to see if any new information has turned up. We cannot afford to let this matter rest, even if the police will not help us. Until we know what happened and why, we must assume others here may be at risk."

"I made coffee," Callie said brightly to lighten his mood. She held the wheelhouse door open for him.

Doc sleepwalked into the cabin.

"Verflixt! What the hell is going on here all of sudden?" Doc cried suddenly, in frustration.

"More than meets the eye, no doubt," the girl said levelly, with a Groucho Marx eyebrow waggle, tapping the ash off an imaginary cigar.

Doc was momentarily speechless at this unexpected display. Then he broke into laughter despite himself. "How have I managed without you all these years?" he said.

"It seems impossible, I know," the girl said.

"There must be someone else who saw what happened," Doc said soberly.

"I saw the ambulance," Callie volunteered. "And that late model Crown Vic our fake detective drove up in. I can't tell you the exact year. Newer cars aren't my thing. They all look the same to me."

Doc shook his head. "I do not want you involved in this," he said firmly. "And besides you are not here. You are in Big Sur, camping. Remember?"

Doc appeared to have an inspiration. He reached for the phone and dialed.

Before long a groggy voice answered and muttered something unintelligible into the mouthpiece. When Doc identified himself the voice became, by turns, more articulate. "Jesus man, what time is it? You know I don't get up before 3."

"I am sorry to wake you, Chico. But something of an emergency has arisen and you were the first person that came to mind."

Chico Fuertas was a car mechanic and the organist in the Beluga Blues Band. He lived in Salinas, but when they were gigging at the Fish Tank, he tended to stay over at a friend's place on a parallel street. "OK. Now that I'm awake, what's up?"

"Did you hear anything around 10:30 this morning?"

"Come to think of it, yeah. I woke up sometime in the morning. Thought I heard somebody setting off fireworks in the neighborhood. Figured I dreamed it and went back to sleep."

"So I have not completely lost my mind," Doc said to himself.

"I heard that," Chico said. "I wouldn't jump to conclusions about that, man." Some of Chico's acerbic wit was returning with consciousness. "So what's the deal?"

"It wasn't fireworks," said Doc.

"No?" said Chico, straining to understand.

"It was Willy Rasp being shot."

There was a rustle at the end of the line as Chico pulled himself into an upright position. "Sorry. It must be the connection. I thought I just heard you say someone shot Wild Bill Willy."

"You heard right, amigo."

"How bad is it?"

"As bad as it gets."

"Shit."

"My sentiments exactly."

"That's fucked up, man. Who'd have it in for old Willy? He never done nothin' worse than overcharge for those fuckin' antiques of his." Chico thought a moment and added, "Maybe somebody took issue with him trying to pass himself off as 'Granny.' I don't see that getting him killed, though."

"Some men posing as cops and medics showed up right afterward and removed the body. When I checked with the real police just now, they were unaware that anything had happened. And by the time they got around to inspecting the crime scene, it had been cleaned up so thoroughly the police were unwilling to open an investigation into the matter. They said they didn't have enough to go on."

"So someone shot Willy and had enough juice to hire a clean up crew decked out as cops and first responders to get rid of all traces of the crime, grab the body and make it disappear. What are you thinking, bra? Cartel? Triad? Mafia conspiracy? What must old Willy have been into to draw down that kind of heat, ese? Drugs, numbers, white slavery?"

"I honestly cannot imagine Willy being involved in any of those things. He was just a retiree turning a modest profit selling antiques, from all appearances. It doesn't make a lot of sense."

"What he charged for those pieces of junk might have blown somebody's fuse. But like I said, I don't see him getting offed on account of that. If overcharging was a crime, half of this town would be in the slammer. And I don't see some crazed tourist bent on revenge going to all this trouble. Hey. I got an idea. Maybe he was in witness protection. He could have been, like, a mob accountant from back east who ratted out his bosses and the bad guys found him."

"Willy? I am sorry, Chico, but I just do not see it." Doc sank into his thoughts. "But who am I to say? Regardless of the causes, unless we turn up some proof of the crime, whoever is responsible gets away with murder."

"Fuckanado, man. So what are you suggesting?"

"Somebody must do something. If the cops won't act, I will. I feel an obligation to do what I can for poor Willy."

"Are you sure about this, bro? Everything seems to indicate you are dealing with some bad hombres here, dude. They'd have to be well financed and well connected to take out Willy and then pull off a charade like you described to cover it up. These were no amateurs. You sure you want to get involved?"

"I do not see that I have a choice."

"Hey, if it comes down to busting heads, you just say the word. I'll back your play, man. You can rely on me."

Chico stood 5' 6" in his Beatle boots. He might have been the toughest Latino north of the border, but Doc had never seen him so much as swat a horse fly. He wouldn't have been Doc's first choice as a backup.

"I know I can rely on you, Chico," Doc said softly. "And you know I appreciate it. We cannot have people getting gunned down in Angels' Keep with impunity. Not if Manfred St. Michel has any say in the matter."

"Manfred who? Who you talking about, man?"

"Me," Doc said, realizing that the band knew him only by his nickname, Doc. "Not if *I* have any say in the matter."

Chapter 7

The small battery-powered clock in the kitchen read 8:15 as Doc went downstairs to collect his guitar and case. He was cutting it close. The Whales, as the Beluga Blues Band was affectionately known, were set to take the stage at the Fish Tank in less than half-an-hour.

"I should be back sometime after midnight," Doc announced. "If you see anybody snooping around before then, call me immediately no matter who they are or what they might tell you. OK?"

"Don't talk to strangers," the girl said listlessly. "Check."

"Hey, no frowning. Understood? You don't want to line your face prematurely," Without realizing it, Doc seemed to have slipped into parental mode. "I will take you with me one of these evenings. I'll arrange it with Lucy. Alright?"

"You promise?"

"I promise."

After pulling up the rickety ladder and laying it lengthwise along the gunwale, Doc took the elevator to ground level. He strode purposefully across the open field to the street, carrying his guitar case. Fortunately, the rest of his gear was already set up and waiting for him at the bar, the advantage of having gigs on consecutive nights during the week.

It had been dark for two hours, but it could have been midnight. The fog was rolling in and the temperature was dropping, winter unwilling to relinquish its grip on the Central Coast just yet. It almost never froze at this latitude, especially this close to the ocean. Even so, the moisture laden onshore breeze could be bracing. Doc zipped his motorcycle jacket to the collar with one hand to ward off the chill.

In the weak light of a nearby street lamp, he could just make out Crazy Eric's blue tarp tented in the otherwise empty lot across the street. The homeless man was referred to by the locals as Eric the Red due to his distinctly Nordic appearance. He had tangled reddish-blond locks that hung to massively broad shoulders, a shaggy red beard, enormous arms and tree trunk legs. These in addition to his 6 ft. 7 inches in height made him an imposing figure, and an individual both town folks and tourists alike went out of their way to avoid. He rarely spoke. Rumor had it he was an Iraqi war veteran who had come back from the Middle East with several screws loose. Doc, perhaps the only one in town not intimated by Eric, had taken pity on the man and had even offered him money on more than one occasion. The latter had declined. It was clear he wanted only to be left alone.

Despite his better judgment, Doc found himself veering off the roadway in the direction of Eric's hovel. He called out, unsure what name the man would answer to. There was a rustling of plastic as Eric emerged and drew himself to his full height, a massive silhouette against the night.

"What can I do for you?" he said mildly, in a deep bass-baritone. It was the first complete sentence Doc had ever heard the man utter, and it brought him up short.

As Eric approached, he seemed to grow ever taller until he towered over Doc. There weren't many men in Doc's experience who could make him appear, if not exactly small in comparison, moderate in size. Doc struggled against the reflex to take a step back. With his imposing presence, his fiery beard, stringy locks, and craggy, weathered face, Eric most resembled a bloodthirsty Viking Beserker who had just stepped off a sixth century longboat.

"My name is Manfred," Doc stammered. "I, uh, live across the street." He motioned vaguely toward the tug.

"I know who you are."

"I regret to disturb you. I am wondering if you happened to notice any unusual goings on this morning--over at Granny's Antiques. Just after 10 o'clock."

"You mean the fireworks. And the car caravans—first the one, then the other. Sure," Eric said. "Could hardly have missed 'em. The circus was definitely in town."

Doc struggled to understand. By "car caravans" he may have been referring to the consecutive visits from the cops, first the fake ones and then the real ones.

"Just between you and me, I don't see that old Willy left 'em much choice," Eric said, conversationally. "The situation was unsustainable. Not saying it was *right* what they did, mind you."

"Who's they?"

Eric's teeth flashed in the darkness as he looked away. "The powers that be, who else?" he said. "The order had to have come down from higher up. I don't see those slugs doin' something like this on their own initiative. They need an angle or the promise of turning a profit just to get out of bed in the morning." The man worked his jaw like he had a bad taste in his mouth. "But the way it was handled stank to high heaven, no two ways about it. It had all the markings of a middle management boondoggle. Bureaucracy's the same wherever you go, but this is the mother of all screwups. It's all there—the incompetence, the lack of imagination, the crappy execution--pardon the pun. Textbook cluster of the first order."

Doc didn't know what to say. He opened and closed his mouth. "You saw something," he said finally, uncertain as to how to get the conversation back on firmer footing.

"Unh hunh. Would have been blind to have missed it. Exhibit A: the car. Straight out of a J. Edgar Hoover G-man fantasy. Exhibit B: the gangland-style delivery. All that was missing was a tommy gun, for shit's sake. And don't even get me started on the cleanup crew. Brain atrophy. Happens when you watch too much network television."

It was clear to Doc that Eric had been hallucinating that morning and was hallucinating still or worse. He was riffing on the shooting, free associating, that much was clear, turning it into something only he could understand in his warped mind.

This had been a mistake. Doc suddenly felt the need to extricate himself. He mumbled something to the effect that he had a gig in a few minutes. He excused himself and turned back toward the street. Tendrils of fog snaked around the nearby streetlamp, while a river of low clouds rushed past overhead. Eric just stood there in his wake, a Mt. Rushmore silhouette chiseled in granite, stationary against the cloud cover. It was unclear if he was even aware that Doc had left.

Doc could hear the sounds of car doors slamming, motorcycles revving, loud talking, laughing and shouting ahead of him, coming from the direction of the Fish Tank. It had never seemed an island of sanity before. But tonight, there was something reassuring about the predictable rowdiness of the mid-week crowd. The meeting with Eric had left him disoriented and troubled.

"Hey Manfred," Eric's voice rumbled out from the shadows behind him, causing him to jump forward reflexively as if physically shoved. "You'd better watch your back. If they could mess up this bad, ain't nobody safe around here."

Chapter 8

The night seemed to be following Doc as he trudged resolutely onward toward the bright lights of the tavern. It loomed up behind him like an inky tidal surge. He tried to shake off his unease but found himself accelerating despite himself. The tension began to dissipate as he reached the parking area, the familiar crunch of gravel underfoot. About forty cars, pickups and motorcycles gleamed under the powerful spotlights that illuminated a couple of acres of parking around the tavern. They promised a respectable crowd for a Tuesday night.

"Hey, guitar man!" someone he didn't recognize near the front door shouted at him to get his attention.

"The doctor is in!" a small bearded man added, a few feet to Doc's right. He was leaning against a vintage red and white '56 Chevy station wagon.

"Crowbar," Doc said, nodding in the man's direction. "How are you?"

"Better now that I'm here," the man said. "It's been one of those days."

"I know just what you mean," Doc muttered, without breaking stride.

He skirted the establishment and entered through the service entrance at the back of the rambling single-story structure. The performer's lounge was empty, he saw, the band already onstage. He kept going. The hallway opened out into the bar proper, next to a raised platform. He bound onto it and made for his gear. His Fender Bandmaster amp was already lit up and waiting. The other three members of the Beluga Blues Band were already in place. Cathy "Catfish" Hunter was engrossed in tuning up her P-Bass. Drummer Roscoe "Kunk" Kunkley was tapping lightly on his snare and Chico

Fuertas was toe tapping the long bass keys on a roadworn Hammond B-3 organ that was reputed to have once belonged to Lee Michaels.

Chico gave Doc a small salute when he arrived. Doc returned the gesture before plugging into his amp. He briefly checked the tuning on his '52 Telecaster and then set about dialing in the sound he wanted on the vintage amp.

There were at least eighty people in the room, about half of them seated at cocktail tables at the peripheries and the other half milling around on the checkered dance floor that occupied the center of the club.

Doc straightened up when he was ready and gave Roscoe a slight nod. The drummer started the four count, and the Whales were off and running, doing a medium tempo rendition of the Howlin' Wolf song, "Killin' Floor."

The evenings blues and R and B offerings were executed competently enough, but only because the band had been playing together so long they could cover for each other when one of them was feeling out of sorts. The fact was, Doc's head wasn't in the game. He kept seeing Willy lying there in a pool of his own blood at the back of his shop not a hundred feet from where Doc lived.

During break time, Doc put out a request backstage that everyone keep an eye out for a dark blue '48 Packard.

"Just let me know if you see it," Doc said earnestly. "Do not go near it. Do not engage the people in it in any way. They may have been responsible for Willy's death."

By now the rumor of Willy's demise had spread through the town. Even the copious quantities of alcohol consumed at the bar that night were insufficient to mask the anxiety that pervaded the club in light of what was purported to have happened to a member of the community. The prevailing sentiment was that if it could happen to someone like Willy, it could happen to anyone in Angels' Keep.

It was with some relief that Doc left the stage that night. Lucy, the owner and manager of the Fish Tank, was in the lounge backstage when he appeared there.

"You look like hell," she informed him affectionately with a peck on the cheek. Doc and the proprietress had been an item now for some years.

"It has been a very strange day," Doc confessed.

Lucy Tang stood 5' 3" and had straight jet-black hair that hung forward along her jaw line and framed a pretty face. She seemed ageless, but Doc was privy to the a fact that she had just passed the four decade mark. They had recently celebrated her birthday in a favorite restaurant of theirs in Pacific Grove. Even though she was born in Missouri and grew up in the states, the daughter of fifth generation Chinese-American parents, it amused her to sound like she'd just gotten off the boat from Shanghai.

"Hey, you want good-time girl?" she said brightly. "Ring bell, two dollah. Ding ding!"

As usual when Lucy's humor took an off-color turn, Doc blushed crimson. "You have heard about Willy?" he managed.

She nodded. She switched off the accent like a sink faucet, saying, "Everyone has by now. I heard you were there when he died. You OK?"

Doc nodded.

"Poor round-eye," she said sadly, lapsing into heavily accent English again. "China girl not like when round-eye Granny bite dust. Need every last customer."

"I am still unable to comprehend it," Doc said, ignoring her attempt at levity. "I saw Willy die right in front of me. And I saw them take his body away."

"People are saying that no body has been found," Lucy said in perfect English.

"The men who took him away, the police and the ambulance people, were fraudulent. It was an elaborately staged charade."

"Who would want to do something like that to Willy—kill him and them make him disappear. He must have pissed somebody off big time. Somebody with resources."

"It was a professional job, no question. Willy was such an unassuming guy. I cannot imagine him getting into the kind of trouble that would have warranted such a response."

"You know the police are denying knowledge of any shooting."

"I think they're afraid people might panic. They have nothing to go on. The cops—the real cops—came to Willy's place this afternoon. They were unable to find anything. But I was there. I saw it happen."

"If you say you saw Willy get shot, that's good enough for me," Lucy said. "For my money, you're one of the sanest people in this town. You say you saw something happen. It happened."

Doc nodded solemnly.

"Round-eye no lie," she said, lapsing into her immigrant persona. "May be western barbarian, but shoot straight."

Doc had been blushing for so long by now that it looked like he had a chronic skin condition.

"So. What are you going to do?" Lucy asked, turning the act off again and waxing serious.

"I am going to talk to Jesus."

For once it was Lucy's turn to be shocked. Doc was not a religious person. Then realization dawned. "You're going to see the mayor."

Mayor Garcia was generally known as "Jerry" to his constituents. But his legal first name was Jesus.

"If you want company, let me know," Lucy said. "I donated a fair chunk of change to his last campaign. Maybe I could smooth the way for you."

"I am grateful, Lucy. But I do not think that will be necessary. I am just going to see whether there are any new developments in the case. I have heard he is a Beluga Blues fan."

There was a knock on the door frame.

Roscoe appeared in the doorway, a frown on his face. "Sorry to interrupt you guys," he said. He turned his attention to Doc. "You know that car you were talkin' 'bout? The Packard? I think it's out in the parking lot right now."

Chapter 9

The lot was virtually empty when Doc ducked out the front door of the establishment. He had to squint to make out the Packard at the perimeter of the parking area through the late-night mist that continued to roll in off the coast. As he approached he could see a small man leaning back against the trunk of the car casually, his arms crossed. He was wearing aviator sunglasses, too big for his face. A solidly built man was planted like an oak tree nearby, legs apart, his hands clasped before him, military style. The two men eyed Doc unwaveringly as he approached. They appeared to be waiting for him.

The smaller man spoke first. Something about the way he carried himself told Doc he was the one in charge. He got right to the point. "It has come to our attention that you been poking your nose where it don't belong." The man had a high scratchy voice. Nails on a chalk board. "That is unfortunate."

He had exaggerated lips that looked like they had been painted on his pasty face. He look uncannily like a ventriloquist's dummy—a sociopathic Charlie McCarthy.

"Unfortunate for whom? What do you know about Willy's death?"

"Let's just say we represent certain interested parties who might be … inconvenienced if you were to continue with your inquiries. My advice? Do the smart thing. Leave it alone. Walk away and don't look back."

"I am afraid I cannot do that," Doc said. "Who are you anyway? What is your part in this?"

The smaller man sighed regretfully. "We're … businessmen," he said. "Not unlike yourself, the way I hear it. We have a job to do, just as you do. You do your job, and we do ours. Everybody's happy. All is right with the world. Ya got it? We don't mess in your business, and you keep out of ours."

"So," said Doc incredulously. "You are suggesting I simply forget about what happened to Willy?"

"That's exactly what I'm suggesting. You ain't as dumb as you look. None a' this concerns you, bud. Let it go."

"And if I don't?"

"It could have serious consequences for your continued well-being."

Doc considered this bald threat a moment. "The only reason I can think of as to why you would wish that I cease my inquiries into Willy's death is that you had something to do with it. Did you murder Willy?"

"Murder," the man said. "Such a strong word. Fact is, you know squat about what may or may not have happened to Rasp. Right now it's a gray area, ain't it? You claim he was killed. But then where's the proof? The cops got bupkis. They got no evidence anything ever happened."

"I was there. I saw Willy die."

"You know zip," the smaller man snapped. "You're way out of your depth here. You got no idea what's goin' on and what your dealin' with." The conversational tone had assumed a more sinister undercurrent.

"Who are you?" Doc repeated.

The small man addressed his much larger partner. "Don't suppose there's any harm in telling him. Won't do him no good." He turned to Doc. "They call me D'Angelo. Pete D'Angelo." Geniality had returned for the moment. "And this is my associate, Carl. We'd like you to rethink your interest in this matter. It would be very unwise for you to persist. That path could lead you right off a cliff. Isn't that right, Carl?"

The bigger man stood still as a statue. "Could be life threatening," he said in a monotone.

"What happened to Willy could just as easily happen to you, see?" the man called D'Angelo said.

Except for the rustling of the bushes and distant hissing of the Pacific against the nearby shore, it was silent. The lot was now empty of other cars. Of the three or four patrons that were milling around the entrance to the bar, none were paying attention to the men facing off in the shadows near the street.

"I get that you are trying scare me," Doc said, trying to keep his voice steady. "But you may find that I do not scare so easily."

The smaller man shook his head almost sadly. He seemed to have a permanent rictus on his face that allowed for a limited range of expression—the result of a botched surgery, perhaps? With a theatrical sigh, he glanced exaggeratedly at his watch. "Can you believe it?" he said. "Look how late it's got."

He straightened and stared implacably at Doc for a long moment from behind his impenetrable aviators. "This unpleasantness could so easily have been avoided," he said. "That's OK. We're prepared to go the extra mile, if that's what it takes. Carl?"

On cue, the bigger man stepped forward.

"I used to play soccer," Doc said, as if he'd just remembered this fact.

This caused the big man to pause for moment, amusement playing on his lips. "And I used to play tackle for the San Diego Chargers before I joined the military," he said. "What's that got to do with anything? I got news for you, bubba, it's going to take more than fancy footwork to escape the shit storm that's about to rain down on you. When I get through with you, you'll be lucky to remember your own name let alone anything else. I'm gonna break you in half."

"Let's just get on with this so we can go home," the one called D'Angelo said in a bored tone of voice.

The man drew quickly nearer, accelerating like a sprinter. He threw a haymaker that Doc easily ducked. The big man's momentum carried him past Doc who pummeled him in the ribs with a quick right-left combination before raking the man's feet out from under him with his heels. The man went down on his belly in a spray of gravel, like a seaplane landing on a pebble-strewn beach.

Carl shook his head and pushed himself slowly off the ground, plucking 3/4 inch pieces of granite off his face and hands as he did so. Beet-red, he lunged at Doc again, trying to grab him in a wrestler's hold, but found himself holding only thin air. Somehow Doc was suddenly behind the man. He pushed him hard with the soul of his boot, sending him careening headfirst into the side of the Packard. His head left a dent in the rear door of the classic car the size of a dodge ball. It was going to take some work to fix, Doc couldn't help but observe. The big guy managed to draw his head out of the dent in the door panel and rotated into a sitting position against the car before he lost consciousness altogether, his head lolling to the side.

The man named Pete D'Angelo watched the display dispassionately from behind his shades. "Hard to find good help these days," he remarked.

"Besides the soccer, I once boxed for the Olympic team," Doc said. "Perhaps I should have mentioned that."

The smaller man ignored him. "Once again the old saying that if you want to have things done right you have to do them yourself applies. I was doin' you a favor by having Carl have the first go at you."

He looked genuinely regretful as he turned his full attention on Doc. There was something preternaturally calm about the man. He exuded all the charm of a cobra about to strike. Unexpectedly, D'Angelo poked Doc in the chest with his forefinger.

It felt like a stiletto sliding in between his ribs. Doc gasped. His legs turned to jelly under him before he even registered what had happened. It was all he could do to catch himself in the last second before he went down. He gazed warily down at the front of his shirt. But the puncture wound he was certain he would find there, was nowhere to be seen. Shirt and chest were intact. However, the searing pain he continued to experience belied what he was seeing.

D'Angelo, meanwhile, was on to other things. Having dismissed Doc as any kind of threat, he was busy coaxing his much larger companion to his feet. He managed to get him into the back seat of the Packard with a steady barrage of taunts and insults before he went on to the front of the car. He slipped behind the wheel, as small as a child as he peered over the dash, and turned on the ignition. Tires spinning, the Packard accelerated backwards toward Doc, stopping just shy of hitting him. Then D'Angelo dropped the column shift into first gear, and the old car fishtailed toward the street.

Doc was left checking and rechecking the front of his jacket and shirt in mystification. He couldn't have been more certain he'd been stabbed. And yet there was no physical evidence to support this. He broke into a cold sweat at the prospect that someone could wield that kind of power. It contradicted everything he believed was possible.

He turned and started back toward the beckoning lights of the bar, bewildered and distraught at what had just occurred and the realization that he knew less than ever about what had happened to Willy and why.

Chapter 10

"Beefy round-eye hunk look pale," Lucy remarked, her brow furrowed. "Require special tonic."

Doc nodded mutely. He had re-entered the restaurant, distracted, still inspecting himself compulsively for the puncture wound he was convinced was there, but couldn't seem to find.

"I'll have Martha and Eduardo close up," she continued in perfect English, handing Doc a brandy. Doc downed it without a word.

"Why don't you and I go for a stroll under the stars? You look like you could use a little fresh air. How about it, big boy?"

Doc allowed himself to be led out the back door, across the rear of the now empty parking lot and down a narrow dirt path which brought them out on the beach, deserted at this hour. The only lights on in Angels' Keep were those that lit the harbor and the streets that converged on it. The businesses there were dark, having closed hours before.

They set out south along the darkened arc of the bay. The wind seemed to have shifted, and a mild breeze blew steadily from inland, blowing the fog back out to sea. Small waves lapped against the sand, the ocean unusually calm. The southern sweep of the bay terminated in the glittering lights of Seaside and Monterey, and at the southernmost point, Pacific Grove. The night was so perfect, so peaceful, it was hard for Doc to reconcile it with all that had happened that day.

"How are things going with the little runaway?"

"Callie is fine. She loves it here."

"She doesn't know you're not her real father?"

Doc shook his head. "I did not have the heart to tell her. She seemed so … hopeful when she arrived. I could not immediately dash those hopes."

Lucy nodded. "How much longer does she have before she has to go home?"

"The camp she is supposed to be attending in Big Sur continues for another week. Then she will have to return to her aunt's in Pacifica. After that she flies back to Detroit. I am thinking of telling her she must go on to Big Sur tomorrow. I do not condone the deception she has undertaken, claiming to be in Big Sur while she is in actuality in Angels' Keep."

They walked on silence for a spell.

"On the other hand," Lucy said. "Didn't you ever do something like that when you were young?"

"I hitchhiked to a rock festival on the Isle of Wight when I was sixteen," Doc said. "I told my parents I was visiting a sick friend near Basel. I was gone for four days."

"That's major!" said Lucy enthusiastically.

"The memory is still one of the highlights of my young adulthood," Doc confessed.

"Listen," said Lucy. "Her parents are on a second honeymoon in Paris. She's in California. As long as they're getting regular updates from auntie, they're not going to be worrying about her. California is like Mayberry compared to Detroit. Maybe there's no harm in letting her stay a few more days."

"I am not entirely convinced," said Doc. "I will give her another day or two here. Then I will pack her off to Big Sur on the bus. She will arrive at the campground in an hour, meaning she will still have a few days time to spend there. That way at least she'll be able to say she was there and not be lying completely."

"Your call," said Lucy.

They continued to walk south along the sand.

"You want to talk about what happened just now. Back in the parking lot?"

Doc ran a hand over the black stubble on his cheeks and then over the equally short black stubble on his head. He was a little self-conscious about his receding hairline and so elected to keep his follicles trimmed close.

"It was the bastards who killed Willy," he said with uncharacteristic vehemence. "I am certain of it."

"My god. Tell me what happened!"

"There was a big ugly fellow. And a small ugly one. Contrary to the dictates of logic, the small one was by far the more dangerous of the two." Doc could still not wrap his mind around what had been done to him.

"What did they have to say for themselves?"

"While they didn't actually admit to killing Willy, they didn't deny it either. They were almost cavalier about the whole business. Cocky. Real gangsters. But they were worried about something."

"The law?"

Doc thought about this a moment and shook his head. "That would seem reasonable. But somehow I don't think so. It was more like they were worried about news of my knowing about the murder getting back to their bosses, or whoever hired them. I do not think they were acting on their own behalf. I believe they are hired guns. And somehow my poking around in what might otherwise be the perfect crime might, I don't know, cause them to lose face or something. Spoil their reputation, perhaps."

"Wow. If that's true, you'd better watch yourself. Maybe you are a loose end to them. I don't want anything to happen to you. Do you know how hard it is to find a decent blues guitarist in this town? You'd be very inconvenient to replace."

Doc couldn't help but smile. He scratched his jaw.

"Did you have a sense of who might be pulling the strings, then?" Lucy pressed.

"No. But I have difficulty imagining it is anybody local. There is nobody here I can think of who could have staged something like this, not to mention wanting to do it in the first place."

"You're thinking organized crime, maybe?

Doc shrugged. "Almost certainly someone from out of town."

"My god," said Lucy, wide-eyed. "The mob. In Angels' Keep!"

Chapter 11

Helga, the name tag read. She had plain features, a stocky build and platinum hair worn short. She was Jesus "Jerry" Garcia's personal assistant. "Please take a seat Mr. St. Michel," she said neutrally. "The mayor will see you shortly."

Doc sat on the upholstered bench that ran along the base of the floor-to-ceiling windows that looked out on the parking lot, the only occupant of the reception room. There were half a dozen cars parked on the asphalt outside, mostly innocuous late model pickups and SUVs. Doc's chromed and gleaming sky blue Harley looked like something that had transported down from a space ship in comparison.

The door opened and Mayor Garcia appeared. At 5' 5" he was considerably shorter in real life than his campaign posters might have led one to believe. Bushy-bearded and paunched he looked like a three-quarter size version of his namesake, the Grateful Dead guitarist. Unlike the late guitarist however, his hair was plastered in place to the point where a good thwack with a mallet might have cracked it. One never knew when the cameras might be rolling.

"Doc!" he said, with apparent pleasure. "Come in, come in."

Doc rose, one-handing his helmet, and strode across the reception area. He shook the proffered hand automatically, unable to return the smile the mayor always had at the ready for any potential voter who might enter his sanctum.

"To what do I owe the honor of this visit?" Garcia asked, going around a desk the size of an aircraft carrier and taking a seat. Doc had once overhauled a 50s Fender Tweed Deluxe amplifier for the mayor, and this seemed to have cemented their friendship forever in the latter's mind. Doc knew enough not to place too much stock in the politician's conviviality, however. He had no doubt that anyone of voting age was a friend of the mayor's.

Doc cut to the chase. "I came to ask you if you might have any new information in the Willy Rasp case."

"Willy Rasp," said the mayor thoughtfully, as if trying to place the name. "The owner of that antique shop on First Street."

Doc nodded encouragement, believing he was finally getting somewhere. He was met instead with uncomprehending silence. "What about Mr. Rasp?" the mayor asked.

"He was gunned down in his shop yesterday morning," Doc declared, barely able to believe the words himself as they issued from his mouth.

Garcia stared at Doc, uncharacteristically speechless.

"You are saying you have no knowledge of this?" Doc's disappointment was palpable. It was clear no one in the mayor's police department had thought enough of his claims to mention Willy's demise to their boss.

"I'm sure I would have been notified of something that serious," the mayor said dubiously. "Are you sure about this?"

"I was there when Willy died."

"Why haven't I heard about it?"

"I filed a report with your department yesterday. Your officers came to investigate the scene of the crime. They claimed they could not find enough evidence of foul play to open a homicide investigation. In the meantime Willy is gone, disappeared from the face of the earth. I was hoping some new information might have turned up by now."

"Well, I'm sorry to disappoint you, Doc. If anything had surfaced to indicate a crime had been committed, I would have gotten word of it."

He lapsed into silence, mulling over Doc's claim about Willy Rasp's demise.

"Can anyone else corroborate any of this?" asked the mayor.

"I am the only eyewitness," Doc said. "As such, I feel it my responsibility to continue looking into the matter."

"Do you know how many murders have been committed in Angels' Keep since they started keeping records a hundred and some years ago?" the mayor asked.

Doc shook his head.

"Zip," said the mayor. "Not one. Zilch. I don't think we've had so much as a mugging in this town since I moved over here from Salinas twenty years ago. It's a safe place. That's one of the reasons folks like to live here."

Doc scratched the stubble along his jaw and then ran a hand over the stubble on his head, a sure indication to anyone who knew Doc that he was flustered, frustrated or otherwise flummoxed. It seemed the mayor was being straight with him. Doc had no reason to suspect otherwise. "Listen," he said finally. "I am not interested in wasting your time, Mr. Mayor. I am as certain that Willy was murdered yesterday morning as I am that we are here right now having this conversation."

"I know you to be an honest man, Doc, a good citizen and a damn fine guitarist. I believe *you* believe you saw what you say you saw. But without further corroboration that a crime has been committed, my hands are tied."

Doc pushed himself reluctantly up from his chair.

"Hold on a minute," Mayor Jesus "Jerry" Garcia said, a look of panic crossing his face. He hated to let a potential voter go away empty-handed. This was quickly replaced by something of the woeful expression that his *other* namesake had in the religious iconography. "If it'll put your mind at rest, I'll put in a call to one of the forensics people in Seaside. Maybe I can get them to send someone up here to go over Willy's place one more time, just to be sure. I can't promise a different result if my team has already been over the scene. But I'll do it if it'll put your mind at ease."

Doc thought for a minute and shook his head. "There is no need," he said. "If there had been something to find at Granny's, your people would have found it."

He thought about mentioning his encounter with D'Angelo and his "associate" and their conversation last night, but thought the better of it. It would just be his word again. He resolved to wait until he was able to produce some solid proof of his claims before he troubled the mayor and his staff again. He needed to retain some credibility here. It would come in handy when he eventually found something of merit.

Chapter 12

"He seemed sincere."

"He's a politician for god's sake!" Callie said. "He does sincerity for a living. Doesn't mean he's telling the truth."

"How did you become so jaded so young?"

"I've been on the internet since I was 3. Santa Claus and the Easter Bunny never stood a chance."

Doc looked at her for a long moment. "Don't you think your aunt is worried about you by now?"

"I've got it covered," said Callie. "I've been texting her every day. Believe me. She's fine." She looked at Doc a moment. "And *you* don't have to worry either. I wouldn't ever tell anyone I was here. Even if they found out I wasn't at camp for whatever reason and waterboarded me. My lips are sealed." She made a zipping motion across her mouth with her fingers. "This is my business, nobody else's."

"I am sorry," Doc said, softening his tone. "I didn't mean to sound like I was questioning you. It's just that ..."

"I get it, alright?" Callie said. Why did adults have to fret over every little thing? It could be really tedious. "Have a little faith."

Doc shrugged. He bent over his beat up Telecaster and strummed a few chords. Unamplified, the sound was quickly swallowed up in the wheelhouse of the tug.

"Why do you insist on playing a guitar that looks like you found it in a rain ditch when you've got all those fine axes downstairs?"

"This is an original '52 Telecaster." Doc said.

"It looks original," said Callie dryly. "It even has the tire marks from the truck that ran over it. See? Here. And here." She pointed carefully at areas on the guitar body where the original varnish had rubbed off leaving the underlying wood blackened from years of direct exposure to the elements. Where the original blonde finish remained intact it was feathered with hairline cracks.

"I would happily choose this guitar over any offering I have downstairs. It has character. It has seen many miles and much playing. The important things are that the neck is straight and the electronics are up to par." He glanced down the length of the neck from the head stock to illustrate and then handed the guitar to Callie, who mimicked him dubiously.

"Unh, hunh," she said, gazing down the neck.

"You are humoring me," Doc stated. "I apologize. Obviously this is something I am very passionate about and which you perhaps find less interesting."

"No, no. I get it. I really do," Callie said, suddenly serious. "It's, like, vintage. And vintage means it has a certain cachet. It's the same with couture. It's easy to tell the real thing, the original, from a copy if you've got them side by side. It's about the materials used. And the dyes. And the quality of the stitching. Those things can't be faked."

"I am impressed," Doc said.

"I've always been into in style," Callie confessed somewhat self-consciously.

To Doc her interest was obvious in the care she took with her "look" from one day to the next. She was always coming up with something unexpected. Today she had on a short canary yellow sweater with small black duck silhouettes all over it, worn over a forest green tunic that came to her knees. Tartan plaid kneesocks rose out of her Doc Martens. Her mohawk haircut was covered by a red beret resting at a jaunty angle on her head. The shaved sides of her head were exposed, giving the impression she was bald under the hat. Like a chemo patient, Doc couldn't help but thinking. He quickly dismissed the notion.

"I love the old stuff," she continued. "Especially from the seventies and the eighties. It's what I look for when I go shopping."

"You shop the secondhand stores?"

"Where else?" she said. "Good luck finding this stuff off the rack at Macy's."

"You know," said Doc, getting into the spirit of the conversation, "it used to be that you could pick up a guitar like this in a pawn shop for a hundred bucks, if you were lucky. But those days are long gone. Believe it or not, this guitar would fetch many thousands of dollars on the market today."

"I totally believe it."

"Have you thought about fashion design as a profession?"

"Hey, I'm just kid, remember? I'm too young to think in terms of 'profession.'"

"You are quite correct" said Doc. "I apologize. It is important not to grow up too fast. I feel I missed much of my youth simply because I had a certain facility with a soccer ball."

"Hey, I'm just pulling your leg. Lighten up a little. In fact, I have thought about it. You'd better believe it."

Chapter 13

"So you were, like, a soccer star or somethin'?"

"I suppose so. A rising star, but only as an amateur. As I continued to grow, brawling became more my thing. I made the Olympic team as a boxer for Germany in '84."

"Wow. A pugilist. That's pretty hardcore. Were you thinking of making a career out of it?"

"I considered it--before I was conscripted into the Bundeswehr, the German military. When I came out a couple of years later, my interests had changed."

"Yeah? How so?"

"In the service it was discovered I had an affinity for electronics. I was put in a training program, and the next thing I knew I was solving equipment problems for the army, mostly in the communications division. I found I rather enjoyed it—both the technical and the theoretical aspects. When it came time to leave the army, I decided to enroll at the university. When I graduated I got a scholarship to study at UC Berkeley. After I completed my degree, I was recruited by a startup in Silicon Valley doing essentially what I had done in the military: troubleshooting hardware problems. I did that for several years. I eventually applied for citizenship and became a US citizen."

"So where did playing music come in?"

"I think I inherited my interest in music from my father. He didn't play himself, but he had a vast record collection and very eclectic tastes in music. He listened to everything from bluegrass to Stockhausen. He had discovered blues music in Paris clubs as a student there in the fifties. A fascination with Chicago-style electric blues rubbed off on me, I suppose. I started playing in gymnasium—your equivalent of high school—and picked it up again after my military service was over. By the time I got to Berkeley, I was good enough to audition with a few bands there. I played everything from Top Forty to metal. I eventually crossed paths with the members of a rock-a-billy outfit who were up-and-coming on the local scene."

"The Real Gone Cats," Callie said. "I know all about it."

"When they found themselves without the services of a guitarist some time later, they remembered me. Before I knew it, I was playing rock-a-billy in clubs all over the state."

"That's when you met my mom," Callie said.

"Yes, I suppose so."

"Passing ships in the night."

Doc shrugged self-consciously.

"So what happened next?"

"I played with the "Cats" for several years, even as I continued to work in Silicon Valley. Then one day it was over. Just like that. I left the band and my job about the same time. My finances were in decent shape. I had done nothing but work and save for years, playing guitar all the while most nights. I had a sizable amount of money accumulated. Or so I thought at the time. I decided to move here."

"How old were you?"

"This was just at the end of the nineties. I was in my mid-thirties."

Callie looked around the cabin. "Let me guess. The money didn't last as long as you hoped," she said.

"You are absolutely correct in that assessment," said Doc, with a dry laugh. "The tech bubble burst shortly thereafter. As a consequence, I was suddenly significantly less rich. I, like many of my colleagues, was left high and dry."

"Literally, I'd say," Callie said indicating her surroundings with a flourish. "OK. So far so good. Why Angels' Keep?"

"I don't know, really. It was an impulse, a whim more than anything. I figured I could live anywhere I wanted to with what I had at the time, and this was the place I chose. I had admired the town from the highway on the many occasions I had passed by on the way to and from gigs along the Monterey Bay. I felt drawn to the area."

"I'm with you on that," Callie said. "It's like living in a postcard here. You've got it all--the view, the ocean, the climate. What's not to like? S'long as you don't mind neighbors gettin' offed now and again."

Doc frowned at her.

Callie grinned back mischievously. "Hey, this place has nothing on Motown. People get killed there 24/7. You were saying?"

Doc was momentarily at a loss. "I have everything I need here," he said, picking up his train of thought once again. "I own my own place free and clear, such as it is. I run a small but respectable business. I have my Harley, that Telecaster you are holding, and a place to play most nights of the week within easy walking distance. Not to mention the affections of the proprietress of said venue. What more could I ask for?"

"You really like Lucy, don't you," said Callie.

"Of course," said Doc. He was hoping Callie wasn't wishing the impossible: that he and her mom might one day get back together again. That simply was not going to happen in this lifetime.

"Yeah," said Callie. "I like her too."

Chapter 14

The store closest to Granny's was just past the lot that Doc's boat occupied. The Treasure Chest was a potpourri and souvenir shop which also sold a few antiques and some vintage wear. Bunny Raft, the store's proprietor, was on the phone behind the counter when Doc entered the shop. Where Willy's store was built like a shotgun shack—long, narrow and claustrophobic. This store was short and wide. The rough natural pine paneling and the large windows that looked out onto the roadway gave the shop a sunny, welcoming feeling.

"And what can I do for you, Doc?" Bunny asked, finally free of the phone. She was in her forties, her hair dyed a flaming red. Her demeanor toward Doc had always been pleasant. But she was reputed to have a temper to match her selection of hair color on occasion.

"Yes," said Doc, clearing his throat. "Perhaps you have heard about what happened to Willy Rasp?"

"My god, I heard!" exclaimed Bunny. "But I didn't want to believe it. Is it true?"

"I am afraid so," Doc said gravely. "I was the one who found him."

"My god!" repeated Bunny. "Shot dead in his own store. Imagine that! Why in the world would anyone shoot Willy?"

"Unfortunately I have no answer to that question," Doc said. "But I am doing my best to find out. That is why I am here."

Bunny put a hand to her mouth, her eyes widening. "I wonder if I should be thinking about beefing up my security. I mean if something like that can happen just down the street …"

"I am convinced there is a reason for what happened to Willy," Doc said, attempting to placate the woman. "It was not a random event. Nor was it a robbery. From all indications it seems to have been something personal. I believe you need not worry about suffering a similar fate." Doc sounded more confident of this than he was. In fact, he wasn't sure of anything at this point.

"What do the police say?"

"Very little thus far, I'm afraid. As far as they are concerned it is simply a missing persons case. They have not been able to locate a body, and thus cannot confirm that a crime has been committed. Until they do, or until a proscribed amount of time has elapsed, they cannot even consider Willy deceased. In the meantime, I seem to be the only witness. I thus feel a responsibility to do what I can to determine what happened to him and why."

"How can I be of help?"

"I must ask you if you saw anything out of the ordinary two mornings ago. Around 10 a.m."

"Did I see or hear anything? Let me think." Bunny wrinkled her forehead as if thinking was an unfamiliar activity. "Well, I was on the phone," she said, reconstructing the scene in her mind. "I did see some cars and people out in the street in front of Granny's. I put the phone down for a minute and went over to the window to look."

"And?"

"I saw a white panel truck. And another car. Out in front of Willy's shop."

Doc asked himself the question he had been asking since the local cops had investigated the crime scene. How could D'Angelo have succeeded in killing Rasp without leaving the slightest bit of evidence? It didn't seem possible that all trace of the crime could have been so thoroughly expunged. "Did you notice anything else?"

"I saw you down there, too, talking to some guy dressed like Sergeant Friday. From that old TV series?"

"Dragnet," Doc supplied automatically.

"I remember wondering what the heck was going on. I couldn't decide if they were filming down there or if something had actually happened that had brought some big city cops to Angels' Keep."

"You didn't hear anything that sounded like shots?"

"Shots? Nope. I saw the cars and the people milling around at the other end of the street. That was all. Later I overheard a customer in the store saying that Willy had been killed."

"You didn't see another car. A dark blue car. A classic, well-maintained?"

"No. No, I didn't," she said.

"What did you do next, if I may ask?"

"I went back to my phone call. When I got off the phone, the street was empty. It was as if nothing had happened."

"Do you remember anything else?"

"No. I'm sorry." She paused a moment and brightened. "You might try Larry."

She was referring to Larry Conner, the photographer who had a small gallery farther up the street, adjacent to the Fish Tank. It also had a direct line of sight to Granny's.

"Yes," Doc said. "That is an excellent suggestion."

"I'm real sorry about Willy," Bunny said. "Folks make out like we had some kind of feud going because we both sold antiques and vintage clothing. But there was no truth to that. We had different clienteles. I catered more to the tourists. And he was more into the antiques side of things. We were never in direct competition."

"I understand," said Doc. "Thank you for your help."

Larry Conner was sitting outside his shop drinking a large coffee. "Mornin' Doc," he said.

"And a fine day to you as well, Larry," Doc replied courteously. "How are things with you?"

"Slow," Larry replied. "But what can you expect? It's the off-season, right? Business will pick up around Easter. It usually does. What else is new, eh?"

Doc nodded sympathetically."

"So what do you need, Doc? You want a print to hang on your wall? I just got some vintage concert posters that might interest you. A Muddy Waters. And a Sonny Terry, Brownie McGee."

"It is tempting," Doc replied truthfully. "Unfortunately wall space is currently very limited in my domicile. There is another matter I wish to speak with you about. Have you heard about what happened to Willy down the street?"

"Wild Bill? Who hasn't?" Larry said. "It's outrageous. It's unthinkable that something like that could happen around here. It's bad enough business is what it is without having shop owners getting picked off. What's that about?"

"You did not happened to see or hear anything down around Willy's place, late morning, two days ago?"

Larry thought it over. "I was out back watching shore birds from the deck around the time it happened. I heard some sort of commotion at Willy's end of the street."

"Shots?"

"No. Just an unusual amount of traffic for a mid-week morning."

Doc nodded for him to go on.

"I made it out to the street in time to see a couple of cars disappear around the corner, heading toward the main highway."

"What kind of cars?"

"There was a late model car, beige. Like one of those unmarked cop cars."

"A Crown Victoria."

"Yes, that's it. I guess they think they look inconspicuous in those things. But hello? Who else but the cops buys those things? Do you know anyone who drives a Crown Vic who isn't a cop?"

"You have a point," said Doc. "And in this case it was a cop. Or someone claiming to be one. Did you observe anything else?"

"Well, there was the panel truck that looked like an ambulance, except that it didn't have any markings either, which struck me as odd. I had my binoculars with me from bird-watching, so I honed in on it as it was driving away."

"Did you happen to see the license plate number?"

"Yeah, I did. That was even stranger. Ambulances don't usually have personalized plates."

"A personalized plate," repeated Doc, rubbing his jaw. "Were you able to make out what it said, by chance?"

"4EXPORT. With the numeral four."

"For export?"

"Weird, hunh?" Larry said. "Somebody at the county hospital has a strange sense of humor, you ask me. Must come from working around stiffs all the time."

Chapter 15

"What you think, big boy?" Lucy asked Doc. He had ducked into the bar after talking to Larry the photographer and had brought her up to speed. Doc's eyes were still adjusting to the marginal lighting after the glaring sun. There were a couple of regulars at the bar busy hoisting tap-drawn Bud Lites, getting a jump on the weekend. Being from Germany, Doc was of the opinion that beer produced for mass consumption in the States was basically beer flavored soda. Even so, it appeared the diminished alcohol content and flaccid flavor of the brew were insufficient to discourage American beer drinkers, even with the addition of several excellent craft brews from the surrounding area to the beer roster. Aside from these early drinkers, the place was as dead as it usually was on a weekday afternoon.

"So," said Lucy. "We still don't have any idea why Willy was killed and why his body was snatched."

"No," Doc replied. "But as of last night we do have a pair of suspects."

"The guys you tangled with in the parking lot."

"Pete D'Angelo and his sidekick, Carl. We just need to find a way to connect them with the murder. If they remain as cocky as they were last night, perhaps they will slip up. I must make sure I am there when they do."

"After what happened last night, I don't want you going anywhere near those creeps, especially that evil little mannequin," Lucy said emphatically. "It's clear he knows some funky ass acupressure."

"I wish I knew of some other way," Doc said thoughtfully.

"Why do you think they went to such pains to make Willy disappear?"

"Your guess is as good as mine. But if the charade was a means to insure they got away with murder, then I would say it worked. At least so far. How or why it was necessary to go to all that trouble, I cannot begin to fathom."

"And the mayor wasn't any help."

"Apparently there was no news. In fact, the mayor did not appear to know anything about the murder. His police department had not seen fit to notify him of my claims. He did seem sincere enough in his desire to help, however."

"He's up for re-election this fall. That guy who owns the army surplus store wants his job."

Doc rubbed the stubble on his chin. "It was very odd going into the store with Garcia's crew. It was as if nothing had ever happened there. It was uncanny."

"Conspiracy take on ominous proportion," proclaimed Lucy with Charlie Chan-like sagacity.

"So what big boy do now?"

"I guess I have to keep asking around to see if I can find a witness to what happened. And to keep an eye out for D'Angelo. I believe he is the only one who can provide us the answers we seek."

"Fledgling, though substantial, PI must promise to exercise caution," said Lucy. "Must not disappear like Wild Bill Willy. Make girlfriend vely unhappy."

Doc couldn't help but grin. "I have every intention of staying alive long enough to get to the bottom of Willy's murder," he said. "And, if I am lucky, a few years beyond."

They sat silently for a time, Doc nursing a ginger ale while Lucy kept a watchful eye on her clientele.

"Chrissie and Callie are about the same age," Lucy said finally. "It's kind of too bad your long lost 'daughter' won't be staying. Chrissie could use a friend." Chrissie was Lucy's teenage daughter. Mother and daughter had moved to Angels' Keep after the divorce from Lucy's former husband had been finalized many years before.

"You are not dismayed by Callie's appearance? You don't think she would be a bad influence?"

"You mean the neon hair, the piercings and the tattoos? Anyone could tell a mile away she's a sweet kid. A nonconformist for sure, but there's nothing wrong with that. The problems usually arise when kids try too hard to fit in."

"You are right. Her appearance is deceiving. I promised I would bring her to the club to see a show while she is here. I will let you know when."

Chapter 16

Alice Stillwater owned the last house on the block. It was a long shot, but Doc decided to interview her as well, to cover all the bases. Stillwater was arguably the oldest living resident of Angels' Keep. Her biography was well known to everyone in town. Native American on her father's side, she had gained notoriety for her paintings, which ran the gamut from dynamic, colorful and occasionally brooding abstracts to meticulously rendered portraits and landscapes. Her art studio was located in the garage next to her one bedroom cottage and was larger than the house itself. The garage was crammed to the rafters with her work--tiny, lovingly executed miniatures tucked in among massive, forceful canvases.

Doc approached the open garage door cautiously. The artist was just inside, standing on a short stool that enabled her to reach the work-in-progress on her easel, her eyes no more than six inches from the canvas. The oil painting was a detailed, hyper-realistic rendering of the beach nearby. The scene was so vibrant and lifelike that Doc had to blink twice to dispel the illusion that the tufts of grass depicted were actually moving in the breeze.

The woman herself was dressed in a full-length, coarse brown tunic. Her gray-streaked hair was tied into two braids that came to her shoulders. She had on a traditional Indian headband that sported a single feather at the back, giving her the appearance of an elder Hiawatha. On her feet she wore beaded moccasins that looked as new as if they had been stitched that morning.

Doc returned his concentration to the matter at hand. He shuffled his feet and cleared his throat noisily as he drew closer to give the artist fair warning that she wasn't alone. He didn't want to startle her and risk having her topple from her precarious perch.

Alice Stillwater turned her crinkly sun-browned face in Doc's direction and squinted at him.

"My name is Manfred," Doc informed her. "Manfred St. Michel." He had never actually met the woman, though he had heard much about her. From the quality of the work he was observing, all the praise was justified.

"What can ah do ya fer, sonny?" said the old woman, leaping off the stool with surprising agility. She seemed to be playing up the Native American part of her heritage with her attire, but she spoke like a prairie cowpoke from the nineteenth century.

"I own the guitar repair shop down the street," Doc explained.

"The boat. I seen it," the woman said tersely, spitting a long stream of tobacco juice onto the weeds at her feet. "Hey, you want some chaw?" She pulled out a tin of Old Abe chewing tobacco and offered it to him.

"Ah, no thank you," said Doc uncertainly. "I do not partake."

"Suit yerself," said the old woman, and the can quickly disappeared into the folds of her dress from whence it had come. "The stuff relaxes me. Helps me concentrate when I'm up on the stool. My balance ain't what it use to be."

"I am sorry to hear it," said Doc, not sure what else to say. "Your work is most impressive."

"Same old, same old," said the woman. "Another day, another canvas. Been doin' this so long, there's no telling what might happen if ah quit. The planet would probally jump orbit and go bouncin' 'round the galaxy like a pinball." She thought this hilarious.

"Alrighty then, buckeroo. Out with it. What brings you out here to the wild and woolly end a' town. Don't believe ah ever seen ya out this way before."

"Yes, well. You may have heard of the shooting," Doc said. "Willy Rasp? The antiques dealer?"

"Holy heavens! Now yer tellin' me folks is gettin' plugged right here in Angels' Keep? What in tarnation is the world comin' to?"

"I was hoping you may have seen or heard something a couple of mornings ago. Unfamiliar people hanging around or strange cars driving by along the street?"

"Everything's pretty unfamiliar to me these days, sonny, I gotta tell ya. Back when I started I was pritteny the only person in these parts. This used to be a quiet town, Mr. St. Michel. You could bank on that back then. Now? I hardly recognize the place. It sure as hell ain't like it used to be. Acourse, what is? Tell me what happened."

Doc told Alice Stillwater the story of Willy's demise.

"Lord take me! Now I heard it all," the woman said after he had finished. "Infamy and dastardly deeds on our doorstep! Why don't I fix us a nice cuppa tea. Got a little hooch in the cupboard I can put in there. Strictly medicinal." She actually winked at him. Doc was aghast at the rapidity with which the old woman had shifted gears.

"No. No thank you," said Doc. "I must be getting back. I am trying to piece together what happened to Willy and why."

"I wish you luck with that, I really do," the woman said. She looked directly at him for the first time. The unexpected bright blue of her eyes caught him off-guard. For the smallest moment, the old woman let her Wild West persona slip, intentionally or otherwise. Was she toying with him? If so, to what end? Willy's death was no laughing matter. He wasn't sure the woman was fully aware of the seriousness of the situation. Maybe she was starting to lose it in her dotage.

"From the look a' you, I'd say if there's anybody can get to the bottom a' this wickedness and see that justice gets served, it 'ould be you." She poked him unexpectedly in the chest, not unlike Pete D'Angelo had done. Doc flinched reflexively, but there was no pain this time. Not even a residual memory of the pain he had suffered the previous night.

She fixed him with her disconcertingly blue eyes. "You look like a man as can handle hisself. Big and strong." There was something unsettling in her appraisal of him, and he felt his cheeks burn.

"I had better go," Doc stammered. "I've taken up too much of your time already. My apologies."

"Hey, don't be a stranger," the old woman called after him with a flirtatious tone of voice. "Come back and visit Auntie Alice any ole time. You heah?"

Chapter 17

Doc stood in the wheelhouse staring out to sea. He was chewing absently on a sandwich he had thrown together as he mulled over his recent meeting with Alice Stillwater. The discrepancy between art and artist was difficult to reconcile. The powerful, masterful canvases stood in stark contrast to the homespun persona the old woman had adopted. Clearly, Lucy wasn't the only one around town who liked to role play. But an old Indian pretending to be a cowboy? What was that all about?

Callie arrived in a yellow one-piece bathing suit that looked straight out of the 1920s, straps slung over the shoulders. She had on a wide-brimmed floppy hat and fifties Cat Eye sunglasses. The variety and quantity of stuff she produced from the pack she had arrived with was staggering. She had at least four changes of clothes in there, in addition to hats, shoes, and enough cosmetics to open her own store. She had a beach towel rolled up under her arm that Doc recognized as one of his own. Not that he minded. He never made use of it himself. Though he lived near the beach, it never occurred to him to actually venture down to the water's edge and spread a towel on the sand there the way visitors to the area were inclined to do.

"Hey," she said, entering the cabin to find Doc rubbing his chin, still staring intently out the window.

"And a fine day to you," said Doc, pulling back from the view and wherever his mental musings had taken him. "What have you been up to?"

"I took a stroll down the beach," replied Callie airily. "Ran into some interesting peeps down there. You woulda loved it."

"Interesting in what way?"

"It was like walking into a time warp, I swear. It was a scene straight out of one of those beach movies. You know, from the sixties. They had this whole longboard aesthetic going on. There were woodies everywhere, beach bunnies with big hair and peroxided dudes. But you knew they weren't real surfers."

"Oh? How could you tell?"

"No one was anywhere near the water, for one thing. And they all looked pasty as the belly on a carp. Buff, yeah, but pale. Like they were a bunch of extras killing time, waiting for the cameras to roll."

"The next thing you are going to tell me is that there was a short Italian looking guy and his buxom Italian girlfriend in the center of the action."

Callie's mouth fell open. "How could you know that?"

"What? You ran into Frankie and Annette? On the beach in Angels' Keep?" Doc laughed at the absurdity of the notion.

"Frankie and Annette?"

"Forget it. It would be impossible."

"Frankie and Annette who?" Callie persisted.

"Frankie Avalon and Annette Funicello. They were the stars of the those beach movies you just mentioned."

"Oh. Yeah. Sure. I remember. I think."

"It would have been way before your time. Ancient history, as they say."

"Hey, I know more than you think. I'm the Queen of Retro, remember."

"The sixties aren't the eighties," Doc pointed out. "This was a long, long time ago. Anyway, there is simply no way. Frankie may still be drawing breath somewhere on the east coast, but Annette is gone now these past few years. MS, I believe."

"How could you even know that?

"I was a fan," Doc confessed. "Once."

"Of those beach movies? You? I don't believe it."

Doc shrugged noncommittally. "You must imagine it from the perspective of a boy growing up in Germany in the seventies. The lifestyle depicted in those films was exotic to say the least. The argument could be made that they may have had a bearing on my decision to come to the West Coast in the first place."

"You are shitting me," Callie said, obviously delighted at this notion. "You are full of surprises, Manfred!"

"Language, young lady. Well. Let's just say it cannot completely be ruled out."

"I'll bet it was this Annette what's-her-name that got you hooked. Am I right?"

Doc blushed. "Funicello. Annette Funicello. She of the gravity-defying black bouffant, always perfectly lacquered into place."

"Check. Definitely one of the chicks I saw." Callie had a sly look on her face.

"It is like I said. It cannot be her. It is not possible. Unless ghosts walk among us here in Angels' Keep."

"So they're not the real deal," Callie said. "They're somebody else pretending to be this Annette … and this Frankie. So what? When was the last time you actually went down to the beach in broad daylight? You don't even know what's going on in your own backyard!"

In light of recent events, this pronouncement struck a little too close to home for comfort. Truth be told, there were too many unanswered questions about what was happening around town these days.

"You'd kick yourself if you missed this. Take my work for it. It's as retro as it gets."

"I don't know," Doc said.

"You've got lighten up a bit, Manfred. This is the perfect opportunity. Come on!" She grabbed a beefy, calloused hand and started tugging on it. "It isn't more than fifteen minutes walk away."

Doc remained as inert as a boulder.

"Please? You seriously look like you could use some diversion. This whole dead Willy thing is getting to you. You've started brooding. You've got bags under your eyes. And I hate to say it, but when was the last time you showered?"

Reluctantly, Doc let himself be dragged toward the deck and the elevator cage. They cut across the parking lot at the Fish Tank to get to the path that led down to the beach. A few more minutes walking and a semicircle of vertical longboards came into view, open toward the ocean.

"I see it, but I cannot believe it," Doc said, only partially in jest. Even from a distance the re-creation of period and place was astonishing.

"You ain't seen nothing yet, homey," Callie said gleefully.

As they pulled abreast of the boards, they came upon a group of a dozen or more kids frolicking in the sand. One was playing a pair of bongos and had a large golden, pirate-style earring dangling from one ear. Doc squinted and blinked. The tanned young man was a ringer for the young Dick Dale, the surf guitar legend who had appeared in the earliest of the Beach Party movies. Frankie and Annette were there, too, or rather their look-a-likes. Vintage station wagons from the forties and fifties gleamed back among the dunes.

Doc angled up the beach to where the Frankie character was seated off to one side, chatting up a couple of girls wearing brightly colored one piece bathing suits.

Doc looked at Callie's own one-piece and said, "You are certainly appropriately costumed for the occasion. Except for the hair, perhaps. But as long as you wear the hat …"

Callie elbowed him in the ribs.

Doc cleared his throat, and asked the Frankie character, "Are you movie people? Is this a historical re-enactment you are staging here?"

"Dig this guy," the Frankie character said aside to the girls with him. "Historical re-enactment. Are you putting us down, man?" It was hard to tell if he was serious.

"No, no, not at all. On the contrary. I am complimenting you on the authenticity of what you have created here. It is obvious all this was done with a great deal of forethought and attention to detail."

"You're blowin' smoke, man," Frankie said casually. "We make the scene here every summer to let off steam. That's all. Nobody's re-enacting nothin'. Been doin' it for years."

"Frankie" looked Doc over. "What are you? Some kind of hodad?"

"No one has ever addressed me as a hodad before," said Doc.

"You know, a greaser, man. A biker. You ride a Harley hog, I'll bet."

"You are quite correct in that assumption," said Doc, with amusement. "I guess in your world that would certainly qualify me as a hodad. I am guilty as charged."

"Hey, it's no big deal, man. We ain't prejudiced. Everybody's welcome here, long as they don't kick sand. You dig? Surfers, hodads, hotdoggers, hotrodders, gremmies, geeks, freaks, whatever. Make yourself at home, man."

"Annette" sauntered toward them, ubiquitous smile in place. "Can I get you folks a soda?" she asked Doc and Callie politely.

My god but she looks like the real thing, thought Doc. "If it is not too much trouble," he managed. He was a little star struck, despite being well aware this wasn't the real former Mouseketeer. This young woman was in her early twenties and "Frankie" not much older. They had had their moment in popular culture decades ago. Before his time even. His first exposure to them had been on VHS.

"Orange Crush OK?" she called over her shoulder as she sashayed over to the cooler.

Doc's eyes tracked her movements involuntarily as she strode up the beach in her black one-piece. He felt a scorpion-like pinch on his arm. He looked down at his arm and then over at Callie. "Hey!" he said.

"Mind your manners, Mr. Hodad," Callie said in a low voice. "Put those eyeballs back in your head."

"My eyeballs are firmly in place," said Doc, a mite defensively. "They are not going anywhere."

After a moment he relaxed and added. "You were quite correct earlier. I have never observed anything like this here before. It is certainly very impressive. These kids have done a terrific job."

The vintage cars brought another issue to mind. He turned to "Frankie" and said, "Have you by chance seen a …" He looked to Callie for help.

It took her a split second to catch on. "A midnight blue '48 Packard," she said, supplying the details. "Original, not custom."

"Yeah," said "Frankie," thinking it over. "Yeah, I have. Seems I remember seeing some wheels like that cruisin' the waterfront a while back. Hey, Bear!"

A tall, broad-shouldered man in his late twenties with a beige fishing hat on his head rose from the sand behind the bongo player.

"'48 Packard," Frankie shouted over to him. "You remember where we saw it?"

The big guy nodded his head slowly. "Out on the service road, a couple hours ago. Who wants to know?"

Frankie turned back to the newcomers.

"Manfred. And this is Callie."

"Cool," said Bear, coming over to join them. "Yeah, there was a Packard. Dark windows. Low and sleek. Almost like they were casin' the joint, now's I think about it."

"I would strongly urge you to avoid that car and the people in it." Doc told him. "I cannot stress that enough. They are extremely dangerous."

"I'm hip, man," said Bear. "There was a vibe comin' off that car. Reminded me of a shark patrolling shallow water. Ya dig?"

Doc nodded. He rose suddenly from the sand. "It is time we got going," he said.

He turned to the Frankie character. He couldn't get over the degree to which this guy and the others looked like their sixties counterparts. Having seen the movies on more than one occasion, he was in awe of the effort expended here in re-creating a particular moment in time. It wasn't difficult to guess at the motivation for it. It was, more than likely, a desire to reconnect with a simpler, more innocent time.

"Annette" arrived with the sodas at that moment. "Hey, you guys leaving so soon?" She seemed genuinely disappointed. "Here, take the drinks with you. Two for the road." She handed them the frosty bottles of soda. "Maybe we'll catch you another time."

"Frankie" seemed to remember something. He pulled a business card out of his T-shirt pocket. "Take this," he said. "Give us a buzz if you ever find yourself in our neck of the woods. You never know."

Doc glanced at the card before pocketing it. The words "Sal's Automotive" were printed on it in bold type. Under that was typed "custom auto repair." At the bottom of the card was a telephone number with a 714 area code. Near Los Angeles, Doc recalled.

"Thanks," he said. "I am amazed at what you have put together here."

"Glad you dig it, man," the Frankie character said.

"Told you," Callie whispered, as they walked back along the sand toward the harbor and civilization.

"I guess where popular culture is concerned, nothing ever really dies in California." Doc muttered in mystification.

Chapter 18

"I haven't seen a big ole smile like that on you in days," Callie remarked. "Fess up. You like having me around."

"Unh-hunh," said Doc noncommittally. "Did you call your aunt?"

Callie sighed. "Yup. Everything's cool."

"She's not worrying about you?"

"Hunh-unh. My cover's secure."

Doc looked at her skeptically.

"What?"

"Is everything alright for you at home. Back in Detroit?"

"Sure."

"How is school?"

"Straight 'A's so far," Callie said, not without a certain pride. "A couple of colleges already have their eyes on me for scholarships and all that. But that's still a long ways off."

"It must be nice."

"Hey, it's no big deal. I'm not even sure it's what I want anyway. I'd like to do something in fashion when I graduate"

"No one is saying you cannot do both. Most jobs require a degree to get in the door these days."

"Whatever," Callie said, exasperated. "You don't know how stifling school can be. It's boring beyond belief."

"What? You do not believe I was young once?"

"Things were different then than they are now"

"You mean at the dawn of the civilization? You believe I am a fossil."

"Not a fossil exactly," Callie said with mischievous smile. "More a relic." She grew more serious. "But that's not an insult. I can relate. It's not like I feel I exactly, like, belong in this time either."

"What? You think you would have liked it better in an earlier period in history? As a young black woman?"

He regretted saying it as soon as it was out of his mouth. But Callie seemed to take the statement in stride.

"Hey, I'm not sayin' I think things were better then than they are now," she said. "It was tough just being a woman back then. I have no illusions about that."

"I apologize," Doc said.

"Don't worry about it. You know, I don't think I've ever felt more at home than I have here in the last few days," she said wistfully, going to the window and gazing out. "This is a town of misfits. I fit right in."

"There are not a lot of kids your age here," Doc pointed out. "There is Lucy's daughter, Chrissie, but no one else really."

"Maybe that's what I like about it," Callie said. "I never related much to kid's my age and what they're into."

"Come on, you must be starting to miss home, just a little," said Doc.

Callie looked at him, her expression unreadable. "Chill, dude. You've got nothing to worry about. I'm not planning on crashing your scene. I'll be around a couple more days, if you don't mind. Then I'll go on to camp for what's left of my time here. After that it's back to Motown, back to school, back to the old grind." She sounded like she was fifty, not fifteen.

"I am sorry if I made it sound as if you were not welcome here. That is not the case."

She looked at him, silently appraising his sincerity for several seconds. "OK, I get it," she said finally. "You don't know how you ever got along without me. Right?" She broke into a big smile.

"Actually, yes," Doc said, relieved that she wasn't offended. "If it weren't for you I would never have met ersatz Frankie and Annette just now, for example."

"Just because I love it here," she said, "doesn't mean I've got it into my head to just hang out and not go back. There's just no way I could do it. Not to my family. Not for my own sake, even." She paused. "Gotta say I enjoy being a PI, though."

"So you are a PI now?"

"Well, you know, your sidekick."

"Ahhh. So *I* am the PI. I see."

"What else would you call what your doing, poking around, trying to solve a murder?"

"I certainly hadn't gotten as far as constructing an identity around it," Doc said with a smile. "One case does not a detective make. Not to mention that so far we have very little to show for our efforts on the one case we do have."

"You know who killed Willy."

"I suspect. I have no proof."

"But what you're doing is what PIs do, right? Asking questions. Doggedly persisting in your quest to uncover the truth at all costs, through thick and thin, rain and shine, sleet and snow ..."

"I get the idea."

"And do you see anyone else jumping in? The po po? The mayor? Is anyone else coming forward to help out? Where's the cavalry?"

Doc shrugged.

"See what I'm sayin'? It's just you and me, Humphrey."

Chapter 19

Doc had an appointment the following morning with someone he knew in the Seaside sheriff's department. They had agreed to meet at the Pelican's Perch, a popular restaurant overlooking the harbor.

Doc was first to arrive. While waiting on his acquaintance, he took the time to admire the view. The large plate glass window framed a scene full of color and movement. This was where the action was during the daytime in Angels' Keep, especially as the weekend approached. From here you could see yacht owners and their families scrubbing down their boats, untangling rigging, unfolding sails, loading coolers and generally making preparations for a day on the water. The last fishermen, whose day usually started well before sunrise, were returning with their catch, while the larger whale watching cruises were just getting underway, as flocks of gulls wheeled overhead. A slough ran inland opposite the entry to the harbor. Here kayakers plied the calm waters with their paddles while seals and sea lions sunned themselves on the jetty rocks.

A medium height, rosy-cheeked, cherub-like man in a khaki uniform approached the table. His name plaque read, Craig Foley, Deputy Sheriff.

"How's it doin', Doc," the man said, pulling out a chair at the table and squeezing his considerable bulk between the armrests.

"Good morning to you, deputy."

"You playin' tonight?" Foley asked after he had caught his breath. Walking appeared to be an exertion for the man. Doc wondered what would happen if he were ever called upon to chase a suspect.

"Of course."

Foley was what could be described as a bike and blues man. He had a vintage WWII BMW R75, complete with attached sidecar in his garage. He and Doc often talked motorcycles when they ran into one another. In addition to which Foley was a huge fan of the Beluga Blues Band and fancied himself somewhat of a player himself. He often had his blond pre-CBS Fender Vibrolux amp in the shop for tweaking and servicing.

The waitress arrived. Doc ordered the "buccaneer" breakfast, which was the works essentially--eggs, hash browns, bacon, sausage and pancakes.

"Just coffee," the deputy sheriff told the waitress. "I already ate," he explained, patting his considerable paunch.

"Sure I can't heat you up a bear claw? They're fresh," said the waitress, whose name was Flow.

"Oh hell, why not?" Foley said, with a minimal pause for deliberation.

"So what's up, Doc?" quipped the deputy when the waitress had departed. He sat back in his chair, folding his hands over his stomach and looked generally pleased with himself. "Hey, I heard somewhere you had a runaway staying at your place. Nothing illegal going on there, I hope."

"No, no. Mein Gott!" said Doc flushing. "It is the daughter of a girlfriend of mine from long ago come to visit for a few days. She is like family."

"Relax. I believe you. Had to ask. In my line of work you pretty much see it all."

"I understand." Doc was aware that deputy Craig could be obnoxious at times, but he was a fairly decent guy underneath the lawman posturing.

"So what was it you wanted to talk about?

"You heard about Willy Rasp?"

"Heard the rumor about his getting himself shot, yeah," Foley said, careful with his wording. "But from my understanding, that's all it is so far. A rumor. Just because nobody's seen him around for a while doesn't mean somebody did him in. For all anybody knows, he went to visit his brother in Minnesota for the summer."

Doc sighed. He was tired of hearing the official police response by now. "There is something else," he said. "A couple of nights ago I had an encounter with a couple of men who all but confessed to killing Willy. Tough guys I had never seen around town before."

"That so?"

"The implication was that they had been acting on behalf of a third party. Someone who was well-connected."

"Can you describe these guys?" Foley produced a small writing pad.

"One was a very odd individual, short in height, pale of complexion. Wore sunglasses even in the dead of night. He was clearly the boss. He said his name was D'Angelo. Pete D'Angelo. I would not recommend approaching him without backup should you locate him."

"That's sayin' something coming from you, Doc. Didn't you box at one time?"

"You must take my word for it, Craig, this fellow is bad news." Doc thought it prudent not to go into more detail than that. It felt like he was finally being taken seriously by a member of local law enforcement and didn't want to jeopardize that. "He had a bodyguard with him. About my size. Name of Carl."

He paused to let Foley take down the information.

"They were driving a restored late forties Packard. Dark blue."

"Can't be too many of those around," said the deputy. When he had stopped writing, he said, "Well, well. That does shed a new light on things. You got anything else?"

"I was talking to Larry Conner the photographer yesterday. He said he saw the ambulance that carried Willy's body away. He even got the license plate. He said it read, 4EXPORT, with the numeral 4."

"4EXPORT? Cute. You sure about that?"

"Larry can confirm it for you. Bunny Raft saw the ambulance, too."

"Really," said Foley, a statement more than a question. "They can both confirm an ambulance?"

"And an unmarked car. A man claiming to be a police detective interviewed me at the scene. I remember thinking at the time that something was not right."

"Description of the cop?"

"Average height and weight. Mid-thirties, probably. Brown hair. Unremarkable, except for his outfit. His suit was old-fashioned. It looked like it had been picked up at consignment shop. It was something straight out of the forties and fifties. And he had on an old style fedora. He flashed a badge, but I did not have time to study it."

Foley grew thoughtful. "A fedora? You kiddin' me? Doesn't sound like anyone from any department around here I know about. So at the very least we've got someone impersonating a police officer. There might be something about faking an emergency response vehicle, too. I'll have to look that one up."

"So you will check into this?"

"It's no sweat to see if the license plate number's legit. I'll follow up on this D'Angelo guy, too. See if there's a sheet on him."

"Will you inform me as to what you find?"

"I can see you've put some time and effort in on this, Doc, and I appreciate it. Sure, I'll keep you in the loop."

"I will make sure you are included on the guest list for tonight," said Doc, which meant the cover charge at the Fish Tank would be waived at the door. The bar generally had no cover during the week, but required a $10 entrance fee on the weekends.

"You're comping me the cover?" said the deputy, with barely concealed delight. "Mind if I bring a friend?"

"Foley plus one," said Doc.

Chapter 20

"I must speak with Pete D'Angelo again. I see no alternative," Doc was back at the tug with Callie.

"S'long as he doesn't give you the finger," said Callie dryly. "Correct me if I'm wrong, but the conversation didn't go so well the first time around. I'm not convinced a rematch is what you need."

"It was some variety of martial arts he employed, I believe. And skillfully at that," said Doc thoughtfully.

"Finger fu."

"Excuse me?"

"You know, Finger of Death," Callie said confidently. "Like in those chop socky movies?" She went into a crouch pose for his benefit, index finger raised ominously.

"It is a fighting technique I am unfamiliar with, in any event," Doc said, regarding her dubiously. "And one I must develop a counter strategy for. Just in case."

"Unh hunh," said Callie skeptically.

Doc let out some air. "They know what happened to Willy. They are our best lead."

"They're our only lead," Callie pointed out. "Unless your buddy on the force can come up with something."

"Perhaps next time I will be able to elicit something closer to a confession from D'Angelo. He acted as if he thought he was untouchable, immune to arrest. If he is careless enough, he may give us something we can act on."

"That's all well and fine, Humphrey. Just don't get too close. Pretend it's a fencing foil."

"I beg your pardon."

"His finger."

Doc grew silent. "I confess I am not exactly looking forward to our next meeting," he said.

"Sorry, buddy." Deputy Sheriff Foley's voice came from the earpiece. "The only Pete D'Angelo in the database died back in the nineties. This guy's alias was "Sneaky Pete" and he had a rap sheet as long as my arm. Everything from extortion and breaking and entering to grand theft and armed robbery. Not to mention being a suspect in several homicides. Never convicted, though. He still ended up spending about half his life inside. He was iced just before leaving prison for the last time. Says here, 1997. And there's nothing on the plates, no California license with those letters and number."

"Thanks for looking into it," said Doc.

"Either the guy you talked to doesn't have a record or he was using an alias. Maybe he ran into this "Sneaky Pete" character somewhere along the line and adopted the name. Maybe they met inside. Maybe they're related. Who knows? And the plates could be faked easily enough. But why use something so conspicuous. You'd think they'd be trying to keep a low profile. Anyway, that's all that's officially known. Wish I could give you more."

"I appreciate your trying."

"In the meantime, there's an APB out on the Packard. Like I said. There can't be many of those roaming the streets."

"Thanks, Craig," Doc said with sincerity. "And please remember what I said about those guys should you find them. You cannot be too careful."

"We'll be taking all the necessary precautions."

"Thanks again. And kindly let me know if anything else turns up."

"You got it," said Foley, a lighter note in his voice. "Catch you tonight at the Tank."

As usual on a Friday night, the Fish Tank was packed. The gig went off without a hitch. Doc still didn't feel a hundred percent, but he was getting used to playing with a percentage of his mind on other matters. Luckily, he could almost do the show in his sleep by now.

Later he and Lucy took a walk along the ocean.

"Big German cream puff distracted," she said, playing the recent emigre as it amused her no end to do. It had remained warm into the night and only now, well after midnight, did the winds start to shift onshore, bringing the scent of seaweed and saltwater with them.

"You have luck?" asked Lucy. "You want to fu ..? Rhymes with luck?"

Even in the dim light from the distant stars, she could see his face turn crimson. Doc's upbringing had been strict. Good manners, gentility and deference toward women had been drilled into him from an early age. Consequently, he had surprisingly delicate sensibilities for one so brawny. Lucy knew this well and it tickled her to tease him mercilessly.

"China girl serious," she said. After a pause to make him squirm, she said, "About the luck part."

He cleared his throat and proceeded to bring her up to date on his talks with Bunny Raft, Larry Conner, and Alice Stillwater. And on his meeting with deputy Foley.

"Dirty dealer use fake name," she said emphatically. "Slippery eel, that one."

"It would be my guess," said Doc. "But why that name in particular?"

"Maybe he long lost relative. Maybe fan of criminal. Want follow in footstep. Or could be coincidence. D'Angelo name not uncommon."

Doc was thinking and didn't say anything.

"What you do now, he-man?"

Doc sighed. "I have been thinking I must speak with this D'Angelo character again. But first, must find."

"You starting to sound like honorable Chinese girlfriend," said Lucy, surprised.

"Honorable girlfriend must be starting to rub off on round-eye," Doc said, turning his head to hide his grin.

"He evil pipsqueak," Lucy said, returning to the topic at hand. "Acupressure pack punch. Must be careful. Take care of noodle." She reached up and patted his head.

"When I find him I will do all I can to keep my noodle from harm," said Doc seriously. "I can promise you that."

Chapter 21

"It's outside. You'd better come look." Callie made the announcement from the top of the stairs, looking down into the workshop to where Doc was bunking in the belly of the tug. She was still in her long cotton nightshirt. It was early Sunday morning. Too early by several hours.

Doc rolled onto his back on the cot, shielding his eyes from the glare from above. "Outside? What is outside exactly?" he asked with a yawn.

"The Packard." The anxiety in her voice was unmistakable.

Doc blinked toward full wakefulness. His first instinct was to calm the girl. "At least we can stop looking for it. What is it doing?"

"It's just sittin' there at the curb. It's like they're waitin'."

"Well, if they are not yet storming the gates, they will have to wait a minute or two longer until I get dressed," Doc said, rising from his makeshift bed. "Close the hatch, if you would be so kind. And make sure the cage is secure. I do not wish to have anyone show up on deck before I get up there."

When Doc emerged topside a couple of minutes later clad in relaxed black jeans, his motorcycle jacket and a clean white T-shirt stretched tight across his powerful chest, the Packard was still out there, parked at the curb. The clock read 7:30. Except for around the harbor area, there was no sign of activity in town.

"Feel free to wash up and get dressed," he told Callie. "I will take it from here."

"What are you going to do?" Callie asked, hands on her hips, tapping her toes. She looked cross.

"I am going to put on some coffee," Doc replied calmly. "And then I intend to make us some bacon and eggs. How does that sound?"

"I'm not hungry," said Callie.

"Maybe later, then," said Doc in what he hoped was a reassuring voice.

"Whatchoo going to do about them?" She indicated the Packard with a toss of her head.

"After I have finished my breakfast I will go down and speak to whomever is in the car. This may be the opportunity we have been waiting for. I do not intend to waste it. Perhaps now at last we will get some answers."

"'I guess you got your wish," Callie said, softening her stance.

"All things come to he who has patience," Doc quoted.

"Don't you think you ought to call in some backup here?"

Doc thought a moment. "Chico is in town today because we have another gig tonight. But I don't want to involve him in this. He might get hurt and I could not live with that."

"*He* might get hurt?" said Callie sarcastically. "What about you? There's a psychopath out there. A murderer. And you're worried about Chico's health?"

"OK, then. There is no reason for the two of us to get our backsides presented to us, if that is how it goes," Doc said. "My hope is that I can reason with D'Angelo, if he is indeed out there, and fisticuffs will be unnecessary."

"You know this is the same guy who warned you to quit looking into Willy's death. Have you stopped looking into Willy's death? No. You really think they just want to talk?"

"That is my sincere hope," Doc said, scratching his beard stubble, the only indication of apprehension on his part. "I wish we knew how many are out in the car." There was a twinge in his chest where D'Angelo had poked him the other night. He knew that if D'Angelo, or whatever his real name was, was out there any additional muscle would be superfluous. It wouldn't much matter how many other enforcers were with him. The net result would be the same. He would be incapacitated. Or worse.

"You could call the cops, you know."

"I need to speak with those people first. With the police involved they would most likely disappear again, or if caught, clam up. I do not pose a serious threat to them, or so they may think, and that may give me an advantage in eliciting more information. This may be my only chance."

"You're just going to go out there. By yourself. You against a carload of thugs."

"I want you to promise me that you will stay out of sight. Do not go outside under any circumstances. I have locked up downstairs. If things go badly, you have my permission to call the police."

"I hope you know what you're doing," said Callie sullenly.

"I doubt they will try anything in broad daylight," said Doc.

"Tell that to Willy," said Callie.

Doc tucked in his shirt and stood. "I'll be right back," he said.

"You'd better," said Callie with a pout.

Chapter 22

With a sense of foreboding, Callie watched from the windows of the tug as Doc strode slowly toward the Packard. The doors opened as he approached. Two large men in suits exited the front doors, the driver and a bodyguard, mostly likely. Carl was conspicuously absent. But the person Doc's eyes were on was Pete D'Angelo, who stepped out of the rear curbside door. He was soon flanked by the driver and the other hulk. D'Angelo positioned himself back against the car, arm's folded, while the two enforcers stood a few feet in front of him, attack dogs straining at an invisible leash. His expression was unreadable behind his trademark aviator sunglasses.

Doc stopped about twenty feet short of the car. "To what do I owe the honor?" he asked neutrally.

"You haven't been listening to me," said D'Angelo, shaking his head slowly from side to side, regret in his voice. "Have I not made myself clear? What's it gonna take to make youse understand?"

"I believe we have been through all this before," Doc said. "If you expect me to simply dismiss what happened to Willy, you will be disappointed."

D'Angelo seemed genuinely distressed. He heaved a long sigh and said, "What if I told you it's not how it looks? Willy had to go. He knew it. We knew it. It had all been agreed upon in advance. Just because he changed his mind the last second, didn't mean he was off the hook. A deal's a deal where I come from."

"He deserved to die? That is your position? You cannot seriously expect me to accept that as a rationale."

"Do I have to spell everything out for you?" D'Angelo said, looking around. He appeared embarrassed. Uncomfortable. He muttered something that Doc couldn't hear.

"I am sorry," Doc said. "Could you repeat that?"

D'Angelo expelled a long sigh. "He neva croaked," he said quietly but clearly. "Ya satisfied? No killing. No crime. Ya follow?" D'Angelo suddenly shut up. He looked around to see if someone might have overheard this declaration. He seemed genuinely fearful. If it was an act, he should have gotten an Oscar.

Doc shook his head. "I saw him die with my own eyes."

"Forget what you think you saw. I'm tellin' you nobody was offed. In fact, just the opposite. He was bein' given a chance at life. When push comes to shove, you'd be amazed at how much that prospect freaks some people out. Dyin' ain't nuttin' compared to livin', it seems. It's enough to put 'em off their feed." He gave a dry laugh. "Right when it's time to start eatin' again. Get it?"

"You must be delusional."

"What I'm telling you is the honest truth," D'Angelo hissed. "Someone dies here, they show up somewhere else. That's how it works. Capisce? What am I doin'? I gotta be outta my fuckin' mind. I ain't supposed be talkin' about any of this to a civilian." He looked surreptitiously up and down the street. As on the day Willy died, there was no activity to be seen. "Why can't you just leave it and go about your business like a good boy? Get it through your thick skull that we're just doing our job here. We're performing a public service already."

"That is all you can say for yourself? That is rather pathetic." said Doc. "Willy is killed. Shut up and pretend it never happened. Is that it?"

"Yeah." D'Angelo said, ignoring the sarcasm in Doc's voice. "Now your gettin' the idea. Don't you understand? I'm doing you a favor here. I don't need to explain any of this shit to you. Whose fault is it if you're dense as a post?"

He looked around and dropped his voice a notch. "You may find this hard to believe," he said in confidential tone, "but I'm actually the good guy here. There's a lot at stake. More than you could ever understand. There are some things it's better not to know about. Alright? Now could you just scram so everybody can get on with their lives?"

"Except for Willy Rasp," Doc persisted. "You have as much as confessed to his murder, regardless of what convoluted reasoning you have employed to justify it to yourself. What I would like to know at this point is for whom you are working. Who hired you to kill Willy?"

"I can see this is hopeless," D'Angelo said. "I've told you too much already. Blah, blah, blah." He addressed no one in particular. "When the other guys do their job, nobody says peep. It's all pats on the back and 'great job there, bunky.' D'Angelo comes along, injects a little flare into the old routine and where's the love? What thanks does he get?"

Doc was momentarily speechless. "Perhaps you should seek professional help," he said. The man was clearly unraveling before his eyes. He was in the throws of some kind of existential crisis, fooling himself with all kinds of nonsense. Maybe the burden of guilt at what he had done was taking its toll. "You are not making a great deal of sense."

"Oh hell, what's the use?" D'Angelo said. "No one can say I didn't try." He looked upward into the low clouds that blanketed the bay that morning. When he looked back down, his tone was steely. "There's another way we can work this," he said. "It's called damage control where I come from. It's nothing against you personally, you understand. You're just a clueless mug. If this is what it's gonna take to shut you up, then so be it. You leave me no choice." He nodded his goons forward.

Doc planted his feet and bent his knees slightly. The guy on the right was half a step closer, so he would be dealt with first. Doc stepped forward, a move that caught both his antagonists by surprise. They had expected him to retreat in light of their superior numbers. Doc stepped inside the radius of the incoming right cross. He caught the bigger man full in the chest with a punch that folded him over. Then he straightened him out with an upper cut that had a lot of shoulder behind it. The big man was out, but he was still on his feet. He went wobbly and stumbled into the path of his associate, who was in the process of charging Doc, tying the latter up for a couple of seconds before he sprawled full length on the hardscrabble, senseless.

The path to Doc now clear, the other man came on like a locomotive. But Doc had already gone over the choreography of how this would play out in his head and was ready for him. He backpedaled, dancing around the man in the way that had been ingrained in him as

85

a young fighter training for the Olympics. Incoming punches found mostly empty space. A few minutes of this and the other man began to fatigue visibly, gasping for breath. Someone with his bulk would have a lot of power, but it would come at the expense of endurance.

Doc noticed the man on the ground starting to come around. Trying to keeping track of both men, caused him to lose sight of D'Angelo for the moment it took for him to slide silently up behind Doc. Doc felt an indescribable pain shoot into his back and explode in his head. It was pure reflex and that enabled him to turn around and thrust the heel of his palm at the smaller man's forehead in retaliation. Oddly, the blow left an angry red impression resembling a birthmark on D'Angelo's forehead. It must have been an optical illusion, Doc reflected later on, but it appeared as if the smaller man's head folded around the place where the blow had landed as if it were made of a pliable substance. There was a stunned look on the smaller man's face.

The next thing Doc knew, he was on his back looking up into the cold gray cloud cover.

Chapter 23

Now that he was down, Doc assumed it was pretty much all over. If he were in the ring, he'd be hearing the count right about now. But there would be no count forthcoming, no mercy shown. In a second, they'd be upon him, pummeling him with their fists and kicking him in the ribs with their steel toe boots.

Instead he heard something unexpected. Someone was yelling something incomprehensible nearby. The sounds of a scuffle came to his ears--fast, ferocious and feral--solid punches landing, grunts, groans, a car door opening and slamming shut, then two more. An engine starting.

A craggy, unshaven face straight out of the ancient mists of history intervened between Doc and the gray sky. It seemed impossibly far away. It took Doc several seconds to identify it and to realize it belonged to Eric, his homeless neighbor. The Scandinavian giant extended a hand down from on high for Doc to grab a hold of. "Hey," he said.

Doc pulled himself up into a sitting position just in time to see the Packard fishtail away from the curb with the squeal of tires and the smell of burning rubber.

"What happened?" Doc managed, trying to piece together a chronology of events leading up to that moment. He was unsuccessful in his attempt.

"Odds were stacked against you," Eric explained casually. "Thought I'd try to even them up a bit."

Doc tried to shake the cobwebs out of his head as he drew himself slowly off the ground, still clutching Eric's paw of a hand. "I do not know how to thank you," he said.

"No thanks necessary. The Weasel's a nasty piece of work," Eric said thoughtfully, crouching down in front of Doc and inspecting him the way a seasoned medical professional might. "He's not someone to trifle with."

"I am afraid I was left little choice," said Doc. "I needed information that only he could provide."

"There's always a choice," Eric said.

"Did Willy have a choice?" Doc challenged him, against his better judgment.

Eric grew thoughtful a moment. "Actually yeah," he said, "he did."

"What? You are saying he pumped himself full of lead?"

"Maybe we ought to have this conversation another time," Eric said mildly. "You need to get your strength back. You're lucky you're not dead. Take my word for it."

"I'm tired of waiting for answers," said Doc emphatically. "I am in your debt. I am well aware of that. But if you have any additional insight regarding Willy's disappearance to impart, I would very much like to hear it."

Eric stood and gazed at him dubiously. "We'd only be covering territory we covered before. The question is whether you're ready to hear it."

"I promise to listen to anything you have to tell me," Doc said. He was in agony, the pain emanating from the point where D'Angelo had made contact. It felt as if every cell in his body were on fire.

Eric sighed. "Well, you know what the Weasel was saying just now?"

"The Weasel? You mean D'Angelo?"

"Like I said, the Weasel," Eric repeated firmly.

"Sorry. Go on. Please."

Eric stopped as if reconsidering the wisdom of continuing. Finally he said carefully, "I believe he really was trying, in his inimitable way, to level with you. I couldn't help but overhear your conversation. From his point of view, he really was just doing his job, or more accurately, his version of it."

Doc just stared at him blankly.

"But hey, I've got to hand it to you," Eric said, brushing the matter aside. "You gave as good as you got. I never expected you to get the better of the Weasel in a straight fight. Never in a million years."

"Wait," said Doc. "I got the better of him? I have no recollection of any such thing."

"You must have a few friends in high places yourself. That or some kickass mojo."

"Mein Lieber," said Doc, remembering his manners. "May I offer you a cup of coffee? I have some Viennese roast upstairs." It was frankly disconcerting to be having a somewhat intelligible conversation with Eric the Red, even if he couldn't have agreed less with what the man was telling him.

"Been trying to restrict my caffeine intake, to be honest," said Eric. "I sleep better at night. But thanks anyway. A word of advice, though. Watch your back. The Weasel can't be too happy about getting his clock cleaned by a civilian." He squinted at Doc for a long moment. The scrutiny made Doc uncomfortable. "At least that's what I think you are. Can't tell for sure. At any rate, he'll be wantin' to settle the score somewhere along the line, that one. You can bet on it. He isn't what you'd call a graceful loser. It isn't in his DNA."

"Well," said Doc reluctant to let the topic rest, but realizing he wasn't in any condition to have an extended conversation. He wasn't going to be able to force the issue anyway, he intuited, dealing with someone like Eric. "Thanks for the advice. And thanks again for your help. I hesitate to think what might have happened if you hadn't shown up when you did."

"Hey, think nothing of it," said Eric, waving him off with a meaty mitt. "That scum have no business around here. They're just a blight on the landscape."

Doc couldn't help but note the irony of such a statement coming from Eric, a derelict of questionable sanity who lived under a tarp.

"Anyway, it's what neighbors do, right?" Eric added, starting to move back toward the street and his domicile beyond.

"If there is anything I can do to return the favor, just name it," Doc called after him. "Do not hesitate."

Chapter 24

"Holy shit!" exclaimed Callie. "That was epic!"

Doc rolled his shoulders and neck. Then he patted himself down to assess the damage done. He was bruised here and there from punches that had slipped through his defenses, but he was in one piece. His back still stung like he'd been attacked by a hive of bees, but the pain was receding.

"You were awesome, dude! You were like Ali out there!"

"To be honest, I am not entirely clear about what happened."

"I can tell you what I saw," said Callie excitedly. "First, it was you against the two knuckle-draggers. You were ducking, jabbing and then dancing away, light as a feather. You put the first guy away in, like, a second. He was knocked out on his feet and didn't know it. It was like Night of the Living Dead."

"I remember that part quite well," remarked Doc. "It's what comes next that is a little fuzzy."

"While you were busy wearing down the other gorilla, the little creep with the sunglasses sneaks up behind you and stabs you in the back with The Finger. He barely touched you, but it looked like you'd been electrocuted. You straightened up and went all pale. I thought you were going to pass out on the spot. But then you spun around on the guy and whacked him upside the head. You hit him right between the eyes with the palm of your hand. It was like some kind of Bruce Lee move. It took the piss right out of him. And, get this, your hand left this red welt on his forehead. He just staggered back toward the car like he was wasted. You fell like a sequoia after that. I could feel the impact up here.

"By this time the other two guys had come around. They were, like, hovering over you, ready to come down on you like a ton a' bricks when the Viking guy from across the street shows up. He started wailing on them like they were the heavy bag at the gym, kicking their asses big time."

"Language."

"You should have seen it! It was a thing of beauty. He walked into that scene like he owned it. He came up and swatted the one guy, cuffed him on the back of the head like he was a misbehaving kid. The guy went down on his knees and just pitched forward on his face. Then he turned to the other guy, the last one standing. He flicked away the guys punches like they were mosquitoes, mildly annoying at best. Finally, he just grabbed the guy by the front of his shirt and tossed him like he was a sack of shi …"

"Language."

"Garbage. The guy flies about ten feet and lands on his back. I felt that one up here, too. Like an aftershock from the Big One. So he just lies there wheezing like a donkey, the wind knocked out of him. In fact, they both just lay there groaning and rolling around for a couple of minutes. Then they managed to haul their butts up off the turf and made for the car. The homeless guy gave them an assist with a couple kicks to the rear end. They wove around like they were plastered and barely made it to the car on their feet. Meanwhile, the evil munchkin was already in the backseat, his head in his hands like he was nursing his wounds. The two other guys climb in the front. One of them starts the car and off they go. Never to be seen or heard from again, I'll bet."

"I remember somebody shouting. And then what sounded like body punches landing," Doc said. "Then nothing until Eric pulled me off the ground."

"That guy you call Eric has hidden talents."

"Funny, that's what he said about me," Doc said "He seemed surprised I'd managed to hold my own against D'Angelo--the little guy. It was like he knew all about him, either personally or by reputation, I cannot be sure."

"That little dude was creepy," Callie said with a shudder. "He looked like he wasn't even real. Like he was one of those ventriloquist's dolls. Charlie …"

"McCarthy," Doc supplied. "That was the impression I had, too." He didn't let on how much the man Eric called the Weasel unnerved him.

"But that big guy from across the way was something else," Callie said with admiration. "He's someone I'd want to have on my side if it all went south and it came to blows. What's his story?"

"I really don't know. All I know is what I have heard, but all that is beginning to seem suspect to me." He took a deep breath. He was going to have to reorder his thinking about crazy Eric. "Rumor has it he is a war vet," he said. "Came back with post-traumatic stress disorder. But no one knows for sure. The couple of times I have spoken with him I frankly was unable to comprehend much of what he was saying. His understanding of the world is very different from mine." Doc paused to consider. "But just now I came away with the odd feeling that he and D'Angelo share a similar worldview. One made as much sense as the other. It was like they were talking in a kind of code. But it was a similar code."

"For instance."

"For instance, what seemed like lame excuses for killing Willy on D'Angelo's part, Eric seemed to take at face value. I do not understand it. It sounded to me inane, gibberish."

"What did he say? I couldn't hear much from up here."

"What D'Angelo was claiming was that Willy's death was somehow justified. It wasn't what it seemed. Killing Willy was a job that needed doing somehow. And it fell to him to do it. And I was somehow interfering in the natural course of events by questioning it."

"And your friend Eric agreed with that hooey?"

"He didn't contradict it."

"Hunh." This new information didn't exactly jibe with her hero worship of the big Scandinavian.

"What seemed to worry D'Angelo was what his superiors might think about his performance. Eric seemed to imply this, too, when I first met him saying he had thoroughly messed up the assignment he had been tasked with completing."

"Killing Willy."

Doc nodded his head. Thinking about it was giving him a headache. He had the feeling that trying to understand D'Angelo's point of view, and perhaps Eric's as well, was going to be a futile exercise until more was known. It would be easy to dismiss them both as crazy. But what troubled Doc was that they seemed to be crazy in exactly the same way.

Chapter 25

Doc paused and gazed out the windows of the wheelhouse, a worried expression on his face.

"What?" asked Callie.

"I am thinking that it might be best if you did not stay here longer." He leveled his gaze at the girl. "After what happened this morning I cannot guarantee your safety anymore. For your own good, I think it is time for you to continue on to camp. Or go back to Pacifica to be with your aunt."

"I can take care of myself," said Callie, obviously hurt. "I know Tae Kwon Do."

"You saw what happened out there—what we are up against," said Doc. "They know where I live and that means you may be in danger, too. Our friend across the street said he did not believe we had seen the last of them."

"You'll protect me," said Callie confidently.

"I wish I could be as certain of that as you are," said Doc. "But the truth is I wouldn't have made it if Eric had not intervened. They killed Willy in cold blood, remember. I doubt they would hesitate to kill again if they believed it was in their interest. I hate for you to end up as collateral damage in this war I seem to be engaged in. It is unacceptable to me that even a remote possibility exists that you might be hurt."

Callie didn't say anything for a long while.

"I'm not ready to leave yet," she mumbled, more to herself than to him.

"Try to understand my position," Doc said. "You are a smart girl. You know I am right.

Callie let out a huge sigh. "OK. I'll go, if that's what you want," she said.

"I will look up the bus schedule for tomorrow," said Doc. "And tonight you go with me to the club. I do not want you out of my sight until I know you are safely on your way either to Big Sur or Pacifica, whichever one you choose. Agreed?"

The girl shrugged. "What choice do I have?"

He felt sorry for her. At her age, it was an adult's world. They called the shots. But that was a fact of life for a teenager. In a few years all that would change. "We will keep in touch. You will see."

"Sure," said Callie without enthusiasm.

"Chrissie, this is Callie."

Lucy's teenager daughter stepped forward dutifully and shook the taller girl's hand. "How do you do," she said.

An awkward silence ensued.

Finally Chrissie said, "Do you want to watch some TV? I've got an Xbox, if you're into video games."

Callie looked at Doc, her expression unreadable. "Sure," she said.

Callie followed the younger girl into the apartment behind the bar at the Fish Tank.

"That went well," said Lucy dryly.

"They will sort it out," said Doc. "They are sure to find common ground. Callie must remain occupied only until I am finished playing. Then I will take her off your hands."

"I get it," said Lucy, then shifting into her alter-ego added, "Asian woman smarter than round-eye think."

"Thanks," said Doc, the atmosphere of awkwardness lingering.

"Now owe one?" said Lucy innocently. "Play giddiyap in bushes?"

Doc reddened. "I had better get to the stage," he said. "Otherwise they will begin without me."

She swatted him on the rear as he departed. "Promise--no bite," she said. "One dollah."

Chapter 26

"Hey Mr. PI," said Chico from his post behind the organ as Doc arrived onstage. "How's it going on the case? Make any headway?"

"I cannot be sure," Doc replied. "The more I learn, the more questions I have. Certainty about anything eludes me thus far."

"If you were into zen, that would mean you were making progress."

"Ha," said Doc. "If not knowing whether I am moving forward or backward is progress, then yes. I must be making progress."

"It's always darkest before light dawns," Chico said, a bemused expression on his face.

"I will try to keep that in mind," said Doc.

"No trace of Willy has turned up?"

"No. And I am no closer to understanding what happened."

"Let's talk about it later, cabron, you and me. OK?"

"Talk about it now," Catfish Cathy, the bassist pleaded. "C'mon. Please? Inquiring minds want to know."

"Yeah," said Roscoe grinning wolfishly from his throne behind the drums. "Throw us a bone, man. We're dyin' for some dish around here. Catfish be needin' her fix a' gossip."

"Screw you, killjoy" said Catfish Cathy, indignantly. "If you weren't hiding behind those skins, I'd kick your butt all the way back to Louisiana."

"You know I never been east a' Bakersfield, girl."

"Well, come on over here and I'll change all that," said the bassist. She pointed meaningfully at her Justin work boots. "A swift kick from these babies should get you as far as the Texas panhandle at the very least."

"If I go, I be takin' you wit me, girl," said Roscoe with a good-natured grin. "I'z gonna need you to ward off them heifer humpin' yahoos."

"Ninos, ninos," said Chico in his most patronizing tone. "Play nice together or no ice cream for dessert. Comprendes?"

During the break, Doc looked in on the girls. They seemed to be hitting it off. They were entrenched in front of the TV screen, game controllers in hand, playing a game that had macho men driving souped up cars through urban landscapes, shooting at villains that appeared around every corner.

"See?" said Lucy. "No problem."

The last set was over at 12:30. Sunday was generally a shorter night for the band because it tended not to be as crowded. Doc packed his Telecaster and headed to the back of the bar where Lucy's apartment was located. He opened the door to find Chrissie asleep on the sofa, the TV still on.

The girl awoke when Doc came in.

"Where is Callie?" said Doc.

"I ... I don't know," said the sleepy girl. "Maybe she's in the bathroom."

The bathroom door stood open. She wasn't there.

"I fell asleep," the girl explained. "I'm really sorry."

Doc met Lucy in the hall. He looked past her toward the open door that led out to the rear parking lot.

"What is it?"

"Callie is no longer in the apartment."

They emerged together from the open doorway to find nothing out of the ordinary in back of the bar. The remaining patrons were heading for a handful of cars scattered around the lot. There was no sign of Callie.

"Scheisse," said Doc vehemently. "Scheiss," he repeated, hands on his hips, piercing the dark corners of the lot with his gaze.

Lucy was at a loss. "I'll look inside," she said. "Maybe she's in one of the club restrooms."

She re-appeared moments later, shaking her head. "She's not here. Want me to call the cops?"

Doc was having trouble getting enough air. He shook his head. There was only one person he could think to talk to.

Chapter 27

That person was standing under the streetlight halfway to Doc's place wearing a faded Hawaiian shirt over army fatigues and combat boots. He seemed to be waiting for Doc. He looked huge, even from 50 yards away.

"They took the girl," was the first thing Eric said as Doc drew up to him. "It happened so fast there wasn't much I could do about it. I apologize."

"What did you see?"

"I was scouting out the shrubbery back of the restaurant. Nice stash of kumquats out there. Spray free. And the back door to the venue being open, I could hear you guys playin' while I was picking. Anyway, after a while the girl shows up at the back door. She's just sort of standing there taking in the air, it looks like. Next thing you know the car's there between me and her. The doors fly open and two guys, like the ones from this morning, grab the girl, put a hand over her mouth, push her into the back seat and they take off. Whole operation couldn't have take more than four seconds."

"It was the Packard?"

"Yeah. The Weasel's wheels. No doubt about it. They tore off outta here and turned right, up toward the main highway."

"How long ago?"

"About ten minutes."

"Do you have a sense of which direction they went?"

"From the sound of it, they turned south," Eric said. He seemed to want to say something more, but stopped himself.

"What? What is it?"

He stroked his scruffy red beard for a moment before answering. "I have an idea where they might be going. It's probably what I'd do in his shoes--if I was dumb enough to kidnap a civilian in the first place and wanted to be sure no one could track me."

"Where is he taking her?" asked Doc anxiously.

Eric ignored the question. "We'll have to work fast," he said. "They've got a pretty good head start by now."

"What do we need to do? Just name it."

"First we'll need a set of wheels. An old truck of some kind would be best. Something that'll blend in. And give us some decent cover, if need be. This could get gnarly."

"And exactly where would we find such a truck at this time of night?"

Eric stroked his beard some more as if weighing the pros and cons of some nuclear option that had just occurred to him. He heaved a sigh. "Follow me," he said.

Doc stood his ground. "Do I have time to put my guitar in the shop?"

Eric looked down at the guitar case in Doc's hand and then back up at Doc's face. "The Tele." It came out as a statement. "Gotta take care of the Tele. No question."

The men covered the open ground to Doc's digs swiftly. Eric waited while Doc placed the guitar case just inside the ground level entrance to the hull.

"Is there anything else we might need?" inquired Doc, holding the door open.

"You got a gun?"

"A gun? No."

"Don't worry about it." Eric produced a massive silver-plated Desert Eagle handgun that gleamed in the moonlight. "This is a .44 converted to .50 AE," he explained. He transferred the weapon to his left hand and reached deeper into the pocket of his army fatigues. "I've got a pea shooter for you."

He drew out a snub-nosed .38 revolver, a detective's special, and gave it to Doc. "You know how to use one of these?"

Doc nodded as he reluctantly took the gun. He had been a decorated marksman in the army. But the occasion to fire at a human target had never arisen during his tenure as a soldier. He preferred to rely on his fists and on his superlative training for self-defense. "Do you really anticipate that we will need such weapons?"

"You have some idea of what we're up against here with the Weasel and his gang," Eric stated. "I hate to say it, but that's just a taste of what might be in store for us tonight, if they're going where I think they're going."

When Doc didn't respond Eric placed the revolver gently in his hands and said, "Best to be on the safe side, friend. Trust me. It could get hairy after we make the jump."

"The jump?"

"You'll see." Eric said, with a wink. He was obviously getting into the spirit of things, starting to enjoy himself immensely. "I'd say we have what we need for the short term. If this turns into a longer stint, we'll improvise. Best to get crackin'. If our window of opportunity closes, we'll have to wait til tomorrow morning to try again."

Doc locked the door and gazed at his dry-docked house for a long moment. He had the sinking sensation that he might not be seeing it again for a while. Then he followed Eric through the underbrush at the back of the property, across a parallel street, and through a couple of backyards, dogs barking as they passed. Finally they emerged on Highway 1. They walked south on the shoulder for a couple of hundred yards. They came to dirt road that ran into the brush off the highway. It deadended after a hundred feet. The was a single vehicle parked on it, barely visible in the ambient light. It turned out to be an ancient panel truck, a rust-colored primer orange. It was more like an old locksmith's van, bigger than a station wagon, but not really a full-sized truck.

Eric produced a key, inserted it in the lock and opened the door in one fluid motion. Doc couldn't conceal his amazement.

"What?" Eric said.

"I was unaware you had … transportation."

"Full of surprises, aren't we," Eric said dismissively. "Just don't tell anyone else. OK? Don't want to ruin my reputation."

"You believe that people will think less of you if they knew you had a vehicle?"

"It's an image thing."

Doc nodded as if he understood, which wasn't quite accurate. There was much he didn't understand lately and he was, perhaps, beginning to accept that as a fact of life. "In that case," he said. "My lips are sealed."

GHOSTS

Chapter 28

Eric pulled the manual choke and gave the accelerator a couple of taps with his thick-soled desert combat boot. He pulled another knob and the engine began to turn over. Amazingly, it caught immediately. Despite its exterior condition, the van was obviously well maintained.

Eric looked over his shoulder and backed the vehicle out of the cul-de-sac, careful to keep to the shoulder of Highway 1 as he did so. He stopped and shifted into first with a grinding of gears. A couple of gear changes later and they were breezing south on the two-lane highway at a fair clip. There was little traffic on the highway at this time of night.

"So where to?" Doc ventured, when the lights of Angels' Keep had disappeared behind them.

"Shipley," said Eric.

Doc wasn't sure he had heard correctly. "You mean the one-horse town on the other side of Prunedale?" He had only ever seen the place marked on the map.

Eric glanced at Doc with amusement. "I know," he said. "Most everyone around here has heard of Shipley, but few have actually been there. There's a reason for that which will become clear once we get there. But we've got to hustle. If we miss our chance now, we'll have to wait several hours to try again. It's not a deal breaker. Like I said, I think I know where he's headed eventually. But I think you'll agree, we want to stay close."

Doc nodded uncertainly. Obviously D'Angelo had a hideout near Shipley, heavily guarded no doubt, and that was where he was taking Callie. Impeccable timing would be required to access the place and effect a rescue. He lapsed into silence pondering this prospect. The .38 felt heavy in his jacket pocket.

They left Highway 1 near Castroville. There was slightly more activity here than they'd seen so far. A couple of bars were open, mariachi music blaring out into the street, and a 24-hour restaurant had a few patrons seated at booths, perhaps trying to sober up before attempting the drive home. No one took a second look at the innocuous rust-colored panel truck that drove by on the main drag.

They made a left on Highway 68, which ran toward the hills in the distance, barely visible in the moonlight. Castroville was soon behind them and farmland opened up around them, dark fields running off into the distance on both sides of the highway as they sped inland.

"What's on your mind?" asked Eric, noticing Doc's reticence.

"I cannot help thinking about what D'Angelo was saying."

"About what?"

"He kept insisting that Willy never died. He said the opposite was true. He was being given a chance at living. What do make of that?"

Eric scratched his jaw. Another couple of miles of farmland slid by the van before he answered. "I guess the cat's going to be out of the bag pretty soon anyway," he said with a crooked grin. "You've got to swear you won't repeat what I'm about to tell you to anyone. I mean *anyone*. Understood?"

"OK," said Doc cautiously. "I swear."

"There's more to Angels' Keep than meets the eye. Much more. The town serves a very important function in the broader scheme of things."

"You mean more important than being a destination for kayaking, whale watching, and fishing?" Doc asked facetiously. Eric was being entirely too dramatic about this, he thought. Whatever it was, it just couldn't be that big a deal.

"Angels' Keep is a way station for disembodied souls headed for incarnation in physical reality," Eric said, trying to gauge how this new information would effect his passenger. "It's kind of like a halfway house for spirits."

Doc didn't know how to begin to respond to that, so he kept his mouth shut.

"The ocean is full of souls," Eric said. "They come in on the big tours you see leaving the harbor each day. There's always more that come back than go out. See how that works? There's never too many at once to attract attention. They wander around Angels' Keep for while, looking like the adults they'll eventually become. They blend in with the tourist population and generally get acclimated to life in the real world. Then they move on."

"Move on to where?"

"To maternity wards all around the planet. They start from scratch in the physical world. Grow up. Grow old and die. And the cycle starts over again."

"So they are in Angels' Keep as …"

"Ghosts of a sort. A shadow of their future selves, you could say. You can't tell to look at 'em. But you'd know it if you shook hands with one. They're kind of squishy."

"Squishy."

"Unlike the more or less permanent residences of the Keep."

"Where does Wild Bill Willy fit into the picture?"

"I'm just about there. See, some souls get stuck in the Keep. They start to forget that the arrangement's only temporary for them. They're there just to get a taste, so to speak, to acclimate, not settle in. They get to the point where they need a little help to move on. Are you seeing where I'm going with this?"

"D'Angelo?"

"Bingo. Though how the Weasel got himself involved, I can't begin to guess. Being a guide is a position of responsibility, and the Weasel's one of the least responsible people I know." He thought about what he had just said for a moment and then added, "But far be it for me to second guess what Universal Intelligence might have been thinking." Eric glanced toward the ceiling of the truck and crossed himself.

"In any case, the Weasel gets recruited for the job for whatever reason and not unpredictably makes a royal mess of it. Instead of gently ushering Willy to the edge of town and sending him on his merry way out of the Keep and into history with a pat on the behind, he gets clever. He guns Willy down Capone-style to show everyone how smart he is, and breaks rule number one: never draw unnecessary attention to yourself. Then he's surprised when you, as a concerned citizen, starts busting his chops, asking awkward questions. Maybe this was the Weasel's big chance to rack up some brownie points up there …" He nodded toward the ceiling once again. "Maybe being a crook isn't as gratifying as it used to be and he's trying to hedge his bets. Who knows? True to form, he blows it big time. Now he's got a witness to contend with. The direct approach hasn't worked on you as well as expected, so he takes the girl in an act of desperation."

Doc had to admit. It all made a twisted kind of sense. It was madness to be sure, but there seemed to be a method to it.

He didn't have an opportunity to delve into the implications of all he'd just heard as they found themselves on a two-lane road just beyond Shipley. There was no trace of electric light to be seen, no streetlamps or friendly illuminated farmhouse windows, no headlights or taillights. Only ominously dark rolling hills against the luminous glow of a moonlit sky.

Chapter 29

The transition, when it came, was surprisingly subtle. There were no flashing lights or noises to indicate they'd made the jump. One second they were on a little-used rural backroad in north-central California, and they next they were in the high desert. The only indication, at first, that anything had happened was a change in the air quality. It was suddenly warmer and more arid. At the same time, the vegetation around them was much more sparse.

Doc cast wildly about. "Was is passiert?"

Eric laid a meaty paw on Doc's forearm to steady him. Doc stared through the window at the barren, cactus-adorned terrain rolling by outside, scarcely willing to trust his senses. The stars were brighter here and more plentiful. The air, being less humid, allowed for more ambient light, and they could see farther in all directions. "What in God's name just happened?"

"We jumped," Eric said mildly.

"Jumped? Where are we are?"

"About 70 miles northeast of Los Angeles," said Eric. "In the desert south of Barstow. When we make this right turn up here, we'll be heading toward the LA basin."

They made the turn onto a wider roadway. There was no traffic in sight.

"How?" was all Doc could manage, as he continued to twist and turn in the passenger seat, trying to take it all in at once. Terror gradually gave way to awe.

"We just ducked through the Shipley portal," Eric explained. "And popped up here."

"Scheisse," Doc said. "No wonder nobody goes to Shipley." He couldn't help but laugh. This was beyond belief. Beyond crazy. Beyond …

Eric chuckled. Doc's laughter was contagious. "You may be right about that," he said.

"This is where you believe D'Angelo went?" Doc said, sobering suddenly.

"That's what I'm guessing," said Eric. "I know he has a place on the coast south of LA. He conducts most of his business out of that location. It seems the logical place to hide the girl."

"I can understand now about it being difficult to track him," Doc said. "Are you the only one besides him who is familiar with this Shipley portal?"

"Far as I know."

"So why kidnap Callie and bring her here?"

"You want to know what I think? I'm thinking you scared the bejesus out of the Weasel yesterday morning during your scuffle. He's used to people going down and staying down after he lays his hand on them. Don't ask me how you did it, but you managed to nail him pretty good before you went out. I don't think that's ever happened to him before. My guess? You've got him worried. He doesn't know who or what you are to pull that off. And I gotta say, I've been wondering the same thing myself."

Doc was busy working things out in his mind. "Portal or no portal, if we can confirm that D'Angelo has got Callie here in Southern California, we can then call in the authorities and they can make the arrest."

But Eric was shaking his head. "There's something else you need to know about," he said.

"It's 1963?" Doc blurted out incredulously.

"You're beginning to understand what's involved. We're going to have to handle this inhouse. Just you, me and the Weasel. But that's not the only wrinkled here. There's something else you have to know before we get much further down the road."

"Let me see if I have this right," Doc said. "We have jumped to the outskirts of Los Angeles in the blink of an eye. Not only that, but you have just informed me we've landed in Los Angeles in 1963. And there is more?" Doc drew a deep breathe and let it out.

"We're not talking about the 1963 a boomer from where we just came from might remember," Eric said. "We've entered an entirely different timeline altogether. One in which the Russians won the Cold War. The United States is an occupied country here and has been for more than a decade."

CAVIAR AND COLA

Chapter 30

They were enveloped in an acrid mist as they descended into the Los Angeles basin. The lights of The City of Angels, usually bright enough to illuminate the skies above Southern California, barely penetrated the blackness. Smoke, dust and debris filled the air. The smell of burned oil, rubber and plastics assaulted their nostrils and lungs, while the road before them became cluttered with chunks of unidentifiable debris in varying sizes. Eric had to swerve to avoid the larger pieces, but inevitably hit a few, challenging the van's suspension system and jarring its two passengers.

"Stink City is what the locals call it these days," Eric said, producing more or less clean rags from behind his seat. He handed Doc one of these to place over his nose and mouth. If the air quality continued to get worse, asphyxiation became a real possibility.

The charred and broken carcasses of vehicles appeared along the shoulder, some military, but most civilian. The American cars that were visible were all pre-fifties in design, Doc noted. He felt as if he were in a bad dream. "Gott im Himmel," he said. "What happened here?"

Eric shrugged. "In this version of history, the Soviets got The Bomb first. They took out a couple of cities to demonstrate its capability. And that was pretty much it. The military moved in. They've been here ever since."

"Scheisse,"

"Yeah. Scheisse is right," Eric said with a humorless laugh.

"So," said Doc, after a moment's reflection. "If what you say is true, Hiroshima and Nagasaki could not have happened."

"That's exactly right," said Eric. "The war lasted a few weeks longer. But the Japanese capitulated anyway, just as they would have in our timeline."

"Which cities?"

"Pardon me?"

"Which cities did they use for their 'demonstration'?"

"Indianapolis and Mobile. It was enough to get the message across."

A tank that sported the distinctive white star of the Soviet army was running on a frontage road that paralleled the main highway across a hundred yards of open ground. It was leading a convoy of trucks in the same direction they were moving in, but at a slower pace. Thankfully, no one seemed to take notice of Eric's panel truck as it sped west on the pitted and potholed main road.

A malignant red glow permeated the horizon before them, while oil fires became visible in the mist, dotting the eerie landscape to the south.

"Vandals," Eric explained. "Red army brats. They set fire to oil derricks for kicks. They're responsible for a lot of the wrecks you see along the road here, too. Of course, no one dares complain."

The drove on in silence, while Doc tried to process what he was seeing.

"You OK?" Eric asked.

Doc shrugged and swallowed dryly. "As well as can be expected," he said, "when the world is stood on its head."

"We're not going to be spending any more time here than we have to," said Eric, trying to sound reassuring. "We're here to get the girl and go home."

"I don't get it," Doc said, peering through the greasy windshield. Eric had the wipers on but they seemed only to smear the airborne oil and polymers that coated it. "Why would D'Angelo choose such a place to live?"

"There's good money to be made here for someone of, shall we say, an enterprising disposition," Eric said sarcastically. "The Weasel pretty much controls the black market in Southern California. He sells drugs, alcohol, cigarettes and any kind of specialty item a bored Russian soldier could ask for, mostly brought in from Mexico."

"It seems it would be difficult to conduct such business under the watchful eye of a totalitarian regime."

"Actually, he has the tacit approval of the provisional government. The brass turns a blind eye because they're willing to do what it takes to keep the troops happy. Illegal drugs and contraband are publicly condemned, but privately tolerated. Items like cigarettes and booze are strictly rationed under the Soviets. They don't have enough stock to meet the demand."

"So D'Angelo is a capitalist in the service of the communists," Doc said.

"I guess economic idealism only gets you so far," said Eric. "But don't get me wrong. There's no love lost between the high command and the Weasel. It's strictly a marriage of convenience."

A loud popping sound was heard and the van began to veer wildly before Eric got it under control again.

"A flat," said Eric. "Dang. That's all we need out here."

He pulled the van into a clear area at the side of the road.

Chapter 31

After rummaging around behind the driver's seat, Eric came up with what he was looking for: a can of Fix-A-Flat.

"This is a temporary solution," he said. "But it'll take less time than replacing the tire while we're out here in the open. We'll still need to jack the truck up."

He produced a car jack of recent vintage from behind the bench seat and exited the old van. After a cursory inspection, he situated the jack in front of the left rear wheel and began cranking the truck off its rim. When the tire was off the asphalt, he connected the can nozzle to the air release valve and squirted foam into the tire. If all went well, the foam would find the leak and plug it.

"Let's hope that does it," called Eric. "Mind checking behind your seat there for something that looks like a battery-powered air pump?"

Doc found what Eric wanted and passed it through the open driver's side door to Eric. A few moments later the tire was re-inflated. Eric handed the pump back through the driver's side window.

The sound of a truck approaching could be heard behind them.

"Stay in the cab and keep your head down," said Eric, silhouetted against blinding headlights, a note of tension in his voice. "We've got company."

Doc kept his head low as he lay across the front seat, lifting it only enough to keep an eye on what was happening in the driver's side mirror. Several seconds later the headlights resolved themselves into a large military transport truck. It downshifted as it passed Eric's van and pulled onto the shoulder a few yards in front of it. Two soldiers wearing gas masks climbed out, both carrying AK-47 assault rifles. One had a flashlight, which he played over the old panel truck.

Eric, meanwhile, was busy removing the tire jack, effectively ignoring the approaching soldiers as if they did not exist. Doc had to admire the man's cool.

"We just need another minute," Eric mumbled under his breath so that Doc could hear, but not the Russian soldiers.

The armed men continued to approach the front of the van slowly, almost casually. Doc was grateful that Eric's vehicle was old even by the standards of 1963. It, in and of itself, shouldn't arouse suspicion. In this hellish version of history, it fit right in.

Eric straightened and called out a greeting in Russian. Eric's sheer size gave the two men pause, not to mention his Hawaiian shirt.

Doc, meanwhile, wedged himself further down under the dash. He prayed the soldiers wouldn't make too close an inspection of the interior of the van.

The Russians answered in accented English. "What is your business?" said the one that had climbed out of the driver's side. "What are you doing out past curfew?"

"Special dispensation," said Eric. "This is a bakery truck. Full of pastries and fresh bread for morning delivery at the commissary downtown. Warm from the oven. You boys hungry? A couple of turnovers and a loaf for the missus wouldn't be missed."

"You show us," the Russian said, after a moment of indecision. He pointed vaguely toward the rear of the truck with the barrel of the machine gun.

"Sure, sure," said Eric, catching Doc's eye through the side mirror. The message was clear: stay down. "Nice night, eh?" he said to the soldier. The statement was absurd considering the toxicity of the air. Not less so in view of the fact that it was made to someone wearing a gas mask.

But the irony was lost on the soldier. "Da," he said curtly.

"You want some smokes?" Eric asked, trying to draw the man's attention away from the interior of the van as he passed. "I'm trying to quit." He fumbled in his shirt pocket and came out with a squashed pack of Camel's unfiltered.

The man proceed to where Eric was standing. Eric offered him the whole pack, which the man snatched away greedily and stuffed in his jacket pocket. He jabbed the air with the nozzle of the sub machine gun threateningly, indicating Eric continue to move toward the back of the van.

Eric put his hands up, like they did in the old westerns. "Keep calm, comrade," he said. "Your patience will be amply rewarded. I can promise you that." He led the soldier around behind the truck, his hands still in the air.

The other soldier was approaching the truck slowly along the shoulder. In another few seconds he would be looking in the passenger side window. Without the steering wheel to shield him, Doc doubted that the Russian would have trouble seeing him curled awkwardly on his side under the dash.

He heard the rear door of the panel truck creak open, followed by a smack that shook the truck and a loud grunt. The sound brought the second soldier to full alert. He stopped near the front of the truck and called out to the first man. When there was no response, he started toward the rear of the truck, his machine gun shouldered. Just as he pulled even with the passenger door, Doc kicked it as hard as he could. The heavy door swung outward, slamming into the soldier. The man flew a good fifteen feet into the scrub brush where he lay motionless.

Eric appeared at the driver's side window. He glanced to where the unconscious Russian lay. "Right through the uprights," he said appreciatively.

"Soccer was more my game," Doc said, trying to calm himself. "I used to be a striker."

"Well, strike one against the opposing team," quipped Eric.

If there were any lingering suspicions in Doc's mind that this time travel business was some kind of hoax, they were now officially dispelled. "What now?" he asked.

"We're changing vehicles. Trading up, you could say." He grinned and looked surreptitiously up and down the road. So far they were alone on the highway. "We'll be less likely to be stopped by patrols if we're in a Russkie truck this time of night."

Eric dragged the unconscious soldier out from behind the truck and left him in the bushes near his partner well off the roadway. "By the time these guys come around, we'll be long gone. Plus without their walkie talkies they won't be able to contact their base anytime soon. Shall we?"

Chapter 32

"Whooooweee!" yelled Eric over the din of the engine in his booming baritone. "I can't get enough of these old transports! Man, they don't make 'em like this anymore!" He pounded the dash with his fist for emphasis. "Bulky, crass as hell and no trace of shock absorption to speak of! It's like the whole truck was chiseled out of a block of granite!" Eric was as happy as Doc had ever seen him.

Gears ground and the old engine rumbled. It seemed more a matter of developing forward momentum than accelerating as it was commonly conceived. Similar trucks passed them now, heading in the opposite direction, and the occasional army tank.

Eric hadn't yet donned one of the gas masks they had found in a cache behind the front seats. But Doc was not going to let macho pride keep him from breathing, so he reached back and selected one of the antiquated masks. He had just situated it on his face when brake lights flashed in the dense haze ahead.

"Checkpoint," said Eric, sobering. It was time to see if the uniforms they had procured from the former occupants of the vehicle would be of use. Unfortunately the biggest of the soldiers had been significantly smaller than Eric. So the shirt barely contained his massive chest and arms. Doc had fared only slightly better with his outfit.

Eric grabbed a gas mask and put it on as the truck came to a lumbering halt. A well-lit kiosk was positioned in the middle of the roadway four truck lengths ahead of them. An official of some kind, judging from his crisp beige uniform, was checking identification. He was taking his time about it.

Eric was drumming his fingers on the dash, nervously casting glances in the rearview mirror. He came to a decision.

"The hell with it," he said, a grim look on his face, and stomped on the gas. The big truck lurched into the oncoming lane, barely clearing the bumper of the truck in front of them. They passed one truck, then another before it dawned on Doc what the big Scandinavian had in mind.

"Find something to grab a hold of," said Eric, as the truck careened straight toward the kiosk squeezed between the line of stopped trucks on the right and the approaching traffic on the left.

They slammed into the kiosk with scarcely a hiccup in their forward progress. It disintegrated on impact in a spectacular shower of broken glass, drywall and wood studs. Luckily, the official on duty had been out of the structure at the time, handing papers back to a driver. They missed him by inches. Even so the air displacement and the explosion of building materials slammed him into the truck with such force he was rendered senseless.

Eric swung the truck back to the right, onto the empty stretch of roadway beyond the kiosk. He peered into the rearview mirror with a satisfied look on his face. "Always hated those damn things," he muttered.

At the next intersection, Eric veered left off the main road, plunging down a two-lane road that led into low-lying hills to the south.

"This used to be Highway 39," Eric explained. "Runs straight down to Newport Beach. And the road we were just on? Route 66, the Mother Road. Now it's the Mother Russia Road." Eric gave a short laugh.

They pulled off the road long enough to get out of the constricting soldier's uniforms. Doc pulled the gas mask off his face and took a couple of experimental breaths. The air quality was much improved since they had left the San Gabriel Valley. These hills, he recalled, were a sea of suburban development in the 21st century. Now, except for the lights of a couple of low-lying ranch houses built in the 30s and 40s, they were dark.

They emerged from the hills unimpeded and began the winding descent into Orange County. A concentration of bright light dead ahead caught Doc's eye.

"The Magic Kingdom," Eric explained.

"Disneyland?"

"Yup. The Reds let Disney build it, believe it or not. In fact, they helped subsidize it. It's as popular under the Russians here as it is under the Americans in our version of history. Maybe even more so."

"Did Disney have to make concessions to the Soviets?"

"They built 'Factoryland' next to Fantasyland," Eric said with a grin. "Aside from that and serving borscht, not much. In the fifties, the Central Committee declared Mickey Mouse, Goofy and Donald Duck friends of the proletariat. It was decided they weren't a counterrevolutionary threat after all. The Soviets are as protective of the Magic Kingdom as they are of their vodka reserves. They serve a similar function, come to think of it. It gives the ground troops something to do on a Saturday night to let off steam. They're in need of diversion as much or more than anyone else around here.

"They love Hollywood in the same way and for the same reasons. Actually, most of what constitutes American popular culture of the fifties and early sixties has survived the occupation. The music, the movies, you name it.

"And yet people are being slaughtered here on a daily basis. The economy and infrastructure are barely existent. And the whole population is brutalized and enslaved.

"It's all about distracting people from their misery, on the one hand, and maintaining military discipline and morale on the other. Hollywood is an incredibly important factor in that equation. It's contradictory as hell and completely perverse. But there you have it."

Traffic spiked as they headed through Anaheim. Businesses abounded for several miles--restaurants, bars, fast food joints, souvenir shops, and the odd gas station. But the lights seemed muted, as if to conceal the fact that the shops and eateries were all rather rundown and dingy. No one paid the truck any heed as it rumbled through town. It was one of thousands just like it which roamed the streets at any time of the day or night.

Eric stuck to backstreets, avoiding other military vehicles and the ubiquitous checkpoints with something akin to a sixth sense. It was likely the comrades they had left in the bushes next to Route 66 had come around, been picked up, and taken back to headquarters with tales of the truck-jacking by now.

When they finally regained the highway heading south, it grew dark again, signs of life fewer and farther between.

"Where is this place you believe D'Angelo is taking Callie?"

"It's south of Newport," said Eric. "Laguna Beach. You know it?"

"Of course. I have done gigs there. In addition, I was a fan of the seminal reality show of the same name that appeared on television a decade ago."

Eric looked over at Doc with a you-gotta-be-kidding-me expression. "Never would have guessed," he said with barely controlled mirth.

"Lucy and I have eclectic tastes," Doc said wistfully. He felt a pang thinking of Lucy and Chrissie. They seemed very far away at the moment.

"To each his own," said Eric with a shrug. "I'm into old episodes of Monster Garage myself."

"You have access to video equipment?" said Doc, shocked at the notion.

"I've got an iPad and a set of earbuds. 4G connectivity. Don't say a word." He shot Doc a stern look.

Doc was dumbfounded.

"Anyway," Eric said, eager to get the discussion back on track. "I'm thinking Laguna is where he'll turn up sooner or later."

Chapter 33

Doc had lapsed into silence. He appeared dazed.

"So what's your full name," Eric asked Doc. He thought it was best to try to keep Doc engaged so as to avoid his being overwhelmed by the high concentration of strangeness he was confronted with. Not to mention his feeling responsible for the girl's abduction.

"Excuse me?"

"Your name?" Eric repeated.

"St. Michel," said Doc distractedly. "Manfred St. Michel. No middle name."

"But people call you Doc."

"To be honest, I do not know how the 'Doc' thing got started. My theory is that it is because I had a certain facility in reviving aging amplifiers."

"The doctor's gonna cure your ills," Eric said boisterously. "Don't need no pills! Know what I think? It's because of the way you bend those strings. People go home feelin' better after hearing you play."

"Kind of you to say," said Doc, savoring the praise. "Quid pro quo. What about you? Are you really Eric?"

"Naw," said Eric, amused. "Not even close. To some people a big, red-haired Scandinavian is automatically Eric the Red, right? My real name's Gunnerson. Gustav Gunnerson. But I'm reconciled to Eric. Looked at from a certain perspective, it's kind of flattering."

"Eric the Red was a titan in the annuls of sea exploration," Doc declared. "A larger-than-life character. The appellation seems apropos."

"Well, the exploration part of it is true," said Eric. "I've been to places and seen things Eric the Red couldn't have imagined in his wildest mead-infused dreams."

"How is it you came to be a time traveler? Have you always known about the portal?"

"It started a few years ago," Eric said without hesitation. "I had what I thought was a psychotic break. I was doing construction in the Central Valley at the time. I was sitting on my back porch, having a Heineken when the world changed."

"In what way?"

"I saw things that weren't there. And knew things I couldn't possibly know. I didn't know it at the time, but I was seeing the overlap--one timeline superimposed over another. It took finding the portal for me to realize that what I had been seeing wasn't an hallucination. These people and places I'd been seeing were real. They all existed somewhere, either in a parallel universe or a different timeline."

"So how did you find the portal?"

"I saw it in a dream. But it was more than a dream. I knew the place I needed to find was somewhere on the Central Coast. But I had to piece together the exact location from maps and topographical charts. When I found it and when I started making jumps, everything started to make sense. It was about this time I discovered Angels' Keep. In my heightened state of sensitivity, you might say, I could see what was going on there from day one. I could see the spirits pouring in from the Pacific, the comings and goings."

"The apparitions did not bother you?"

"Naw. It was a beautiful scene, actually. Amazing. As natural as can be. Eventually my vision cleared and I could function again like a more or less normal human being, though I still get flashes of what you might call insight now and then. It's OK as long as I'm not behind the wheel when it happens."

Just great, thought Doc, as they sped toward the coast in a stolen Soviet-era military vehicle. "Would you rather I drive?" he asked plaintively.

"Not to worry," said Eric. "Hardly ever happens anymore."

"So when you are not in Angels' Keep, you are jumping to different times and places," said Doc.

"That is correct."

"And what do you do there?"

"Pretty much what we're doing now. I'm what you might call a problem solver."

"And how is that?"

"It's just the way it is. I tend not to end up on white sandy beaches on uninhabited alien worlds. Whenever I jump, it's usually jumping into the fray. There's usually some kind of conflict taking place. And consequently there's almost always a role for me to play. A job to be done."

"What kind of job?"

"Odds to be evened out. Someone who needs the kind of help I can provide."

"And what kind of help do you provide?"

"Look at me. I'm big for a reason. And I'm a fighter, like you. Diplomacy and negotiation are not my strong suits. I call things the way I see 'em. And then I do what it takes to sort things out the way I know how. The way I see it, my job is to balance the scales a little. I basically help those who aren't able to stand up for themselves."

"That is very noble."

"Somebody's gotta do it," said Eric, with a self-effacing shrug.

Chapter 34

Demonic fireworks lit up the gloom in the distance to their right. A muted rumble of explosions followed that could be felt through the chassis of the truck.

"Long Beach, probably," said Eric. "The Russians rousting some rebels. Or maybe it's just a random shelling to remind everyone who's boss."

The bursts of light, dirty yellow in the haze, tapered off as they continued south toward the coast.

"Slow down for a second," Eric said. He was in the passenger seat, having let Doc take the wheel some minutes before, much to Doc's relief.

A transport not unlike the one they were riding in was parked on the shoulder. Doc braked as they passed it. In the headlights of the stationary vehicle a couple of teenage kids were being prodded and bludgeoned by the barrels of automatic weapons wielded by four Russian servicemen. The soldiers paused long enough to acknowledge the passing Russian transport with a jovial salute before resuming tormenting their hapless prisoners.

"Kids," said Eric. "Out after curfew. Here's good."

Doc pulled the transport to the shoulder some distance ahead of the other truck and the one-sided confrontation that was taking place.

Eric tucked the Desert Eagle handgun into his waist band at the small of his back. "I'm like you," he remarked. "Don't like to use the hardware unless absolutely necessary."

"And you don't think it will be necessary under the circumstances?"

"Nah," scoffed Eric. "You stay here. I'll be right back."

Eric was gone before Doc could switch off the engine, set the handbrake and disembark the truck. In the side mirror he saw Eric call out a friendly greeting to the soldiers in Russian. The beatings paused as he approached, his Hawaiian shirt flapping in the breeze over his army fatigues.

Doc open the driver's side door and climbed out just in time to see Eric take a machine gun away from one soldier, and with the speed of a cobra striking, hit the second full in the face with the butt of the rifle, poke the third and fourth soldiers in the abdomen with the gun barrel, effectively knocking the wind out of them, before coming back to the man he had taken the rifle from. He handed the man back his rifle before decking him with a quick jab to the jaw and took the rifle back again as the man went down. Then he turned his attention to the men who were trying to straighten up, still holding their stomachs, and rendered them unconscious with measured taps to the forehead with the stock of the automatic rifle. The fight was over in seconds.

Doc opened his mouth to volunteer his help, but closed it again. It was obvious the big Scandinavian had no need of assistance.

Eric sent the boys, bruised, bloodied, but still standing, off with an admonition never to violate curfew again, probably unnecessarily considering the punishment they had received at the hands of the now reposing Russian soldiers.

"Probably got stopped sneaking home from their girlfriends'," said Eric gravely, as he watched the traumatized boys crash noisily into an orange grove adjacent to the highway.

Eric then bent over the unconscious soldiers. Patting their uniforms, he found a pack of cigarettes in the shirt pockets of two of them. The cigarettes disappeared in his fatigues.

"You smoke?" asked Doc, surprised.

"Universal currency," said Eric. "Works better than money. Ruble's not worth a damn around here. Cigs are more effective if you want to get things done. Doesn't hurt to have a ready supply."

The horizon was lightening behind them by the time the Pacific Ocean came into view. Only the bare bones of the suburban sprawl that would one day characterize Orange County were in evidence. Development here had ceased at roughly World War II levels. Small towns came and went, separated by large open areas and miles upon miles of Orange County's eponymous citrus groves.

The pollution that they'd encountered in the San Gabriel Valley coming into LA the previous night was no longer in evidence as they arrived at the crossroads of Pacific Coast Highway and the Newport peninsula. The harbor area before them exhibited little of its 21st century opulence and exclusivity. The high-priced yachts that jutted out from the peninsula and Balboa Island in the new millennium like quills on a porcupine were virtually nonexistent in Russian-occupied Southern California, circa 1963. Instead, the boats they saw were utilitarian—fishing trawlers mostly--with modest rowboats and skiffs moored among them, while Newport itself resembled nothing so much as a small fishing village on the Eastern seaboard.

"The Party frowns on what it calls the trappings of the bourgeois elite," Eric explained. "And then there's the fact that just about everybody but the party bigwigs is piss-poor these days. Start accumulating too much stuff and you're bound to get noticed. Nobody wants that."

They pulled off the roadway onto a turnout located on a bluff overlooking the peninsula and the island of Balboa. Never a fan of urban development, he couldn't help but admire this simpler version of the town, despite his awareness of the circumstances that had caused it to remain in this stunted state well into the sixties.

"I know" said Eric, reading his thoughts. "There are always pluses involved, no matter how bad things get. Right? Besides the lack of overdevelopment, there are other benefits. Civil rights? Women's rights? They both got a big boost under the occupation. Skin color and gender tend to take a back seat when you're fighting for survival against a common enemy. Not to mention the whole Vietnam thing was a non-starter."

They sat and admired the view for few minutes.

"Sitting here it is difficult to believe that what we saw last night exists," said Doc.

"Life is way better here on the coast, that's for sure," said Eric. "And the further south you go, the better it gets. If you keep your head down, the Russkies pretty much leave you alone to go about your business. The beach communities tend to be self-reliant, for the most part. The fishing's good. Everybody grows their own veggies and makes their own clothing. The Reds like to roll through every now and again to collect a tribute and generally raise some hell. But the advantage to a hand-to-mouth existence is that there's never a lot left over to give to the Reds. Not giving to the regime is a point of honor around here."

"No one stockpiles food and necessities?"

"Oh sure. There's a lot of trading and bartering going on behind the scenes. But it's kept under wraps. It could go pretty badly for a community if somebody gets caught."

"People get killed?"

Eric nodded. "If the Russkies feel threatened in any way, the Air Force gets called in and the offending community disappears from the face of the earth."

"That is extreme."

"The Russians are paranoid about an uprising happening. It's a sensitive area for them, you might say. They did it to the czars back in the good old days when they staged their Bolshevik revolution. They're scared to death of it happening to them. So they tend to be pretty ham-fisted in their response to threats. The Soviets have never been noted for their subtlety."

Chapter 35

The view of the ocean worked like a balm to sooth the memory of the jarring events and revelations of the previous night. When a fair amount of time had elapsed, Eric shifted the old truck into reverse and pulled back from the overlook. Then he swung the utilitarian vehicle in a wide arc that brought them back to Coast Highway. Traffic continued to thin out as they headed south along the seashore. They passed a couple of transports heading north, but that was the extent of it.

"The US is a large country to occupy I imagine, even for the Soviets," Doc remarked.

"It's enormous," Eric agreed. "I'm not sure the Reds knew what they were getting into. They've got a couple of million soldiers on the ground here, but that isn't nearly enough to effectively patrol a country this size. And the fact is, they probably couldn't maintain control without the Sword of Damocles approach. It's an old story. Plus, they figure they have The Bomb to fall back on. Things got out of hand in Minneapolis early on and guess what? No more Minneapolis."

"That's unthinkable," Doc said, aghast.

"You're right about that," said Eric solemnly. "Even so, none of that has prevented a pretty well organized underground resistance movement to take hold. They conduct small operations in towns and cities across the country. Localized urban guerrilla warfare. If the rebels can attack and then disappear in areas where the Russians are thick on the ground, there's less chance of a disproportionate response, such as an indiscriminate bombing campaign. It's a tricky balance though, knowing how far to go before innocent people start getting lined up and shot."

"Does it do any good? Resisting?"

"These are Americans we're talking about. Doing something is better than doing nothing, even in the face of overwhelming force. But hey, this is better than some other alternatives I've seen."

"Like what?"

"Like the one where the Nazis won the war."

"No."

"Yup."

"You seem to have a lot of knowledge concerning D'Angelo."

"I know him mostly by reputation. Hard to spend any amount of time here and not hear about the Weasel. And I've caught sight of him a time or two in my travels. But our paths have never really crossed. Until now."

"Were you tracking D'Angelo back in Angels' Keep?"

"No. Nothing like that. D'Angelo was the last person I expected to show up in the Keep. Not normally his kind of place."

"So why did you choose Angels' Keep, if I may ask a personal question."

"Convenience. It's close to the Shipley portal. And for the peace and quiet. It's the perfect place to decompress between jumps. Good weather. Clean air. Good music." He gestured toward Doc with deference. "Not a lot happening—most of the time."

"You do not mind living in a field under a tarp?"

"I love it. After some of the stuff I see in my travels and some the places I end up, there's nothing better than to be out in the open under a starry sky."

"Well," said Doc. "Now we are here, surrounded by Russians, preparing to rescue a damsel in distress from a slippery, psychopathic thug with superhuman powers," Doc said.

"What could be better?" replied Eric happily.

THE BEACH TOWN UNDERGROUND

Chapter 36

Laguna Beach during the occupation looked a lot like the Laguna of the early fifties. Located along one of the most picturesque stretches of waterfront in Southern California, Laguna remained as appealing as ever. As far as construction was concerned, the clock had stopped at the time of the invasion: August 3, 1952. But what was there was well-preserved and well-maintained. Civic pride apparently still ran high here.

"Never been strafed," Eric explained as the truck lumbered down the long hill toward Main Beach. The Laguna Hotel shone brightly in the midday sun. The cars on the street, though sparse, were of forties and early fifties vintage. The scene reminded him of pictures he'd seen of Havana in the decades after Castro had taken over—the sense of a culture frozen in time. Like the houses and buildings visible, what cars there were were lovingly maintained.

"The American auto industry was shut down when the Reds took over," Eric said as they drove into town on Coast Highway. "Still, most folks tend to prefer the trusty old Detroit products to the newer Russian models. Not that I blame them. Never could get too excited about the Volga or the Trabant myself."

"Why did the Russians not just continue production in Detroit? They would have had everything they needed."

Eric gave Doc a wry grin. "It's a great example of ideology trumping pragmatism. The success of the American auto industry of the forties and early fifties was a symbol of everything the commies were against: freedom, style, individuality, the profit motive."

"It is not quite as glorious in our time. But I see your point," Doc said.

"Even now, a dozen years after production ceased, American cars are still all over the place. Every American car still running out there is a slap in the face to the Reds. So there's lots."

The hulking transport drew resentful looks from drivers and pedestrians alike as they arrived at Main Beach. They found a small turnout and pulled off the road.

Eric checked the mirrors. People were giving the truck a wide berth.

"While this vehicle may have been useful to us further north," Eric declared, "it unfortunately makes us just a little conspicuous down here."

Doc glanced in his side mirror, acutely aware of the hostility the truck provoked.

"If we plan to be here for any length of time we're gonna have to arrange for alternate transportation," Eric said, voicing Doc's thoughts.

"Do you know anyone who might help us?"

"Down here? Unfortunately, no."

A thought came to Doc. He almost dismissed it out of hand. But then none of what had happened to him since the previous night seemed any more plausible than the notion that had just occurred to him. He reached into his jeans pocket and rummaged around for a second before he found what he was looking for.

He handed Eric a business card.

"Where'd you get this?" Eric asked, raising an eyebrow.

Doc described his and Callie's encounter with the Beach Party reenactment troop in the dunes near Angels' Keep, complete with custom cars, old long boards, and the Frankie Avalon and Annette Funicello lookalikes.

"It says here "Sal's Automotive," Eric noted. "What makes you think this can help us?"

Doc turned the card over in Eric's hands and showed him what was handwritten on the back.

"'Party Crashers.'" Eric couldn't suppress a laugh. "Cheeky. I'll grant them that. If they actually do hail from around here. And that's a big "if." Eric turned the card back over. Something caught his eye. "See this area code here--714?" Eric pointed to the contact number at the bottom of the card. "Once upon a time it covered most the area south of Los Angeles. Where we come from it's still in use, but now it only applies to a small area north of here."

"What is the significance of that?"

Eric tapped the card. "See this?" he said. "I happen to know that's a Laguna Beach prefix."

Doc considered what Eric was telling him. "So you are saying that this area code, coupled with this telephone number, could only have existed in the past."

"Specifically here and now," Eric said. "Which could mean what you thought was a re-enactment wasn't. Those people you saw, or at least some of them, could actually have been from around here somewhere."

Doc was struck by an even more absurd notion. "You're saying that ersatz Frankie and Annette …"

"Could have been Frankie and Annette," Eric completed Doc's thought.

The two men looked at each other for a long moment.

"There's only way to find out," Eric said.

Chapter 37

Eric moved the transport to the curb in front of the still majestic Hotel Laguna, ignoring the hateful stares directed their way. The hotel was located at the southern end of Main Beach. While Eric kept watch from the driver's seat, Doc climbed down from the cab and entered the shade of the seasoned though well-appointed building. He found a pay phone to the right of the hotel entrance. He deposited a ten cent piece in the slot and prayed for a dial tone, unsure if 21st century dimes were compatible with the old machines. Providence was with him, it appeared, because a loud buzzing sounded from the earpiece of the receiver. He glanced at the card and dialed the number listed there.

"Sal's automotive," said a voice at the other end.

"Pardon me," Doc said haltingly, not sure how to phrase what he had to say without immediately getting hung up on. "I am looking for the Party Crashers. Do I have the correct number?"

There was a pause at the other end. "Who is this?"

"My name is Manfred St. Michel," said Doc. "I believe I may have met a person or persons in your organization as recently as a couple of days ago on a beach in northern California. They gave me a business card."

A long silence ensued on the other end. Then, "Big guy. Biker. Snake tats on the forearms."

"That is correct."

"Well, ain't this a surprise. Where are you?"

"Downtown Laguna Beach. I am in the lobby of the Hotel Laguna."

"OK," said voice at the other end, somewhat tentatively.

"But before I continue I have to know something," Doc plowed ahead. "Are you *the* Frankie Avalon? The singer of 'Venus,' 'Bobby Sox to Stockings' and 'DeDe Dina?'"

"Last I checked. What's going on, man. What can I do for you?"

To Doc, the conversation was taking on a surreal quality. Not only was he talking to the fifties teen idol, but five decades and 370 miles separated their encounter in Angels' Keep from their current conversation in Laguna Beach. And yet here they were talking as if this were the most reasonable thing in the world. "Something has come up," said Doc.

"Let me guess," said Frankie. "It has something to do with that '48 Packard you were warning us to be on the lookout for."

"Actually, yes," said Doc. "How did you know that?"

"There happens to be a Packard like the one you mentioned right here in Laguna. It's owned by a lowlife named D'Angelo. I didn't put that Packard and this one together until just now. So what's he done this time?"

"Yes. Well. He has made off with a friend of mine."

"As in abduction? Kidnapping?"

"Unfortunately, yes. Do you remember the girl who accompanied me on the beach that day?"

"The one with the hair? She's kind of hard to forget. You're saying he took her?"

"He was trying to get to me," Doc said. He drew a deep breath. "It's a long story."

"Hey, I got all afternoon, chum. Lay it on me."

Doc paused to collect his thoughts. "I witnessed a murder that this D'Angelo committed. Or I believed he had committed. In any case, he clearly did not want his part in the matter to become general knowledge. As a last ditch effort to secure my silence, he took Callie."

"And you're here to get her back."

"Precisely."

"This D'Angelo is not a cat you wanna mess with. Not unless you have a death wish. Or a private army backin' you up. You dig?"

"There is just two of us. But we are sizable."

"Who's your amigo?"

"Gustav Gunnerson," said Doc. "Also known as Eric the Red."

"Who hasn't heard of Eric the Red?" said Frankie, with genuine awe in his voice. "The guy's a legend among jumpers. Hope for the oppressed. Relief for those in need. All around champion of the little guy. But I got to tell ya. Eric the Red or no, you're going to be heavily outgunned going up against D'Angelo and his crew."

"My hope is not to engage him directly if possible," admitted Doc, still smarting from the psychic wounds he had incurred in his confrontations with the man Eric referred to as the Weasel. "Perhaps there is another way. I confess we do not know enough yet about the situation. We have only just arrived."

"Hang on a minute," Frankie said. A hand was clamped over the receiver and indecipherable muffled voices were heard.

Frankie came back on the line. "Listen, why don't we meet up. You said you were at the Hotel Laguna?"

Doc confirmed this.

"Let's say Main Beach, near the lighthouse, in fifteen."

Doc agreed, and they hung up.

He relayed the essence of the conversation to Eric in the truck a short time later.

"We need to get this truck off the main drag regardless," Eric said, "The Russians probably have an all-points out for us by now." Shoving the transport into gear, he maneuvered the big truck into the relatively light traffic heading south on Coast Highway. He signaled immediately for a left hand turn. They drove up the side street and made a right at the next intersection.

Eric pulled to the curb and switched off the engine. "This'll have to do for now," he said. "Main thing we're out of view of the main road."

The time travelers departed the truck and headed back toward the beach.

Chapter 38

Frankie looked just like he had when Doc first met him on the Monterey Bay a couple of days earlier. With his disbelief suspended, nothing could have been more obvious that this was the singing star himself and not an imitator. His curly brown hair was impeccably coiffed and looked as if it could withstand the full force of nature's wrath. He stood 5' 8" in his flip flops. He was wearing faded Levi cutoffs, a yellow T-shirt, and a toothsome smile. At twenty-three he was already a show business veteran, having cranked out hit records since the mid-fifties. He was surrounded by teenagers and was busy signing autographs as they approached.

When he saw Doc and Eric, he told those assembled, "Time to scatter, kids. Let's pick this up later. I've got some business to take care of."

The kids in question didn't need to be told twice. They backed away, an expression of awe on their faces as the two big men arrived, eclipsing the sun.

Frankie took Eric and Doc aside and, in a voice that couldn't be heard by anyone else, remarked, "Heartthrob by day, freedom fighter by night." He laughed self-deprecatingly and led them off down the beach.

"You're with the resistance?" Eric asked, unable to keep the amazement out of his voice.

"I lead a cell here," said Frankie quietly. "As an entertainer I get to move around more than most. That means I have a better chance of getting my hands on the things that are needed. It's not just guns and dynamite. I've got sources for medical supplies, clothing and food for those who need them. It may not look like it, but there's a lot of people hurting around here. I guess we all do what we can with what we got."

Frankie Avalon, a leader of the underground resistance? Why was that so hard to believe? Obviously under these extreme circumstances, even the ubiquitous faces of popular culture could hide unexpected depths.

Frankie explained to them that they had just wrapped shooting on what would be the first of the sixties Beach Party movies.

"The one with Dick Dale in it," said Doc, with an appreciative nod, "And Robert Cummings."

"You've already seen it," said Frankie. "Why doesn't that surprise me?"

"On DVD," Doc explained. "My lady friend, Lucy, and I saw the whole series one weekend."

Frankie nodded as if he knew what a DVD was, or could guess. "No spoilers, OK?" he said. "And I'm allergic to reviews. I'd just as soon bask in my delusions of grandeur a while longer, if you don't mind." He laughed again.

"If it helps, I liked them," Doc said. "I especially liked the original Beach Party movie. The one you just completed."

"I like this guy," Frankie mugged. "I make it a point never to look up my own my stuff when I'm hanging out in the Promised Land. But if there are more movies after this one, it means I stayed alive long enough to make 'em. Right?"

"The Promised Land?"

"It's what we call the place that you come from. The place where the Russians didn't win."

"By the way, this is Eric," said Doc stepping back and drawing Eric forward.

The two men shook hands, Frankie squinting up at the big man as if studying the summit of a distant mountain.

"I'm honored to meet you," said Frankie. "I gotta thank you right off for everything you've done for us."

Doc felt he was missing something.

Frankie noticed his confusion and, sotto voce, said, "Oh, yeah, this guy has done loads for the resistance. He's helped our guys out of some dicey situations. He's been a one-man cavalry riding to the rescue on more than one occasion."

"Is that true?" Doc asked the red-haired giant.

Eric, who was obviously uncomfortable with the praise, remained silent.

"And those of us who have made the jump know he's done the same kind of thing in a lot of other times and places."

They continued walking toward the cliffs at the north end of Main Beach.

"I gotta ask you a question," Eric put in unceremoniously. "We had to jack a Russian transport last night to get down here and will probably need to ditch it soon."

"A transport? Jesus. Where is it?"

"Back there," said Eric with a toss of his tangled red locks. "On a side street."

Frankie suddenly looked genuinely concerned. "We'd better see about stashing it pronto," he said, "before it starts attracting attention. It could bring down a lot of heat if the Russkies found a stolen truck of theirs around here."

"I know, and we're sorry for the hassle and for the risk," Eric said. "It was the best we could do under the circumstances."

"I dig, man. I've been there more than a few times. When the enemy's breathing down your neck and your options are limited, you have to grab what's handy.

"Now let's go get that truck before somebody else beats us to it," Frankie said, leading them back toward the Coast Highway.

"There's going to be a real beach bash here tonight," Frankie said as they crab walked across the sand. They were walking as fast as they could without actually running. "It's a wrap party for the movie. Bonfire, booze, broads, music, the works. Annette'll be there along with the rest of the cast, including Dick Dale." It amused him to watch Doc's eyes light up. "I pegged you for a music lover," Frankie said with genial laugh. "Maybe more than that. You play?"

"Guitar. Electric blues."

"Wild. You'll dig it. Guaranteed. It's invitation only. And as of right now you guys are invited."

"I would be honored," Doc said. "You are not afraid of the authorities?"

"Actually, it's a Party-sanctioned event. The Russkies have a soft spot for American movies and music. You may have heard."

Eric threw Doc an I-told-you-so look.

"Party Crashers," said Doc thoughtfully. "What you wrote on your card. I like it."

"Says it all," said Frankie.

They reached the sidewalk and forward progress became easier.

"Considering all that is happening here, why don't you just stay in what you call The Promised Land? What is to keep you here?"

"This is where home is, man. This is where we're needed."

"Yes," said Doc. "It makes sense."

"Right now we've got a few hours to kill. I say let's get this truck of yours and and ditch it. Then we'll make tracks back to my place. You guys look hungry. When was the last time you ate? If you've been up all night, you might want to take a nap before we come back into town."

PARTY CRASHERS

Chapter 39

To everyone's relief the transport was right where they had left it. Eric climbed behind the wheel and fired up the truck while Frankie went to retrieve his wheels. His car, it turned out, was a customized red '32 Ford.

"A Deuce Coup," Eric noted admiringly.

"One of the perks of stardom," said Frankie, with a self-deprecating grin. "A guy I know who does props for the movies built this for me. It screams, too."

"Very nice," said Doc, sliding onto the bench seat next to him.

They were off in a blue cloud of burned rubber, Eric following them in the lumbering transport as they worked their way up Laguna Canyon. The houses soon thinned out, and they found themselves on an unpopulated two-lane country road. It was a far cry from the Laguna Canyon Road Doc remembered from occasional tour stops to the area.

"I confess I am not sure I understand," said Doc.

At this pronouncement Frankie burst out laughing.

"Did I say something amusing?" said Doc, not sure whether to be offended or not.

"Just the way you said it, man," Frankie said. "All earnest and all. We got nothing *but* questions about what's going on. We found it helps not to overthink things. Where the jump is concerned, it's easy to get bogged down looking for the whys and wherefores. But, hey, I'll give it a shot. If I can answer your questions, I will. What's on your mind?"

It took Doc a moment to find his train of thought again. "That day we met on the beach up north, were all those people you were with from here?"

"No. Just Annette, Dick Dale, Bear, and I. We've made some connections over the years and that's who you saw. Not everybody can make the jump."

"Why not?"

"I couldn't tell you. I even tried to bring my wife once. No go."

"I didn't know you were married," said Doc. "I thought you and Annette …"

"A lot of people think that," Frankie interrupted with a laugh. "The studio doesn't discourage it. They figure it makes for good PR. Whatever sells tickets, right? But the truth is, I got married a few months ago."

"Where is your wife?"

"I've got her in a cabin in the mountains southeast of here, out towards the desert, well out of harm's way. You can bet I'm up there every chance I get. But there's a lot to do down here. Sometimes I don't see her for longer than I'd like."

"So you and Annette and Dick Dale and your friend, Bear, are able to make the jump without difficulty. You are among the chosen few."

"Ain't that a kick? Probably for the best. Otherwise there'd be traffic jammed up for miles, people looking to blow this crazy scene. And what if the Russkies got hip to it? I wouldn't even want to imagine that. No time or place would be safe from those ratfinks. Could you picture it?"

"Is there more than one rabbit hole?"

"Oh yeah. They're scattered all over. We're going to one now, near my house in the canyon. It's the best place I can think of to stow the truck so no one else will find it."

Chapter 40

"That's my place up there," Frankie said, nodding toward a Victorian-style house, barely visible among the palm trees on a hill to their right. They passed the turnoff to the house. "Where we're going is just up ahead."

It looked like Frankie was going to steer the car into the tall bushes along the shoulder, but as he turned the wheel a narrow dirt track appeared, etched into the brush. Frankie checked the rearview mirror to make sure that Eric was still behind them. Satisfied, he returned his attention to the dirt road. It was overgrown with tall wheat-colored grass that swept the undercarriage of the car. The road ran up a gully that wound into the hills. A half a mile later, it straightened out.

"Used to be a fire road," explained Frankie, pulling off on a flat expanse of grass.

He turned off the engine. Eric pulled up next to them in the transport.

"It's another hundred yards or so farther up this trail," Frankie told Doc. "I'll go with your friend. This shouldn't take long."

"I'll come with you," said Doc. "Why not?"

"Your choice," said Frankie, frowning. "Where we're goin' will be nothin' to write home about, if I'm reading this right. But it'll do for our purposes."

"What do you mean?"

"How much do you know?"

"I know nothing," Doc said. "Last night was my first jump."

"It's like this," said Frankie, reconciled with the fact he was dealing with a novice. "Every portal leads to twelve locations—twelve different places in space and time. It opens to a different one of these every half hour. Meaning it takes 6 hours to cycle through all the possible options. Then the process starts all over again."

"Is Shipley one of the destinations?"

"Nope. As far as I know there's only one that goes there and that's off of 66 in the desert near Barstow. We stumbled on it when Annette, Dick and I were driving back from doing a show in Vegas one night. This particular portal has eleven destinations that no one in their right mind would want to visit and one that's OK. Right now it doesn't much matter where we end up. We just need to go through, park the truck and come back as quickly as we can."

They exited the coupe and joined Eric on the bench seat in the cab of the truck.

"Where to now, Captain?" asked Eric from the driver's seat.

"Straight ahead," said Frankie.

The shift in topography was less subtle this time, no doubt because the place they found themselves in was so unlike the place they had just left. They beheld a landscape so bleak they could have been on another planet. This is what the world would look like in the aftermath of a nuclear conflagration, Doc reflected. The ground in every direction was scorched black. The sky was soot colored, dense, and close to the ground. The air was thick with grit and the visibility was poor. There was not a living thing, plant or animal, to be seen as far as the eye could see. Massive chunks of broken concrete sprawled before them, festooned with twisted rebar, broken piping, and ripped out wiring.

"Holy shit," said Eric.

"The Riviera, it ain't," said Frankie cheerfully. "As a place to ditch the truck? It'll work."

"I can't argue with you there," said Eric slowly.

"Anywhere up ahead will do," Frankie said. "I don't think it's going to matter much where you leave it. Parking tickets aren't going to be an issue around here."

Eric put the truck in gear, and they rumbled toward a jumble of steel girders clumped a hundred yards away. They found an opening in the mountain of rubble before them, just wide enough for the truck.

"This oughta do," said Eric with a certain satisfaction. He pulled the handbrake and switched off the engine. Besides the sound of the wind gusting among the girders, silence reigned. They climbed out of the truck and set out for their point of entry.

They had traversed about fifty yards when Doc stopped abruptly

"What is it?" Eric asked, suddenly on the alert. "You see something?"

"There was somebody over there by that boxcar."

"What did they look like," asked Frankie, apprehension creeping into his voice.

"It looked a person. Sort of."

"Pasty white?" Frankie said. "Eyes that glow in the dark?"

Doc nodded.

"Shit," said Frankie. "Morlocks."

Chapter 41

"Morlocks?" Doc said. "As in the H. G. Wells book, *The Time Machine?*"

Frankie nodded. "I only ever saw the movie," he said. "The one with Rod Taylor in it. But you get the idea."

"Is this really a mutant species that lives underground?" asked Doc in a whisper.

"I don't know about underground," Frankie said. "But the rest of it fits. I've only ever seen one before. And he didn't strike me as the friendly type. I didn't hang around to shoot the breeze, if you know what I mean."

There was the rustle of metal behind them. When they turned at least a dozen weirdly luminous pairs of eyes peered back at them, apparently floating, disembodied, in the darkness. Without requiring further prompting the trio broke into a sprint for open ground. Eric had the Desert Eagle revolver out in an instant.

Doc was considering drawing his own weapon when they were besieged by a ragtag army of alien-looking beings. They scurried down out of the hills of rubble like rodents. There were hundreds of them. And they were fast.

The trio ran toward where they hoped the portal would be. Behind them the horde of ghostly, bedraggled entities was closing steadily.

Eric fired two shots into the air as they ran. The loud report of the huge handgun gave their pursuers pause. But the reprieve lasted only an instant before the specter-like mob began to close the distance as before. The first of these was now only a couple of steps behind Eric, who was covering their retreat.

"It's got to be here somewhere," Frankie shouted over his shoulder. He promptly vanished.

Doc was next through the portal. He found himself on the now familiar stretch of dirt road in the hills of Laguna, Frankie a few feet in front of him. They both doubled over to catch their breath like sprinters at the end of a mile run.

"Where's your friend?" said Frankie between gasps.

Doc look around. Eric was nowhere to be seen.

Doc drew a breath, turned on his heel, and charged down the dirt road in the direction they had just come. The sky darkened almost immediately, and he found himself back in the post-apocalyptic nightmare he had left moments before.

There was a commotion twenty yards in front of him. He couldn't actually see Eric, but guessed he was there somewhere in the midst of a swarm of the wraith-like troglodytes just ahead of him. As Doc looked on, he caught glimpses of Eric fighting like a madman in the midst of the horde. He was twisting and turning his torso, using his elbows and fists in a corkscrew motion to keep his attackers at bay.

Doc fumbled for the revolver in his jacket pocket and fired off a couple of rounds. They served to draw attention away from Eric for moment, which was all the big man needed to wrench free. An echoing chorus of muffled shots was heard from within the group. The assailants clutching at Eric fell away, screaming, obviously wounded. Eric made a beeline for Doc like a pro football fullback running for the goal line, dragging a half a dozen of the creatures in his wake. Doc crouched and laid down cover fire until the .38 clicked on empty chambers.

Eric crossed the distance to where Doc was standing in a few long strides. When he reached Doc he grabbed him by the collar and pulled him backward through the portal with him. The two men collapsed in a heap on the fire road. They were alone, except for Frankie who was staring back at them in amazement.

"You guys alright?" Frankie said.

"Good thing those creatures couldn't follow us through," Eric remarked, gasping as he inspected his wounds. There were gashes and scratches on all the exposed parts of his body. His face and throat were bleeding, as were his hands. Fortunately, none of the abrasions seemed to be life threatening.

"Nothin' a little iodine won't fix," Eric said matter-of-factly. He brushed himself off as if this were all in a day's work.

"I'd recommend tetanus shots when we get back," the former teen idol remarked.

Chapter 42

"Mein gott. What was that?" Doc asked.

Frankie shrugged. "You mean Crispy World back there? My guess? The Bomb. I'd say we were looking at a version of this planet where the full-scale war that hasn't happened here, at least so far, did happen."

"And those creatures?"

"The Morlocks? Mutants most likely, like you said. Too much radiation. Remind me to ask them next time I see 'em."

There was a scraping sound behind them.

The trio turned to find one of the ghostly pale creatures sprawled on the ground. It appeared to be a smaller version of the things they had encountered in what Frankie called "Crispy World"--a juvenile perhaps. It drew itself up into a sitting position, casting about in terror.

"Where am I?" The words, though heavily accented, were recognizable.

Everyone was too stunned to speak. Doc, Eric and Frankie had a chance to get their first good look at a Morlock. What they saw was a child, smeared in white paste from head to foot, bare-footed and wearing a loin cloth. He had on a pair of goggles that gave off a greenish glow--night vision glasses of some kind, most likely. The child, a boy apparently, pulled the goggles away from his face and continued to look anxiously around him. From all appearances he really was a human child.

"Is this Before Time?" he asked, blinking at the trio in front of him.

Frankie looked at his companions who were towering around him like citadels and decided he might be the best ambassador under the circumstances. He approached the boy cautiously. "I'm Frankie," he said in a calm voice. "Who are you?"

The boy tried to scurry backward at Frankie's approach.

"It's alright, kid. We're not going to hurt you." He stopped a few feet away from the boy.

The boy looked Caucasian under the body paint and goggles.

"We just want to know who you are and where you're from. This is Laguna Beach. My name's Frankie, and these are my friends, Manfred and Eric. What's your name?"

"Turk," said the boy.

"As in 'young turk?'" said Frankie, a note of amusement in his voice.

The boy didn't catch the humor of the statement. "I am young Turk," he said. "Is this Before Time?" he repeated.

"Before the time of what?"

"Before the war," said the boy.

"There was a war where you're from?"

The boy nodded.

"Who were the people who attacked us just now?"

"Angelenos," said the boy. "We are Angelenos."

"From Los Angeles."

"Yes."

"Why were you trying to kill us?"

"Hungry," said the boy.

Frankie almost laughed out loud, but stopped himself when he saw the boy was deadly serious.

"You eat other humans?" he asked.

The boy nodded. "Hungry," he repeated.

Frankie turned to Doc and Eric. "I've got some candy in the glove compartment," he said. "One of you mind getting it?"

Doc strode back to the car. Eric followed him.

"What do you think?" asked Doc quietly, so as not to be heard by the boy. "Have you ever seen anything like this before in your travels?"

"Not like this specifically," Eric said. "But I've seen variations. The post-apocalyptic scenario shows up in one form or another in a worrisome number of alternate versions of reality. I don't think people appreciate how close we are to annihilation at any give point in time, even in the 21st century."

"A cheerful thought," commented Doc.

"War, climate change, overpopulation, disease, plague …"

"I believe I get the idea," Doc interrupted him as they reached the deuce coupe. He rummaged around in the glove compartment and came up with three Hershey chocolate bars.

"The American candy industry still seems to be alive and well under the Russians," he remarked as they brought the bars back to where Frankie was talking to the boy. "I can only assume dentistry is thriving as well."

Doc gave the candy to Frankie, who extended it to the boy. The boy snatched the candy away and began to wolf it down, wrapper and all.

"Hungry," Frankie informed the others, with a knowing nod.

"Candy bar," said the boy appreciatively, his mouth full of chocolate and wrapping paper. "Candy bar," he repeated before resuming his ministrations.

"I believe he rather fancies it," Doc said.

"What kid wouldn't?" Eric said.

"He must be one of the 'chosen few,'" Doc said to Frankie as they watched the boy eat.

"Gotta be, if he made the jump," replied Frankie.

"Maybe he'll become some kind of religious leader when he grows up," Eric put in. "He Who Walks Between Worlds or something like that."

"Do you think he holds it against us that we had to shoot some of his people trying to make good our escape just now?" Doc wondered aloud.

The boy looked up and stared directly at Doc, chocolate in his teeth.

"More food," he said.

"He wants more to eat," said Doc.

Eric looked at the child. "I don't think that's what he means," he said slowly. "I think he's talking about any dead bodies we may have left behind us."

"More food," Doc repeated in a disembodied voice

The boy nodded enthusiastically.

"Christ," said Frankie. "I guess these Angelenos aren't the sentimental type."

After a long moment Doc said. "What now?"

"We can't just leave him out here for the Russkies to find," Frankie said. He looked at the boy to get his attention. "You want to come with us, Turk? We could get you a real meal. Get you cleaned up. How does that sound?"

At the mention of getting cleaned up, the boy looked fearful. He scooted backward and promptly disappeared through the portal.

Doc, Eric and Frankie remained standing on the roadway, contemplating the strange encounter.

"Hard to swallow," said Frankie.

Eric gave Frankie the thousand yard stare.

"Something to chew on," Frankie said, undeterred. "No accounting for taste."

Before Eric said or did something he might regret, Doc broke in. "Should we be concerned about others coming through?"

"Doubtful," said Eric. "In my experience less than one in a million can make the jump. And that's being generous."

"I don't know about you," said Frankie amiably. "But I'm starved."

Both Doc and Eric turned away in disgust and headed for the car.

Chapter 43

Frankie made the turn to his house off Laguna Canyon Road. He started up the bumpy dirt road that climbed to where the turn-of-the-century two-story house stood in an oasis of palms. They passed a sign that said Sal's Automotive Repair.

"Who's Sal?" Eric asked.

"Guy I bought the business from," said Frankie. "I'm a car mechanic moonlighting as a movie star, if you want to know the truth."

"You were an icon of the early rock 'n roll era," Doc stated authoritatively from the back seat. "A pop sensation."

"Nice of you to say so," Frankie replied, amused. "But you know how it is in the business. Here today, gone tomorrow."

"It was you who sang, "'Just Ask Your Heart', 'Why' and, of course, 'Venus.' Those are classics.'"

"You've got a long memory, man. Where did you say you were from?" said Frankie, with a laugh.

"I am serious. You must be aware of that—traveling back and forth in time as you do."

Frankie sighed. "I have the distinction of being the first of the manufactured pop stars. Did you know that? I'm lucky to be a footnote in the history of pop in your time. And I've picked up enough making the jump to know that the beach movies are a joke to most people."

"I have considerable affection for those beach movies," Doc said with consummate earnestness. "You are considerably more than a footnote—in my book."

Eric was conspicuously silent on the matter.

"You're one of the few, man," said Frankie jovially. "But thanks just the same. I don't take it personally. It was a gas making this movie,

I can tell you that much. The fact is, my music career was in the tank before this gig came along. Dig this. Did you know that they offered the role to Fabian first? They couldn't picture a short Italian guy from Philadelphia in the role of California beach boy. Can you believe that?" He laughed good-naturedly. He didn't seem to mind poking fun at himself and his image.

"But the movie caught on," Doc pointed out. "And it spawned, what? Twelve more films?"

"Sounds like you know your movie history," said Frankie admiringly. "I should call you The Professor."

"Like the Robert Cummings character in your current movie," Doc said. "I am flattered. You are aware of that much, then. That you made a dozen beach movies and spin-offs?"

"Yeah," said Frankie. "I cheated. I promised myself I wouldn't do any, ah, research on my life or career. But someone in the group up north had one of those flat electronic gizmos."

"A PDA?"

"A tablet, I think they called it. They waved it in my face. It would have been bad manners not to take a peek."

"Did Annette look up her statistics?" Doc asked before he could stop himself, recalling Annette had died not too long ago.

"Nope," said Frankie. "She's always been the one with the self-control." He looked at Doc and added soberly, "I guess there's some things it's better not to know. It was foolish of me to do it in the first place."

After a dinner of sandwiches and potato salad, Doc fell asleep on the sofa in front of a large window that looked out over the valley. Undeveloped rolling hills extended for as far as the eye could see in all directions. He dreamed of being in a bleak landscape, like the one east of Los Angeles, fires burning, acrid smoke, burned out vehicles. Morlocks seemed to be closing in on him from all sides. But they could never quite reach him. He was in a bubble of some kind that acted as a barrier against the violence and the carnage all around.

When he awoke the drapes were drawn, and it was dark outside.

Frankie appeared next to him. "Alright Rip Van Winkle, time to make tracks--if you're coming," he said.

Doc felt compelled by his breeding to apologize for dozing off.

"Don't mention it," said Frankie. "I have the feeling you didn't get a lot of sleep last night. Listen, I know you want to find your friend as soon as possible. I understand that. But we're not going to be able to do anything tonight."

Though he tried to hide it, Doc was sick with worry about Callie. What would he tell her parents if anything happened to her?

"Listen, if you'd rather not come that's fine," Frankie said. "I understand completely. You're welcome to hang out here. Catch your breath."

Doc thought it over. What he needed right now more than anything was a diversion, he concluded. Waiting around would only drive him crazy. "And miss the opportunity to meet one of my guitar heroes, Dick Dale?" he said, sitting up on the sofa. "And the fetching and talented Annette Funicello? I would never forgive myself."

"We won't stay late," Frankie assured him. "I need to put in an appearance with the rest of the cast and crew. Stand for a few publicity shots. Like that. Believe it or not, I'm not much into parties myself."

"Says the star of *Beach Party*," Eric remarked drolly from behind him. "Who says irony is dead?"

Chapter 44

The bonfire was easy to spot when they arrived on Main Beach. The blaze was sending cinders high into the night sky in the center of the rock-lined alcove that constituted the north end of the crescent. There were at least a hundred people gathered there. Except for small groups of middle-aged men in business suits--movie execs probably--most of the attendees were kids gyrating to the sounds of surf music being pumped through speakers attached to a record player, all of which were powered by a gas generator droning in the background.

"Meine guete, is that not Dennis Wilson?" Doc said, noticing the bleach-blond drummer of the Beach Boys holding court near the base of the cliff.

"Hunh?" said Eric, momentarily distracted by the ubiquitous bikini'd bodies.

"And there is Dick Dale!" Doc exclaimed. "Is it possible he was ever so young?"

"You wanna meet The King of the Surf Guitar himself?" Frankie said with a smile. "It can be arranged, man. Come on. It's cool."

Doc had to steady himself as they approached. Dale, for his part, was a little taken aback as he beheld the two burly time travelers that Frankie had in tow.

"I am a great admirer of your music," Doc managed as he extended his hand. "And I am especially enamored of those old 100 watt single Showman amps that you developed with Leo Fender," he effused. "The ones with the 15 inch JBLs in them. They are true vintage." He realized he was rambling and abruptly caught himself.

"Old did you say?" said Dick Dale, a bemused look on his face. "Those are the latest, man. They just came out. But it sounds like you know your electronics."

"I repair amplifiers and electric guitars for a living," said Doc. He was about to say the word "vintage" again, but pulled himself back from the brink at the last moment.

"There aren't that many guys around that know their way around the new Fender gear," Dick Dale said. "I'm looking for an equipment manager. You have a number?"

"Unfortunately, I am not from the area," said Doc, with genuine regret. He was reluctant to inject the topic of time travel into the conversation at this early juncture, even though he knew Dick Dale was an experienced jumper. So he sidestepped the issue. "Perhaps Frankie here could give you my details," he said diplomatically. "I would be honored to work with you. Tube gear can be a bit temperamental, I know. I have a few suggestions offhand for stabilizing performance which I would be happy to share with you."

"I'd like to hear 'em," said Dale. "Let's make it a point to get together."

Doc and Frankie took their leave after shaking hands with Dale, Doc still in a daze.

"You've been here five minutes and you've already gotten a job offer," said Frankie. "Not bad, guy. Hey, there's Bob Cummings. Did you know that he was the only one of us who could surf worth a damn? He learned in Hawaii. And he was supposed to be playing the square in the movie, right?--the guy who wasn't supposed to know one end of a board from the other." He laughed. "Leave it to Hollywood. And there's Dorothy Malone. Plays his long-suffering assistant in the movie."

"I remember," said Doc.

"Everybody here is in awe of her and Bob. They're legends around Tinseltown."

With the exception of Cummings, Malone, the studio execs, Doc and Eric, everyone was in their twenties.

A middle-aged man who looked like a used car salesman approached them. Frankie stepped forward to intercept him. "Sam, I'd like you to meet Eric and Manfred," he said. "Manny and Eric, this is Samuel Arkoff, the producer on our picture."

Arkoff seemed to be looking past the two big men as if eyeing some faraway landscape, one on which limitless possibilities abounded. "We've got a Viking piece in development," he said, around his unlit cigar. "Swords and horns. You guys would be perfect for it. If you're looking for work, come down to our field office here in Orange County. Frankie knows where it is. We'll talk." He turned to Frankie conspiratorially. "Wouldn't even need to spring for a wig for this one," he said, nodding at Eric. He seemed to find his pronouncement extremely amusing. Frankie gave Eric an apologetic shrug that seemed to say: They're suits. What can you expect?

"That's a very generous offer, Mr. Arkoff," said Frankie in a conciliatory tone. "I'm sure they'll give it their full attention. Hey, there's Annette!" He steered Doc and Eric away from the money man before trouble ensued.

"You guys interested in a career in Hollywood?" Frankie whispered when they were beyond hearing range. When both men shook their heads in the negative, he laughed out loud. "Why am I not surprised," he said.

Chapter 45

"I'll let you in on a little secret," Frankie said confidentially, as they walked up the beach. "Annette was asking about you after you showed up the other day. She's got a thing for older men. Especially if they also happen to be built like Sherman tanks."

Doc could feel his cheeks turn crimson.

Annette was talking to a pair of female cast members who departed uncertainly as the trio approached. She dazzled in a summery-looking evening dress.

"Nette, you remember Manfred, from the beach the other day?" Frankie said. His voice dropped to a whisper. "You know, on our last trip up north?"

"Sure," she said cheerfully, extending her hand. "Nice to run into you again."

"Likewise," Doc managed.

"And this is Eric," Frankie said.

Annette took a step back to look up at the big man. "I see you take your One-A-Days," she said soberly.

"Eric. As in Eric the Red," Frankie told her confidentially.

Annette's face transformed at this revelation. "Oh my!" she exclaimed. "I am very honored to meet you. Frankie and I have heard so much about your amazing adventures and all you've done for folks. Wow!"

Eric the Red was turning redder than usual.

Noting the big man's discomfort, Frankie pulled him aside. "Hey, you heard of Morey Amsterdam?" he said. "He's right over here. Funniest guy you'll ever meet."

Frankie led Eric away, leaving Doc alone with Annette feeling like a high school freshman at his first school dance.

"C'mon," said Annette, taking the initiative by grabbing Doc's hand and pulling him back toward the base of the cliff. She found a perched on top of a boulder and dangled her legs over the side. She indicated for Doc to join her with a pat of her hand. "So what's up Daddy-O? Tell me a little about yourself. You certainly look like you could handle yourself in a pinch."

Doc colored slightly. "Let me see," he said, trying to order his thoughts. "I am from Germany originally, from near the French border. I play electric blues in a band called the Beluga Whales--in the beach town on the Central Coast that you and Frankie visited the other day."

"Electric blues. How exotic."

"Otherwise, I spend my time fixing guitars and amplifiers. I have my own business."

"You sound like a model citizen. And here I thought you were a bad boy," said Annette. "A greaser without the grease. A biker."

"This is not incorrect," Doc said. His German accent always got thicker when he was nervous. "The biker part at any rate. I do in fact possess a Harley Davidson motorcycle."

"You should talk to Harvey—Harvey Lembeck. He knows a thing or two about Harleys. Especially after this movie!"

Doc broke into a grin and did a fair imitation of Lembeck's biker character's signature fingersnap-and-point from the movie.

"Hey. You've got that down," Annette said, genuinely impressed. "How did you …? Oh right. I get it. Where you come from this movie's ancient history. Here nobody knows a thing about it yet. It won't be released for another month. This time travel business is, like, weirdsville. The Twilight Zone. Dig?"

"I definitely dig," said Doc earnestly.

They were silent for a moment, observing the fire and listening to the music. Doc identified a surf instrumental by a group called the Challengers playing. It would be used decades later in the soundtrack to the movie Pulp Fiction.

"You know you're really lucky," Annette said finally. "Coming from where you come from. Everything's so beautiful there, so … peaceful. There's none of this madness you see going on here."

"Then why do you stay?" Doc asked. "You could leave through the portal any time you wanted to and never return."

Annette seemed to consider this question soberly for a second. "My life is here," she said finally. "My career is here. If I had to start over where you're from, there's no guarantee there would be a place for me. Could I make it in the entertainment business in your world? I'm not so sure."

It was clear the girl had wisdom beyond her years, Doc thought. Tastes were fickle. Countless styles and trends had come and gone in the preceding five decades. Whether she could make a name for herself with her talents in his time was an open question.

"See? That's what I mean. I don't know who I'd be anywhere else. Who else out there would care who Annette is? Maybe nobody."

"It seems impossible that someone with your energy, talent, and enthusiasm would not make a name for herself in any temporal context whatever," he said. "On the other hand, I understand your misgivings. It might not be a challenge you would want to undertake."

"As bad as it gets here sometimes, everything lines up in my life. Everything makes sense. You see? I know who I am here. I have a clear purpose."

"And how do you perceive that purpose, if I may ask?"

"To keep the darkness at bay," she said seriously. "To take people's minds off what they have to confront every day. Look. I know I'm selling fluff. I don't have any illusions about that. But if I can offer kids even the teeniest hope that things might be better someday, then I'm fulfilling my purpose. That's the way I see it."

Chapter 46

"Frankie told me about your friend getting kidnapped," Annette said, after a moment. "I'm truly sorry. D'Angelo is not a nice guy. They say he's got some kind of weird voodoo powers. He touches you, you croak."

"Yes," said Doc. "I have gone a couple of rounds with him already. Believe me, I know what you are talking about."

"You survived?" said Annette in amazement.

Doc nodded. "Barely," he said.

"Big, strong and modest, too," said Annette admiringly.

"Despite my rugged external appearance," he managed to joke, "I am really a softie underneath. Or so I have been told."

"So much the better," said Annette. "I can't tell you how tedious the tough guy act can get." She hugged one of his massive arms and leaned her stiffly sprayed bouffant against it.

Doc started to panic, wondering how best to extricate himself without giving offense.

Annette herself provided him relief from his quandary when she sat up abruptly and straightened her dress. "So tell me what you're going to do. About your friend."

"I must find her first," said Doc. "Then I will do what I must to retrieve her. The sooner I get her away from her captor, the better."

"Well if it's any consolation, you and your friend over there look to be the right guys for the job." She nodded toward Eric who stood next to Frankie near the bonfire. At 5' 8" Frankie wasn't exactly small. But he looked like a child next to the big Scandinavian. "If anybody could pull it off, my money would be on you two. And then there are the stories."

"Stories?"

"Your friend there is a bonafide hero to a lot of people in a lot of places," said Annette. "He's known far and wide for helping those in trouble. I've heard tell he's not above knocking heads if he has too."

"Yes, I have seen evidence of his pugilistic skills," Doc allowed. "Until yesterday, I had no idea of what he was capable. I had formed a rather unflattering opinion of him based on appearances and local hearsay, I must confess. But he has astounded me on several occasions since we embarked on this quest. Without him as a guide, I would never have gotten this far. Now there is at least a ray of hope that we will find Callie."

"Well, you're in good company with that one," Annette said, indicating Eric. "He's a man of his word, they say."

"You have done much jumping?"

"A fair amount. The place you're from is by far my favorite. It's like a little slice of heaven."

"You have visited bad places in your travels?" Doc inquired, thinking of Crispy World.

"I've seen ghastly kinds of places. I'm talking wastelands where mankind is reduced to fighting for scraps. I've barely escaped with my life on a few occasions." She shuddered visibly at the thought. But the sly grin on her face told Doc she wasn't entirely adverse to the risks involved. She secretly relished the excitement. There was definitely a wild side to America's sweetheart.

"So," said Doc circumspectly. "Are you also affiliated with the group that Frankie belongs to?" He wasn't sure if he was stepping outside the bounds of propriety with the question.

"The Party Crashers," Annette said in whisper, ducking her head and looking around. There was no one within earshot. "Yup. And you have good reason to be careful mentioning that name around here. These people you see may all seem as American as apple pie and ice cream, but there are commie spies everywhere."

Doc found himself imagining her in camo gear, wielding a machine gun. He shook his head to clear it.

"So are you, you know, involved with someone?" she continued, changing gears seamlessly.

"Back home?" said Doc. "Yes, in fact I am."

"What's her name?"

"Lucy."

"But you're not married," said Annette. "I don't see a ring."

Doc shrugged. "It is enough that we know what we are to one another," Doc said.

"I dig. Getting hitched can be, like, squaresville. Especially if it's done for the wrong reasons. Like just because it's something everybody else does."

Annette, rebel and a budding feminist? Who knew?

"Whether you're hitched or not shouldn't matter," she said, "if you really and truly care about each other."

They fell into silence, watching the fire and the people bobbing up and down to the music in the distance. A slight off-shore breeze and the radiant heat from the fire kept the evening chill at bay.

"Well I'm glad you, you know, made the scene," Annette said. "You don't expect to have people you meet in other times and places just showing up out of the blue. It's not that common. Jumpers are a rare breed."

"I honestly have no idea why I have been accorded the honor," Doc confessed.

"Nobody knows why they can or can't do it," said Annette. "And take my word for it, it'll just give you a headache trying to figure it out. I believe there are certain things we're not meant to know."

They continued to watch the pageant from afar: the dancers, the bonfire.

"I'm sure you'll find a way to get your friend back," Annette said finally. "And if there's anything I can do to help, don't hesitate to let me know. I mean it. We jumpers have to stick together."

Chapter 47

After Annette had left to rejoin the party, Doc must have dozed off. He dreamed he lay helpless on train tracks with an invisible locomotive bearing down on him out of the night. At the point of impact, he jerked awake to discover the thundering noise he thought was part of his dream was in fact the rumbling of motorcycles. A group of ten motorbikes had left the coast highway and were now streaking across the sand toward them. Near the bonfire Frankie was motioning him over with some urgency.

"It's members of the RSMC," Frankie explained when he arrived. "The Red Star Motorcycle Club. You know how in the olden days bikers were the outlaws? Times have changed. These guys are an arm of the establishment. They're commie thugs that do the jobs even the Red Army wants no part of. And since they have the blessings of the high command, they can do pretty much anything they want to."

"What do you think?" Doc asked Eric. The first of the motorcycles was now fifty yards away.

Eric didn't respond at first. He seemed to be assessing the situation, mulling over various options. "Let's hang back and see what develops for now," he said finally. "There's too much potential for collateral damage. I say we keep our heads down and stay as inconspicuous as possible for the time being."

His beard and wild hair flowing, Eric stood a full head taller and a foot broader than anybody else on the beach except Doc. He was anything but inconspicuous, but Doc thought it prudent not to point this out.

The bikers started weaving recklessly as they approached the bonfire, ripping up the beach with fits of acceleration. By the time they arrived, the festivities had ground to a halt. The engines were switched off, and a tense silence settled on the scene.

The leather-clad riders were obviously inebriated. They wielded bottles of vodka as they dismounted and staggered up to the fire, hurtling abuse in Russian at those gathered.

"They like to think they're real tough guys," Frankie said under his breath. "But without the support of the Party they'd be nothing."

"They look tough enough to me," Doc remarked.

"They're hoods in leather. Bullies."

At this point the drunken riders were chasing shrieking, bikini-clad girls around the beach. It was a scene straight out of an American International B-movie. Life imitating art, if you wanted to be very generous in your definition of the latter. Doc could picture the sequence of events that would unfold. The local guys would be pushed to the limits of endurance by the antics of the surly intruders and the inevitable rumble would break out as the young men rushed to defend the honor of their women.

In reality, no move was made by the males present to intervene. In their defense, it likely would have been suicide to try. The evening air continued to be rent with Russian cursing and the shrieks of women. Doc saw Annette slug a guy twice her size in the jaw. Her adversary looked daze for moment, rubbing his face in wonderment before resuming his bull-like charge. But he was sluggish and slow with drink, while Annette moved like a gazelle in comparison, easily outmaneuvering him and staying a few steps ahead of him at every turn.

It took Doc a moment to realize the beach was emptying. There were concrete steps etched into the cliff in a corner of the cove, all but invisible in the dark. A steady line of party-goers was filing up the stairs, gripping beach towels, coolers, and jackets before them like refugees. On the cliff above, those who had already retrieved their cars urged them on, waiting to whisk them to safety. Within moments only a handful of terrified women remained on the beach, dodging the bikers.

By now Doc had decided he had seen enough. He strolled casually over to one of the unoccupied bikes, a vintage Indian motorcycle from the early forties, as if to admire it. It really was in superb condition, he couldn't help but note.

Eric seemed to sense what Doc was thinking. He selected a target of his own: a 500cc Triumph. He swung nonchalantly into the seat, taking a moment to familiarize himself with the controls. Frankie wanted to say something to dissuade the husky time travelers from taking action, but Eric preempted him. "You don't want to be a part of this," he told Frankie evenly. "You live here. You don't want to mess things up for yourself or anybody else around here. Stay cool. We'll figure out a way to meet up with you later."

Frankie backed away reluctantly, finally turning on his heels and following the others up the cliff face.

So far the Russians were unaware that two of their motorcycles were in the process of being commandeered. But that quickly changed when the sound of the bikes firing up exploded above the curses and screams near the fire.

As they heard their own motorcycles come to life, the Russian bikers quickly forgot about the girls. Outraged, they made a beeline for Eric and Doc who patiently awaited their arrival straddling the rumbling and revving bikes. The girls meanwhile took advantage of the distraction to slip away unimpeded, their honor intact. At the approach of the mangy, swaggering and swearing Russians, Doc and Eric continued to hold their ground, gunning the loud two-stroke engines provocatively as the bike's owners stumbled drunkenly toward them, their faces black with rage.

Doc, who had nearly as much experience with motorcycles as he did with tube amplifiers, gunned the Indian bike he was on and spun it in a tight circle, spraying the approaching men with stinging sand. He reversed direction and did it again. And again. The Club members were sprawling on the ground by this time, covering their heads to avoid getting sandblasted, while Eric and Doc wheeled around them repeatedly and unrelentingly.

"How does it taste, comrades?" roared Eric above the din the bikes made. "A little gritty maybe? Here, have a little more, there's plenty to go around. Remember this the next time you decide to harass a bunch of kids."

"We will get you," shouted one of the Russians in heavily accented English, trying futilely to rub the sand out of his eyes. "You are dead men!"

"Don't count on it," retorted Eric. "If you're interested in getting your bikes back in one piece though, you'll sit on your hands and let us ride away. You'll find your rides around the corner there in front of the Hotel Laguna, but that's only if you're good boys. You get impatient and come chasing after us, all bets are off. You'll never see your bikes again. Are we clear, comrades?"

There was stunned silence. No one had ever stood up to them before. They were having difficulty processing this turn of events and adjusting to the new reality. Meanwhile, Eric and Doc resumed their motorbike balletics, sustaining the barrage of sand and dirt for a several minutes longer to get their message across. "Are we clear?" bellowed Eric at the top of his lungs, coming in for another pass. "I can't hear you!"

"Da, da," came the resentful, dispirited replies, as the men saw they had no alternative but to comply. The stood watching helplessly as the two men raced away toward the glittering lights of town.

Chapter 48

They'd made it round the front of the Hotel Laguna just as the first of the motorcycles back at the bonfire started up. Shielded by the structure, they extended the kickstands and dismounted the borrowed bikes. Frankie appeared curbside in his coupe. The two men needed no prompting. They ducked into the custom car, Doc in the back seat and Eric riding shotgun. The vehicle lurched onto Coast Highway heading south, leaving clouds of smoking rubber in its wake.

A block later Frankie braked so hard his two companions had to brace themselves to avoid going through the windshield. Doc was left reflecting on the wisdom of seat belts, which hadn't yet become de rigueur at this point in history, while Frankie made a hard left and headed inland. They were soon on Laguna Canyon Road winding north away from the beach. Eric, who was closest to the door, kept his eye on the side mirror. So far there was no sign of pursuit.

"Those RS guys ain't geniuses on their best days," Frankie remarked with a grin. "Let alone when they're in the bag."

The trio rode into the blackness that was Laguna Canyon in this day and age. There was no traffic in either direction, no lit signs indicating commercial enterprises or houses. Only the ghostly silhouettes of the hills, which rose around the road, were visible against the stars overhead.

Frankie downshifted when they approached his driveway. He made the turn, scattering gravel as he navigated the road up the hillside. The house was dark and still when they arrived.

They went in a rear entrance which brought them into a short hallway leading to the kitchen. Once there, Frankie flicked on the lights. There was a dining area directly ahead of them, separated from the kitchen by a diner-style countertop complete with gleaming chrome and bright vinyl barstools.

"Make yourselves at home," Frankie said. "But I'd advise against turning the lights on in the front room. We don't need to remind the Soviets someone lives up here. Thugs like the ones back on the beach aren't the only ones we need to worry about at night. Red Army soldiers like to burn down houses just for a kick when they're wasted and can't think of anything better to do."

Frankie took a seat in the booth beneath a window along the far wall. Doc and Eric sat down across from him at a lapis blue Formica table that matched the bar and stools. Frankie pulled a bulky, black corded phone over and started to work the rotary dial. Doc, meanwhile, seemed mesmerized by the unbroken blackness visible through the side window. Any indication of urban sprawl was nonexistent.

"Danny," Frankie said into the mouthpiece. "What have you got?" He listened for a while, grunting once or twice. "No," he said after a moment. "It's cool. You done good."

He and hung up the phone.

"I had a couple of friends stake out D'Angelo's place tonight while we were at the beach," he explained. "They said he showed up just before sunset. He had the girl with him. She looked OK, they said."

"Are they sure it was her?" Doc said, excitement in his voice.

"Yeah. They said she was hard to miss. Young Negro chick with white walls and bright green hair."

Doc had to grin at the image. Callie was here, he thought. Apparently unharmed.

"Listen," Frankie said, leaning forward. "I've been working on an idea to get you guys past D'Angelo."

"Yeah?" Eric said mildly. "What did you have in mind?"

"There's a custom car show happening tomorrow afternoon downtown. It happens once a month. I know for a fact D'Angelo never misses a chance to show off his Packard when he's in town. So while he's at the car show, you slip in behind him. You get into his house and get the girl out."

"He's still going to have a bunch of his guys guarding the house," Eric pointed out.

"I been thinkin' about that, too," said Frankie, obviously pleased with himself. "Check this out. I get some of my people and dress them up like Red soldiers. I've got access to every kind of getup under the sun through my connections at the studio. You head straight in, like you're conducting a routine inspection. You find the girl and bring her out. But here's the catch. We'll need a truck to make it look legit. And the only authentic Russian army truck I can think of that we've got access to right now is where we parked it earlier today." He let this sink in.

"Back in Crispy World," Doc said, not bothering to hide his chagrin.

"We'll take extra fire power this time," Frankie continued enthusiastically. "I've got a stash of AKs we can use. We dip our toes in the water first, see if there's anybody around at the portal site. If it looks clear enough, we break for it. We grab the truck and haul bananas back out of there. What do you say?"

Frankie's excitement was hard to resist. Both Doc and Eric were nodding their heads wordlessly.

"If there's no alternative," Eric said. "Why not?"

"The thing is," said Frankie, "we'll have to get the truck tonight, so you can be ready to move in the morning. I'll make a few calls to line up what you'll need for tomorrow, and then we can make tracks."

Eric and Doc looked at each other.

"Let's do it," said Eric.

Chapter 49

The necessary calls made, Frankie disappeared down a stairway hidden at the back of a broom closet at the rear of the house. He reappeared a moment later with three sub machine guns and three belts of ammunition. He passed the guns around and motioned for the guys to follow him outside. They situated the weapons in Frankie's car and climbed in. In a matter of minutes, they were parked on the dirt road that led to the portal.

Frankie turned off the engine, and they climbed out.

"Everybody ready?" he asked, as the three gathered in the middle of the roadway.

Doc heaved a sigh, looking down at the automatic weapon.

"You know how to fire one of those?" Eric said.

"Actually, I have some experience with this model," Doc said mildly.

"I'll bet he's got trophies back home from firing these babies," Eric told Frankie. "He's an expert at just about everything else."

The threesome moved up the road. The portal, as usual, was invisible. All they could see was the outline of rolling hills in the ambient starlight.

"If we're lucky," Frankie said, "they're all at home in front of the TV and we'll have a clear field to the truck." He grew more serious and said, "Let's take a peek at what we've got on the other side."

They took a step forward and found themselves in the now familiar post-apocalyptic landscape they had encountered earlier that day.

Unfortunately, they were not alone. The path to the truck was obstructed by a sea of wraithlike figures identical to the ones they had previously encountered, their eyes glowing in the dark. There must have been a couple of hundred of them gathered around the portal, murmuring among themselves like an audience waiting for the featured performance to begin.

The trio raised their guns, ready to defend themselves against the impending onslaught.

After a moment, Doc said. "Something is not right here."

It was true. They had been standing in the open surrounded by Morlocks for several seconds now and no move had been made to attack them.

"Don't shoot!" came a familiar high-pitched voice.

From out of the crowd before them Turk, the young man who had followed them through the portal the first time, appeared. He had dispensed with his night vision goggles so he would be recognizable to them. He held up his hand and the murmuring around him was hushed.

"We're only here for the truck," Eric said in a booming voice to those assembled. "We mean you no harm."

A conversation between Turk and the adults closest to him ensued. The words "candy bar" and "chocolate" surfaced more than once during the discussion.

Then, a remarkable thing happened. The crowd before them parted, creating a clear corridor for them to pass through.

Eric, Frankie and Doc lowered their weapons.

"What are we waiting for?" said Frankie, already moving in the direction of the truck. "Let's go before they change their minds."

Doc followed close behind Frankie and Eric brought up the rear.

"Doesn't this beat all?" Eric said, bemused. "I have a new respect for Hershey products."

THE OPERATION

Chapter 50

Doc awoke the next morning infused with an unreasonable sense of well-being. He was so startled, when he opened his eyes, to find himself on a sofa in an unfamiliar house that he almost ended up on the floor. It took a moment to sink in that the house belonged to a former teen idol named Frankie Avalon and that the year was 1963.

"Care for a cup a' joe?" It was Frankie peering in from the kitchen area. "We've got breakfast on in here. Come and join us when you're ready."

Doc pulled himself up from the couch. "Yes, thank you," he said. "I will be there in a moment."

Frankie withdrew while Doc took in the view through the parted drapes. He admired the open country spread out before him. There was presently no traffic on the canyon road below. The only sounds beside bird calls came from the kitchen. The clanking of dishes and silverware reached his ears along with the sounds of hushed conversation. The sun streamed in through the side windows of the house at an angle that suggested it was late morning.

Doc pushed the door open and found Frankie and Eric wedged in one side of the booth opposite a radiant Annette.

"It's Sleeping Beauty," Annette remarked good-naturedly, making a space for him on the bench next to her. She had on white pedal pushers, a dark-blue floral blouse and sandals. Not a hair on her perfectly coiffed head was out of place.

Doc struggled to come to full wakefulness. "My apologies," he said. "I had no idea it was so late."

"We're show people, remember?" Frankie said amiably. "Day, night, night, day. It's all the same to us. There's no set schedule around here, better believe it."

"However, if you were hoping to try some of Frankie's world-famous Italian omelet," Annette said, "then it's a good thing you showed up when you did."

"It smells fantastic," Doc said, taking a seat gingerly next to Annette.

Frankie jumped up, leaving Eric tucked into the corner of the booth, and went to retrieve a plate of food that had been warming in the oven.

"I think it's still edible," he said, placing the plate in front of Doc and taking his former position on the bench next to Eric. "We've got the stomach pump ready just in case."

Frankie watched him expectantly as Doc dug into the mountain of seasoned eggs, simmered onions, peppers and tomatoes. After a minute he nodded his approval and said, "Excellent." It didn't hurt that he was as hungry as a bear.

Satisfied, Frankie went on to the business of the day.

"I called my guys this morning," Frankie began. "They're standing by, ready to put on a convincing show for D'Angelo's guards. They'll be here in a couple of hours to pick up the transport. If you want to go into town early to check out D'Angelo's place, you're welcome to come with me. Annette and I are doing a sound check downtown in a few minutes. They've got a stage set up on the beach. We'll be doing a couple of numbers to promote the picture this afternoon at the car show. Part of the contract. It's a shame you'll be tied up. There are going be some familiar faces on stage today."

"Like who?" Doc wanted to know.

Frankie shook his head sadly. "It'll only distract you from your purpose if I told you," he said. "Don't worry, I'll give you the play-by-play afterward. How's that?"

By now everyone at the table was grinning, except for Doc, who muttered something in German under his breath.

"Anyway, back to the nuts and bolts," said Frankie. "You'll be in good hands with my guys. They know what needs to be done. They've done it all before. But if D'Angelo decides to stick around today, you've got to promise me you'll pull back. We don't need anybody getting aced if we can help it. Best to live to fight another day, if that's what it takes. Are we agreed?"

Chapter 51

Less than an hour later Eric and Doc were strolling casually past D'Angelo's compound on foot. The majestic single-level Spanish-style villa D'Angelo and his men occupied followed the contours of the hillside directly above downtown Laguna. A paved driveway led in from the street past a wrought iron gate framed by cypress trees. The street made a sharp left above the driveway, running parallel to it and the back of the mansion before turning uphill again. A high, ivy-covered stone wall shielded the house from the roadway above it. The driveway itself split as it came up to the front door, which was located at the southern end of the mansion, the right fork looping behind the house to what was probably a service entrance in back.

Through the bars of the gate, they caught a glimpse of five men in dark suits and sunglasses, sporting automatic weapons. D'Angelo's distinctive Packard was pulled up to the front door, while several other vehicles were parked off to the side. To keep from being noticed, the pair marched past the entry, heads down, and moved swiftly up the street. The roadway expired a quarter mile later at a wide firebreak.

The spot offered a stunning view of the idyllic beach town and the sun reflecting off the Pacific. The hillside was so steep they felt as if they were hovering in mid-air over the town, close enough to reach out and touch it. In the distance Catalina Island was sprawled on the horizon.

The stage Frankie had mentioned faced inland toward town from Main Beach. The two men found they had a perfect view of it from their vantage point. Directly across the coast highway a shady street that ran perpendicular to the beach had been closed off to through traffic and was quickly filling up with with rods and custom cars of every style and vintage, as well as restored antiques dating back to the Model T era and beyond.

They found a boulder to sit on to wait out D'Angelo. From here they had an unobstructed view of the mouth of the driveway. Little of the house itself could be seen from this perspective, shielded as it was by the stone wall that ran along the back of the property. The street leading past the house was visible for some distance above and below the villa.

They settled in, on the lookout for Frankie's boys in the transport and for the hoped for departure of D'Angelo from his lair.

"Not bad," Eric remarked, taking in the view. "Now we wait."

Families and herds of teens continued to arrive on Main Beach until all the available space along the waterfront appeared to be occupied. The throng spilled into the street in front of the stage and merged with the car show crowd from across the way until there was an unbroken sea of humanity stretching from the middle of town to the water's edge. Armed Russian soldiers had cordoned off Highway 1 along Main Beach, routing traffic inland and around the town. One had to assume that a Party boss or two and their families might be in attendance.

Before they left that morning, Doc had managed to coax the music lineup for the show out of Frankie. Consequently, he was now torn between wanting to get Callie out as quickly as possible and hoping the transport might be just a little late. The thought of seeing such an assortment of legendary performers in their heyday was enticing to say the least.

"So," said Eric. "Don't tell me you're really as big a fan of those old beach movies as you let on. I mean, c'mon."

"I would not be disingenuous about something like that," said Doc sternly. "As I said, American popular culture has always held a particular fascination for me. Isn't there something from your own past that you have an inexplicable and equally indefensible fondness for?"

"Sure," Eric said. "Some of that fifties stuff I can get with. Brando, Dean, Presley, Jerry Lee. Hard rock, sure,--Zep, AC/DC, Grand Funk Railroad. Nothing against Frankie. The guy's got guts. No doubt about that. And a social conscience. And I gotta say, Annette's more than just a pretty face. She's a decent kid. She's got a good head on her shoulders. Who would have guessed?"

"It is no surprise to me."

"That's another thing about you, my friend. You've got a willingness to look past the obvious. Even with people who would be very easy to dismiss. There's nothing wrong with that. It got us this far. Without the help of Frankie's people, I wouldn't like our chances of getting your girl back. To be honest, we're still going to need a shitload of luck."

Chapter 52

Dick Dale and the Deltones were due to take the stage first, followed by a short set featuring Frankie and Annette. The Beach Boys were on after that. The latter had yet to attain the level of national and international notoriety that they would achieve in the next few years.

Dick Dale and his band did their distinctive reverb-drenched set. They did not disappoint. Dale's fiery, machine gun-like double picking crashed on the beach town like a tidal wave. Frankie and Annette's short set of songs from the movie was disarmingly sweet, but milquetoast in comparison to what went before. The Beach Boys arrived on stage and did several tracks from the only two albums they had released to date,—Surfin' Safari and Surfin' U.S.A.

Eric and Doc passed a pair of binoculars Frankie had loaned them back and forth between them. Doc couldn't wipe the grin off his face. Here was a lanky, handsome Brian Wilson who looked fresh out of high school, years before the infamous breakdown, singing the falsetto parts and playing Fender bass. There was a cherub-like Carl Wilson on lead guitar, and the only real surfer in the band, bleached-blond Dennis Wilson behind the drums. They all wore beige stovepipe Levis and plaid Pendleton shirts like the ones they would appear in on the cover of the upcoming Surfer Girl album. It doesn't get much better than this, Doc thought.

Eric was more reserved in his enthusiasm. Even so, he never turned down a go at the binoculars.

When the Beach Boys left the stage, there was a lengthier lull in the entertainment. A couple of hours had come and gone by now, and the Packard had still not moved from the compound. There was nothing to be done but continue to wait and hope for the best.

Despite Frankie's assurances, it was beginning to look like D'Angelo might not be making an appearance at the custom car show after all for reasons unknown.

Doc tapped Eric's arm. "Look," he said.

"The transport's here, at least," Eric said.

They watched the truck lumber slowly up the hill. Eventually it drew up before them in a cloud of diesel fumes and the squeaking of brakes. They tensed reflexively when they saw that the truck was loaded with Red Army soldiers. They slid slowly off the rock they had been sitting on, ready to go in opposite directions down the draw behind them if necessary.

"At ease," the driver called out, with a friendly wave from the side window. "We're on your side. We're with Frankie."

Doc and Eric straightened sheepishly and walked up to the truck. They cautiously regarded the man behind the wheel and his partner riding shotgun. "Nice outfits," said Eric, finding his voice. "Convincing."

"Helps to have friends in Hollywood," the driver said matter-of-factly. "American International has got outfits for every occasion. We could have had you believing we were Martians, if that's what the script called for."

"I believe it," said Eric with a chuckle.

"Eric," Doc said urgently, suddenly on full alert. "It is D'Angelo."

Sure enough the Packard had just nosed out of the driveway and was now cruising slowly downhill away from them.

"Your timing couldn't be better," Eric informed the driver. "How many guys you got?"

"Eight, me included."

"Should be enough," Eric said. "If all goes well you won't need anything but your charm to get in, wearing those duds."

The driver, whose name was Stan, gave him a crocodile-like smile. "Russian military is a role we're reeeal familiar with," he said. "Trust me."

"You speak Russian, too?" Eric inquired.

"Enough to get by," said the driver.

Chapter 53

Since they were only ones not in costume, Eric and Doc climbed in back where they would be hidden among the others. Stan left the big truck in low gear and let its momentum carry them slowly downhill. The vertical exhaust pipe belched black smoke at the sky and the engine rumbled and roared loud enough to announce their arrival well in advance of their making the turn into the driveway at Casa D'Angelo. Stan steered the truck up to the wrought iron gate and pulled the handbrake. The truck rocked and settled. Three of D'Angelo's well-dressed goons approached from the house, brandishing automatic weapons.

Stan appeared unfazed, bored even, as he sauntered slowly around to the rear of the truck and let out the rest of the Party Crashers who were dressed, like Stan, in full Red Army combat regalia. They climbed out in practiced formation and with the clatter of boots on concrete took up positions in front of the gate, clutching what looked like real Kalashnikovs across their chests and gazing straight ahead. It was an impressive display.

As Doc and Eric looked out tentatively from behind the truck, Stan approached the gate and said something in Russian in an authoritative tone of voice. The guards were defiant, answering back in American English. More rapid-fire Russian followed. Whatever Stan had said worked because the surly guards moved to open the gate. He then returned to the truck, slid in behind the wheel, and put the truck in gear. They lurched through the opening and stopped just before the front door of the hillside mansion.

Stan then came around the back of the truck where Eric and Doc were laying low, waiting.

"We'll go look for the service entrance while you and your guys go in the front," Eric told him. "That way we've got the bases covered."

"Sure thing," said Stan. "Meet you back here in, say, ten?"

"You got it," said Eric.

The truck was parked in such a way that it afforded Doc and Eric cover as they ducked out of the back and down the service driveway toward the rear of the house.

Behind them the ersatz Russian soldiers were shouldering their way into the entryway.

Doc and Eric spotted the service entrance and, finding it unlocked, entered a commercial-size kitchen. They encountered no one as they proceeded briskly past the stainless steel countertops and emerged in a long hallway that separated the kitchen from a stately dining room. Floor-to-ceiling windows offered commanding views of the town, the ocean, and Catalina Island in the distance. Hearing a commotion and raised voices toward the front of the house, Doc and Eric turned in the opposite direction, toward the rear of the villa. The hallway became dimmer and quieter as they entered an area where several bedrooms were located.

"If she's anywhere, she'll be back here," Eric whispered.

There was still no one in sight. They followed the hallway as it loped to the right. All the activity was behind them near the entrance to the house. So far no shots had been fired.

Eric stopped outside the first door. Hearing no sound behind it, he turned the doorknob and pushed the door slowly open. It was apparent at a glance that the room had not been used. It was made up with the cool efficiency of hotel room maid service.

They tried three more rooms and hit pay dirt on the fourth try. The room they entered was strewn with teen magazines, notable for the fact that in place of the usual advertisements for hair and skin products there were hammers and sickles throughout, underscored by communist slogans. Among the magazines on the bed was the beret Callie had been wearing the night she was taken. Doc checked the closet and found Callie's purse there and her faux leather jacket.

"She was here," Doc said.

Chapter 54

"The Weasel must have taken her with him just now," Eric said. "She's probably in the car with him as we speak. Damn."

Doc and Eric retreated down the hallway the way they had come. The shouting match they had heard earlier had subsided. They could hear the rustle of uniforms and the thud of jack boots on the carpeting down the hallway before them.

They decided not to wait for Stan and his guys to show up. It would be easier all around if Stan didn't have the presence there of two civilians to explain to D'Angelo's security detail. They ducked through the kitchen and out into daylight at the service entrance, arriving back at the truck without incident. This time they climbed up into the cab from the shielded passenger side. A couple of minutes later Stan and his outfit emerged from the house. His "soldiers" climbed in back of the truck.

"Cocky bastards," Stan said to Doc and Eric when he was behind the steering wheel, checking the mirrors as he backed the transport out of the driveway.

"It's probably a toss up whether they wanted to incur the wrath of the Soviets or risk pissing their boss off," Eric remarked.

"In that case, it's lucky for us they're still slightly more afraid of the Russians and what they're capable of," Stan said. "The Reds wouldn't hesitate to level this town to set an example. After they got their own people out, of course."

"That's a credit to your performance, then" Eric said. "You make damn good Russians."

"Thanks, I think," said Stan. "So where to now, guys? Can I drop you somewhere?"

"You can let us out in town, if you don't mind," said Eric. "If we're lucky our girl is there somewhere. If need be we'll see if we can ride back with Frankie."

"I've heard tell this D'Angelo character is one scary sucker. You sure you don't want some reinforcements?"

"I figure we'll have a better chance if we keep it low-key," Eric said. "Better if it's just the two of us going in. But thanks for the offer."

"What'll you do when you find her?"

"Improvise," Eric said.

Stan pulled the truck over to the curb as close to the festivities as they dared to get and let Doc and Eric out. Frankie wasn't hard to spot. He was standing next to the stage, signing autographs as usual. Instead of interrupting him, Doc and Eric scanned the sea of gleaming antique and custom cars that extended inland along the shady street. The Packard was not among them.

"Perhaps he is elsewhere in town," Doc surmised.

Eric nodded, still craning his neck in hopes of glimpsing the Packard there. "You may be right about that," he said. "Let's circle around back."

They found an alleyway that ran parallel to the street the car show was on and ventured inland, away from Pacific Coast Highway. The noise of revving car engines and the ubiquitous murmur of the crowd quickly receded as they marched up the narrow, vacant one-lane road. When they arrived at a cross street about a quarter of a mile inland, they turned right and walked cautiously towards the main drag.

Coming up on a street corner, Eric motioned Doc to stay back while he peeked around the side of a building. The cordoned off part of the road occupied by the cars participating in the show began about 50 yards away. In this part of town it was business as usual, mundane cars parallel parked along both sides of the street. Families strolling. Groups of teens roaming around.

"You have a look," Eric said, as he made way for Doc.

Doc carefully studied the scene before him.

"I think I see something," he said.

He and Eric moved quickly out from their hiding place and walked at a brisk pace along the sidewalk in the direction of the car show and the beach beyond. As they proceeded, the distinctive contours of the Packard began to come into view. It was parallel parked at the curb just ahead of them not far from where the car show began. They slowed down in unison, aware that they would soon be visible in the rearview mirror if someone inside the car were paying attention. They were well aware they needed the element of surprise on their side if they hoped to get the drop on D'Angelo.

So far there was no indication that they had been seen. In fact, there was nothing to indicate that the car was occupied at all. There was no sound nor sign of movement from inside the dark, sleek automobile. The opaque tinted windows were of no help to them in determining who was or wasn't inside.

As nonchalantly as possible, Eric plucked a fire extinguisher from a wall adjacent to the entrance to a nearby pharmacy. He moved quickly and surely out into the street, while Doc continued to move cautiously along the sidewalk toward the passenger-side door.

Stopping for a beat at the rear bumper of the Packard, Eric took a breath and nodded meaningfully at Doc. He then closed the distance to the driver's door in two long strides and unceremoniously smashed in the side window with the fire extinguisher.

"Hey!" someone shouted from inside the car.

It was Callie.

Chapter 55

She was alone in the car.

"You OK?" Eric asked her through the shattered window. He inspected the interior of the car. "Where's D'Angelo?"

"They'll be back any minute," she said. "They're tryin' to get into the car show."

Eric reached for the door handle through the window but discovered that the doors could not be opened from the inside.

"The doors are rigged so you need a key to get in or out," Callie said. "They figured it was safe leaving me."

Eric nodded and threw the fire extinguisher to Doc over the roof. "You'll need that to get in," he said matter-of-factly.

Doc nodded, and with obvious regret, smashed the passenger window.

Eric grabbed the upper part of the door frame and hoisted himself through the driver's side window. Doc did the same from his side. It took some doing for the big men to squeeze through. But after a few seconds, they were side by side on the front seat of the car.

"Showtime," Eric said, feeling under the dash for the ignition wires.

"We are stealing D'Angelo's car?" Doc asked, incredulously.

"We need to get out of here fast," Eric replied. "You have a better idea?"

Doc shrugged and fell silent. He turned in his seat and addressed Callie in a gentle tone of voice. "How are you, my dear?" he said. "Are you hurt?"

"I'm fine, if being bored out of my mind doesn't count," she said. "I'll be better once we're far away from that evil little twerp. Talk about creepy."

"We are here to take you home," Doc assured her.

"My God! What took you guys so long?" she asked. The smile on her face contradicted the accusatory tone in her voice. Obviously her sense of humor remained in tact.

Eric was already stripping the ignition wires with a pocket knife he produced from one of the many pockets of his army fatigues.

"Just messin' witchoo!" said Callie. "I've never been happier to see anyone in my life."

She hugged Doc from the back seat and looked warily over at Eric, who was hunched over the steering wheel, working the wires under the dash. "Isn't this the guy from across the street?" she asked Doc. She wasn't exactly disappointed that the big Scandinavian was on board.

"Oh, you have not met," Doc said. "Eric, this is Callie. Callie, Eric."

"How do you do," said Callie, in very ladylike fashion. "I saw what you did to those guys outside of Manfred's the other day. Nice work."

"No big deal," said Eric, reddening slightly at the praise as he worked on the wires. "Pleased to finally meet you, too. We've come a long way to find you, little lady."

"Don't think I don't appreciate it," Callie said, settling back in the rear seat. She indicated the scene outside the front window of the car. "What is this? Retrotown USA? I'd swear we're back in the fifties."

"Sixties, actually," Doc said. "It's a long story."

"You gotta be kiddin' me," said Callie. "No way. We're in the sixties?"

"We kid you not," mumbled Eric, still working under the dash.

"You guys did come a long way to find me!" Callie said with a huge grin. "Way longer than I thought."

THE ESCAPE

Chapter 56

Doc studied the street before them. He spotted D'Angelo and two hulking bodyguards walking toward them from the direction of the car show. So far their angle of approach prevented them from getting a clear view of the Packard. Nevertheless, D'Angelo must have sensed something was amiss because he stopped suddenly. He tilted his head like a hunting dog testing the air for the scent of its prey. With a gesture from their boss, D'Angelo's men were suddenly sprinting toward them at full speed.

"Here they come," Doc warned.

"Almost there," said Eric.

The car's engine began to turn over. The starter motor was still cranking ineffectually when the bodyguards arrived on opposite sides of the car. Guns were produced.

As if they had rehearsed the move, both Doc and Eric threw their doors open, clipping the two men and sending them sprawling.

Eric returned his attention to the wires under the dash. The big men outside of the car got groggily to their feet just as the engine caught. Eric slammed the Packard into gear and it rocketed away from the curb.

Eric fought the wheel to straighten the car out as they fishtailed toward D'Angelo who was now standing in the middle of the street directly in their path. He defiantly held his ground as they accelerated toward him. Eric swerved at the last moment, grazing their outraged nemesis as they sped past him at full throttle.

From the middle of the street behind them D'Angelo shrieked impotently at them, a startling, inhuman sound, his face contorting in a way that recalled Edvard Munch's "The Scream." He quickly receded in the rearview mirror, fists raised in impotent fury.

At the first intersection Eric veered left and then left again a block later so that they were pointed inland. In a matter of seconds the town disappeared around them, and they were roaring up the canyon road.

"Can someone fill me in on what's going on here?" said Callie from the back seat. "What's the Russian connection? I saw a bunch of soldiers back there in old-fashioned Russian army uniforms. And then there were those creepy teen magazines back the compound, with the hammers and sickles all over 'em."

"You were kept indoors the whole time?" asked Doc.

"Yeah. They blindfolded me after they grabbed me outside the bar. I know I shouldn't have gone outside. I'm sorry. I couldn't help it. I needed to breathe some fresh air. I took, like, two steps out the back door, and there they were."

"Do not concern yourself over that now," Doc said. "What's done is done. I can't tell you how relieved I am that we have you back. Go on. What else do you remember?"

"Not much really. I was blindfolded the whole time. We stopped once after about twenty minutes. It sounded like D'Angelo was dropping off his bodyguards. Then it was just me in the back seat of the car and him driving."

"He must've recruited his posse from up north," Eric remarked. "He and Callie were the only ones who could make the jump, and he must have known that."

"How did you know that I could do it when we started out?" Doc asked him.

Eric glanced at Doc. "I just knew," he said.

"You and D'Angelo share a similar intuition, then, as to who can and cannot make the jump," Doc mused.

"I don't like to think I have anything in common with the Weasel," Eric said with distaste.

"And then there was this godawful smell," Callie continued her story from the back seat. "It was like a fire in the county dump. Everything you could imagine—rubber, upholstery, paint, plastic, oil, grease and anything else you can name, burning. I almost passed out.

Then the air got a little better, and when we finally stopped, there were other guys there taking orders from D'Angelo. They locked me up in a bedroom and kept me prisoner for I don't know how many days. There was nothing to do but thumb through these weird teen magazines full of, like, communist propaganda. It was sick. There was no cell service, no cable, no WiFi, nothing."

"We will do our best to bring you up to date once we have put some distance between us and D'Angelo," said Doc, eyeing Eric. "We promise."

He thought but didn't say, If we get out of this alive.

Eric, in the meantime, was nosing the Packard through the twist and turns of Laguna Canyon Road, his eyes intent on the stretch of highway before them. The few houses in the canyon were a blur going by. He checked the rearview mirror from time to time.

"It won't take the Weasel long to commandeer another vehicle and come after us," Eric said. "I thought his head was going to explode back there."

"My guess is he has never had his car taken from under his nose before," Doc remarked with some satisfaction.

"You just may be right about that, pard'ner," Eric said, with a grin.

"So what do we do now?"

"We've done what we came to do," Eric said, glancing back at Callie. "Now it's time to go home. What do you say?"

They reached the turnoff to Frankie's house and passed it without slowing. They rounded a bend, and suddenly a wall of Russian tanks and trucks appeared on the road before them, taking up the entire roadway. It was a military convoy bearing down on them.

"Shitsky," said Eric. "Time for Plan B."

The phalanx of military vehicles loomed ever closer, an impenetrable wall from one side of the road to the other. On the right, the familiar dirt track appeared—the one that led to the access point they had used to make the army transport disappear.

"Hang on," Eric said mildly. He braked hard, sending the car into a four-wheel drift that presented the driver's side to the approaching convoy. The tires caught a few feet from the first of a line of massive Russian trucks, and they plunged off the main road into the brush, raising a plume of dust and dirt like a rooster tail in their wake. Eric kept his eye on the mirrors. But thick clouds of dust made it impossible to tell if anyone had bothered to follow them or not.

"Time to pull a Houdini," Eric said. "Should be coming up any second now."

Doc, seeing the look of incomprehension on Callie's face, said, "Stay calm. We are getting out of here. You will understand in a moment."

There was a flicker, a change in the light, as the Packard made the transition.

A second later, Eric brought the much abused Packard to a sliding halt on one of the most beautiful, pristine white sand beaches any of them had ever seen.

Chapter 57

Callie stared, speechless, out the back window of the car. There was no trace there of the place they had just left. No dust, no dirt road, no Russian convoy. Instead there was the beach, as unmarred before them and as it was behind them, just a gentle arc of sand that vanished from view around the bend in both directions. Turquoise water lapped amiably on the shore, while to their left palm trees swayed, yielding to a climbing verdant hillside which terminated in a black volcanic peak. There was no sign of civilization to be seen.

The stunned silence stretched on until Callie said, "Would someone mind telling me what the heck just happened?"

Doc opened his mouth to speak, but at the last moment decided to defer to Eric. His own expertise in these matters left a lot to be desired, he realized.

"We made the jump," explained Eric simply. "We jumped, and this is where we ended up. It's a crap shoot when you're using a new access point. But I'd say this is an improvement over what we've seen so far." He glanced knowingly at Doc.

"Frankie mentioned there was only one location from that portal worth visiting," Doc put in. "This must be it."

Callie nodded, understanding nothing.

Eric thought it prudent to let the radical change in their circumstances sink in a moment. "This is OK," he said finally. He seemed to be making an effort to remain upbeat. "This is good. When the coast is clear, we can jump back."

They all looked out at a cerulean sky dotted with puffy white clouds, at the calm, inviting water, at the palm trees waving in a light breeze back from the beach and at the land rising steeply to the top of the mountain in the distance. There wasn't another living soul around.

"So then." Doc said. "Any speculation as to where we might be this time?"

"None," said Eric. "I don't have the slightest idea," he said. "The Indian Ocean? The Seychelles? The South Pacific, maybe. Your guess is as good as mine."

Doc, like Callie, nodded. They could have been a pair of bobble head dolls.

"You have never been here before," stated Doc after a minute.

"There's no end to the places I haven't been. New portal. New possibilities."

A lone cloud passed over the car, and it started to rain--first a sprinkle, and then a downpour. The rain coming in through the shattered windows felt warm. No one seemed to mind. Eric turned on the windshield wipers.

In it a couple of minutes the rainstorm had ceased, the sun came out, and the skies were clear once more.

"Hey," said Callie brightening. She pulled out her cell phone and switched it on. Her face fell as she soon realized there was no signal.

"We could try the radio," Eric said doubtfully. "Maybe there's a station nearby." He turned on the ancient in-dash radio and turned the tuning dial all the way backward and forward a couple of times. There was nothing but static. He switched it off again.

"No reception," he said. "Could mean a couple of things."

"Like?"

"We happen to be out of range of the nearest broadcast station. Or."

"Or?"

"There's no one out there transmitting to begin with."

"What? Why?"

"We could have landed in a non-technological era. Pre or post, take your pick. It's happened to me more than a few times. You gotta watch out for critters when that happens."

"What kinda critters?" Callie asked warily.

"Dinosaurs," said Eric.

He noticed her consternation. "Oh yeah," he confirmed.

"I don't think that's going to be a problem here though," he went on, gazing out the window. "If this is an island, odds are there won't be any large reptiles or mammals runnin' around here to worry about. They'd need a larger contiguous landmass to survive."

"What?" Callie said, as if she were suddenly hard of hearing. "What are you talking about?" She looked around her again and blinked. "How is any of this possible?"

"Ever heard of teleportation?" Eric said casually. "Time travel?"

"Like on the Syfy Channel. And in movies and books. Sure."

"Bingo."

"We're in a sci-fi movie?"

"If it helps you to understand the concept," Eric said.

"No, really. What happened? Teleportation and time travel aren't real. They're fiction."

"Guess again," said Eric. He seemed mildly bored. It was obvious he had had this conversation one too many times of late.

"But …" Callie fell silent studying their new environment. It was the best argument in support of what Eric was claiming. That they were in a vastly different place from the one they had been in moments before could hardly be denied. It was only a relatively small step to postulate they might be in a different time as well.

"OK," Callie said, sitting up straight on the back seat. "Let's start at the beginning. D'Angelo grabs me at the Fish Tank. He has me blindfolded and stuffed into his car. The next thing I know I'm in a bedroom somewhere."

"D'Angelo is an adept time traveler," Doc explained. "He wanted to take you where he was certain no one could follow. What he hadn't counted on was that Eric here is also an experienced time traveler. We followed you through a time portal near Prunedale on the night you were abducted. And our pursuit eventually led us to D'Angelo's compound in Laguna Beach, where Eric believed you would be kept."

"Laguna Beach? It didn't look like Laguna Beach. When I was a kid I used to watch the show. All the cool kids did."

Doc gave Eric an I-told-you-so look.

"Laguna Beach in the year 1963."

"1963?"

"Not only that, but it was a parallel universe to the one we know. One in which the Russians had won the Cold War and taken over the country."

"The army uniforms," Callie said quietly. "And the magazines." Is if coming to her senses, she said, "This is crazy."

"Indeed," agreed Doc. "Nevertheless it is the truth."

"My head is starting to hurt."

"Quite understandable."

Chapter 58

"Eric is quite proficient at time traveling," Doc said. "From what I have heard he is a legend among the select few who are able to make the jump."

"Oh yeah? Who else is a member of this exclusive club?" She addressed Eric for his input.

"Besides D'Angelo? And now you and Doc? Frankie and Annette. And Frankie's friend, Bear. And Dick Dale."

"You're shitting me."

"Language," Doc said. "Those really were younger versions of themselves that we ran into on the beach that day," he said. "They were not merely lookalikes. They often come to Angels' Keep. For recreation."

"And you would know this how?"

"Eric and I succeeded in contacting Frankie in Laguna Beach. He invited us to stay at his place while we were attempting to devise a plan to rescue you."

"Really."

"Really."

Callie considered Eric in silence for a moment. "So, the big guy here is just slumming it under the tarp in Angels' Keep, pretending he's a homeless person?"

"Technically speaking, I am a homeless person," Eric said. "And I have never intentionally misled anyone about who I am. People tend to make certain assumptions when what they're hearing doesn't mesh with their own experience. It's easier to believe the other guy's crazy than to concede their own knowledge might be severely limited. I just never bothered to correct their misconceptions."

"I get it why people think you're crazy," Callie said, "if this whole time travel, wormhole orientation is where you're coming from."

"Who could blame them?" Eric said, with twinkle in his eye.

"OK. So here's this superguy time traveler hiding in plain sight."

"Who's hiding?"

"Exactly," said Callie, with satisfaction in her voice.

Looking out at the ocean and the sea of palms was hypnotic.

"So what now?" Callie asked, rousing herself.

"We go back the way we came," Eric said. "The convoy back there is probably gone by now. So barring any unforeseen circumstances, we should be back in the Keep in a few hours."

"But D'Angelo is back there, too," said Callie. Her eyes grew wide. "Do you think he knows about this place? Could he follow us here?"

Eric shrugged, his brow furrowing. "It's best to assume he can. This access point is right in his backyard. That's why the sooner we get out of here and on our way the better."

"But you do think he'll come after us."

"The Weasel? Count on it. He'd have to, after what we just did to him and his precious wheels."

He started the car and turned it around so that they were facing the way they had come. He pressed the accelerator, following the car's tire tracks in the sand to the point where they started from out of nowhere.

"Almost there," he said.

Everyone braced for the transition.

The car traveled past the point were the tracks first appeared. Nothing happened.

"The hell?" said Eric.

He turned the car around and tried again. There was still no change. The beach stretched on before them and behind them as always.

He pulled to a stop and scratched his head.

"What is it?" asked Doc.

"I hate to say this," Eric said. "But it looks like we're stuck."

Chapter 59

"On the bright side," Eric said, scratching his beard. "If we can't leave, the Weasel can't follow us here either."

"You do not suppose there might be another portal around here somewhere?" said Doc.

"In my experience they're not thick on the ground," Eric said. "But you never know."

The sun was just above the horizon line. It would be dark soon. "Perhaps we should decide where to spend the night," Doc said.

Eric turned the car toward the palms inland from the beach. He found a clear area where the land began to rise and the terrain grew rougher. He stopped the car and turned off the ignition. "This is about as far as we can go in the car," he said. "Like I said, it's a long shot we'll find another portal around here, so don't get your hopes up."

"What happens if we don't find a portal?" Doc asked, somewhat apprehensively.

"You can start building that grass hut in the tropics you always dreamed about."

"Seriously?"

"I am dead serious, man. This may be what retirement looks like for the three of us."

"For you and me, maybe," Doc said. "But for her?" They had just rescued Callie from D'Angelo only to become prisoners of this island.

"Hey, don't worry about me" Callie said. "I like it here just fine." In fact, she was tickled at the prospect of hanging out in this exotic locale indefinitely. The place was a travel poster come to life. It beat Detroit by a mile on its best day.

"Yes, but think about how your parents will react if you do not show up back home when you're supposed to."

"You adults always need something to fret about," Callie said. "Enjoy the moment, dudes!"

"I wish I could," Doc said frowning. He turned to Eric. "Has this ever happened to you before? A portal just disappearing like this?"

Eric was scratching his beard. "You know. Now's you mention it … there was this one time. In Bhutan."

"What happened?"

"I'd gone to do some trekking in the high Himalaya. I'd hired a Sherpa as a guide. So here we are on this mountain pass that's not more than a foot wide, nothing but solid rock on one side and a thousand-foot drop on the other, when we happen upon this access point right in the middle of our path. Didn't know it was there until we stepped through it. It was a desert on the other side. Sand dunes as far as the eye could see."

"I believe a pattern is emerging here," Doc remarked humorlessly. "Limited human habitability."

"Unfortunately, that's true of a lot of the places you end up when you're jumping. They won't out-and-out kill you. You don't end up in deep space, for example. But for the most part they're not, shall we say, very user-friendly. Survival skills are definitely a plus for a jumper."

He resumed the story where he had left off. "So here we are stuck on this rock face with our only alternative being to hike the three or four days it would take us to get back to civilization. And did I mention we had supplies for maybe one more day?"

"Go on."

"My guide leaned against the rock wall, closed his eyes and started chanting. After a while he brushed himself off and walked back up the path to where the portal was. This time he just kept going along the path. The portal had just disappeared. When I asked him about it, he just pointed downhill. I didn't speak the language, but the upshot clear. He'd somehow managed to move the thing out of our way and into the valley a thousand feet below us."

Everyone was silent as they contemplated Eric's story.

"So," said Doc finally. "Are you thinking something similar may have happened here? Someone may have moved this portal intentionally? But why?"

"I'm just telling you what I know from personal experience. There may be any number of explanations for this phenomenon that I'm not aware of. The world is full of surprises."

"That's the understatement of the year," muttered Callie.

"As far as the portal is concerned we're all novices. Besides, we haven't seen anyone here, let alone someone who could have pulled something like this off."

The silence closed in. Doc leaned back against the passenger side door of the car and gazed up at the volcano, a faraway look in his eyes. "Perhaps tomorrow we can do some exploring," he said.

Chapter 60

They slept where they sat in D'Angelo's Packard: Eric in the driver's seat, Doc next to him in the passenger seat and Callie curled up in the back. After the day's excitement sleep came quickly.

They awoke shortly after daybreak. With Doc and Callie in various degrees of wakefulness, Eric took off for the beach on his own.

A chop had arisen on the ocean. The white froth atop the waves was a splendid contrast to the deep blue of the sea, which in turn blended with the azure of the sky.

He retraced the car's tracks on foot, relieved to find that no unfamiliar markings had appeared overnight. He walked down the beach to the point where the tracks started and kept walking. Still nothing. The portal had not magically reappeared with the dawning of the new day. He took his time on the way back, reconciling himself with the fact that they might indeed be there for some time. He paused to admire the majestic sweep of the volcano that had doubtless given rise to the island millions of years before. It appeared to be dormant at least. A steady wind was blowing out of the east. Perhaps there was a storm kicking up out there somewhere, he reflected.

Callie and Doc were seated on top of an lava stone outcropping a short distance from the car when he returned. They had been observing his progress from afar for some time.

"No luck?" Doc said.

Eric shook his head.

"Ready to hike?" Doc asked.

Callie jumped down off the rock. "Let's go," she said.

After about fifteen minutes the trio found themselves on an overlook. It offered such a commanding view of the coast and the craggy mountain behind them, they decided to pause there.

"I could really see myself, like, living here," said Callie.

"Without electricity and running water?" said Doc.

"You underestimate me, buckeroo," said Callie somewhat indignantly. "I can forage with the best of 'em. Remember I am a ..."

"A decorated Girl Scout," Doc finished for her. "We may all have to avail ourselves of your wildcraft expertise if we are destined to remain here for any length of time. My preference, of course, is that we find a way back to Angels' Keep and get you back to your aunt's place before anyone realizes you are missing."

If Callie had been traumatized by her captivity, she was hiding it well.

"Look at all this!" she said, gesturing broadly with her arm. "It's like dreaming with your eyes open."

"Even this could grow tiring after too long," Doc said, sounding to his own ears like a typical jaded adult.

They trudged on in silence, Callie with the energy of a young colt leading the way. The path climbed gradually toward the blackened summit still several hours away.

"Hey, check this out!" she said.

Doc and Eric drew up next to her. They were standing in a wide clearing where the earth was raised to form several mounds.

"It could be a burial ground," said Eric. There were no inscriptions. No writing of any kind. Even so, there was something about the feel of this plot of land, located on an exposed shoulder of the mountain, that inspired a certain reverence.

"This must mean there are peeps around here somewhere," Callie effused excitedly.

"Or where at one time," Eric interjected. "I don't know. Seems pretty quiet so far."

"Do you think there are spirits here?" Callie asked, eyes wide.

"As much as anywhere, I'd guess," Doc volunteered, with bemusement on his face.

Callie couldn't suppress a shudder.

"This place does seem to have a sense of abandonment about it," Doc said soberly. "These graves, if that's what they are, are old--ancient probably. They could be the remnants of a culture that died out long ago. Like Easter Island."

Eric just shrugged and said nothing.

The three of them stood in the brilliant sunshine, a brawny middle-aged man, his adoptive daughter and a latter day Viking who lacked only a shield, a helmet and a spear, each lost in his and her own thoughts for several minutes, while a gentle breeze continued to blow in from the east and rustled the vegetation around them. It sounded, for an instant, as if voices were chattering away in a some long forgotten language. But it was just the wind and the silence.

CELESTIAL LOGISTICS

Chapter 61

It took a few moments before they realized they were not alone.

A small brown-skinned man had appeared out of the thicket behind them. He carried a staff and was naked except for a loin cloth. His skin was painted with elaborate white markings that made him look like a skeletal apparition. He could have been an aboriginal tribesman.

When Doc had recovered from his shock, he nodded toward the man and said, "Good day."

"English," said the tribesman.

"You speak English?" Eric asked hopefully.

The man raised his right hand and brought the thumb and forefinger close together, in what could only be construed as the universal sign for "a little bit."

There was an awkward silence before Callie blurted out, "Where is everybody?"

The old man nodded toward the mounds.

"Everyone's dead?"

"Dead," the man repeated. He pointed toward himself and shook his head.

"Except for you," said Callie slowly. "What happened?"

The old man thought a moment. Finally he said, "All gone."

It looked like they weren't going to get any more when the old man said, "Greed sickness."

"Greed?" asked Callie incredulously. It seemed the woes of the outside world had intruded even here in what should by all rights have been paradise.

The old man nodded solemnly. "All gone," he said again.

Though he was obviously from a culture far removed from the one Doc, Eric and Callie hailed from, he seemed unsurprised to find them there. One would have thought from his reaction that this sort of thing happened all the time.

The tribesman took stock first of Doc and then of Eric. He pointed at both men and said something unintelligible. Noting the incomprehension on their faces, he found a stick and began drawing in the soft earth. He drew something that looked like a bird. He pointed again at Doc and then at Eric and finally at his artwork. It was clear he was trying to make some kind of connection between his drawing and the hulking foreigners.

Doc scratched the stubble along his jaw as he was wont to do when stumped. "My name is Manfred," he said. "This is Eric. And this is Callie."

The old man nodded at each of them in turn. Then he poked his staff at his drawing one last time, pointed at Doc and Eric and repeated, "Manfred. Eric."

"Maybe you know something about what happened to the portal," Eric said. He drew a circle in the air with his hands and mimicked stepping through it.

The man nodded, indicating he understood the question. He drew another figure in the sand. It was demonic looking. But the resemblance to Pete D'Angelo, complete with aviator sunglasses, was unmistakable. He said a word they couldn't understand.

"He knows about the Weasel," said Eric flatly.

"D'Angelo has been here previously," Doc agreed.

"Listen," Callie piped in. "What do you wanna bet this guy deliberately moved the portal to prevent D'Angelo from following us. This guy is like Eric's Sherpa."

They considered this.

"Well if he can take it away, maybe he can bring it back long enough for us to get out of here," Eric said.

The tribesman shook his head at this and motioned for them to follow him.

Another hour of climbing brought them to a clearing just above the tree line at the base of the final sweep toward the summit of the volcano. There was a large cavern before them that ran back into the vertical rock face. The could see the entire east-facing side of the island from here, an uninterrupted blanket of green beneath them extending all the way to the water's edge. The party was momentarily stunned by the view, shielding their eyes against the glare of the ocean in order to take it all in.

"Wow," said Callie. "It'ould take a while to get used to *that*," she said giving Doc a dark look.

After an appropriate interval for the appreciation of the vista, the man motioned them forward into the yawning entrance to the cavern. It was even larger up close, about thirty feet high at its highest point and about the same distance wide. There was a small fire flickering in the center of the antechamber. Their guide lit a torch from it and started toward the rear of the large outer room. From here the cave dimensions shrank quickly until they were marching through a tunnel barely large enough to accommodate Doc and Eric in single file. A few moments more and another smaller room opened up before them.

The old man lit more torches here, these attached to the walls, and the visitors got their first good look around them. Water trickled out of the rock to the right and seeped into an Olympic-sized circular pool. Flagstone steps led across the pond from front to back. To the left side of the room there was an alter, a huge stone slab, supported horizontally by boulders of lava rock. The center piece was a fair-sized chunk of ferrous oxide meteorite, from the look of it. Around it were smaller stones and crude stone carvings of animals and birds. Incongruously, among the assembled pieces was an automobile carburetor.

"Looks like Pete maybe had some car trouble here once upon a time," Eric said drolly.

Chapter 62

The tribesman motioned Doc toward the pool.

"Got your Speedos?" quipped Callie. "I think you're going for a dip."

But their host instead indicated the stone steps that ran across the pond toward the far wall.

"He wants me to cross," said Doc uncertainly.

The old man seemed adamant. To appease him, Doc tested the first of the flat stones. It seemed anchored well enough to support his weight without shifting. He took a second step. And a third.

At the fourth step he disappeared.

"I'll be damned," said Eric. "It *is* another portal. It's gotta be."

They waited for several minutes. When Doc did not reappear, Eric said, "It must be OK. Otherwise he would have come right back through."

Callie was the next up. She looked to Eric for guidance, clearly frightened. The prospect of teleporting was new to her and not something she was exactly comfortable with.

"You'll be alright," Eric encouraged her. "Remember, if you don't like what you see on the other side, all you have to do is take a step back. OK?"

The girl nodded and turned resolutely to the stone pathway before her. She took two more tentative steps and, like Doc before her, vanished.

When after a couple of minutes nothing further happened, Eric turned to the old man. "I'm thinking they're alright," he said.

The tribesman just looked at him, his eyes twinkling.

Eric, the grizzled veteran jumper, didn't hesitate. He'd seen enough not to be intimidated by an unfamiliar portal. He was confident there would be nothing at the other end of this one that he wouldn't be able to handle.

"Adios, partner," said Eric to the old man, doffing an imaginary hat. "See you next time around."

Chapter 63

They found themselves standing, transfixed, in a white room. But "white" wasn't entirely accurate. The room was beyond white. It's walls, floors and ceiling literally glowed from within. It was impossible to tell exactly where one ended and the other began or even how big the room really was. But it was the *sensation* of being there that was the most astounding. It was as if they were suddenly lighter than air, floating, all the burdens and cares of the world lifted. The place was at once thoroughly alien and at the same time intimately and overwhelmingly familiar. It was like coming home again after a long, long time away. Callie was sobbing quietly. A tear rolled down Doc's cheek. And Eric too was trying hard to rein in his emotions. Even so, he sniffled and cleared his throat.

A very tall, slender woman of regal bearing and indeterminate age appeared before them. "Welcome, travelers," she said with warm voice. "It has been a while, hasn't it?"

"Where are we?" Callie managed. Eric surprisingly produced a small package of Kleenex from out of his fatigues and handed it to her.

"You can call it what you will," said the woman. "I call it headquarters. It's where everything in the universe starts, and where it all ends. My name is Thea."

"My name is …" Doc began.

"Oh, I know very well who you are," said the woman. "All of you. You don't remember me, do you? No matter. It is lovely to see you all again."

"Are we dead?" Callie wanted to know.

"No," the woman smiled. "Nothing like that. You've made a slight detour in your travels, is all. We might as well make the most of it. Eh? Why don't we walk a bit."

She started for the far wall, which elongated into a hallway as they approached it. There were windows along one side of the corridor. Through them they saw what looked like a bustling corporate office.

"Celestial Logistics," the woman named Thea explained. "This is where the portals are monitored. They do not exist only on earth, you see. They are scattered through the entire universe. As you can see, they require a sizable staff to oversee and maintain."

It took a moment for this concept to sink in.

"May I ask a question?" Doc asked finally.

"Of course."

"How is it determined who can pass through these portals?"

"A certain threshold of divinity needs to be present," said the woman. "You all surpass that mark."

"What of this man, Pete D'Angelo, then? Do you know of him? He seems also to possess this ability to travel across time and space. And yet divinity is hardly a word I would associate with him."

"Yes, of course we know about Pete," said Thea wryly. "Everyone here does. That he is a very naughty boy cannot be disputed. And yet he does possess his share of divinity, though he has worked hard to suppress it over the millennia. He was once the Supreme Being's favorite, you see. So despite his controversial history he remains, in essence, of noble pedigree."

The three sought to reconcile this news with what they knew about the man Eric called the Weasel from personal experience.

"What the hell happened to him?" Eric blurted out.

"What often happens to a child of privilege who has been coddled and doted on in excess," she said, making clear her position on the issue. "They begin to think the whole universe revolves around them. Suffice it to say he developed an inflated sense of self-worth, which infamously led to his eventual banishment. It has been his single purpose since that incident to subvert and pervert any and all of our most highly cherished principles and intentions for mankind."

"He sounds a lot like Lucifer," Callie piped in.

"Clever, girl. Let's just say they are of a similar lineage. Just as you two share a common provenance with some of the most elevated powers in the celestial hierarchy." She indicated Eric and Doc. To Eric, she said, "Your service has been invaluable, sir. Do not think it hasn't been noticed."

Eric blushed.

"Oh please," pleaded Callie. "Tell me who they are really. Are they, like, archangels? Michael? Gabriel? I'll bet Manfred is tough-guy angel Michael. His last name *means* Saint Michael already. And Eric could be an ass-kicking Gabriel. Am I right? I mean, come on. They live in Angels' Keep, fer chrissake. They gotta be angels."

Thea had that Mona Lisa smile again. "To confirm or deny this would only detract from the validity of who they are now, and from the important work yet to be done. It would serve no useful function."

"What work might that be?" Eric put in.

"Your destinies have become intertwined with that of Pete D'Angelo," said the regal woman. "That may prove useful. To be quite honest, the Supreme Ruler of the Universe has grown rather weary of Peter's antics. You and Manfred may be in a unique position to … assist Pete in seeing the error of his ways. If there's anyone in the world who could provide Pete D'Angelo the necessary impetus for change, it is you." She leaned forward conspiratorially. "Just among ourselves, I would not be alone in welcoming such a change. But I warn you. The path is fraught with danger. You must not lower your guard."

"Why does the Supreme Being do it?" Callie asked. "I mean let someone like D'Angelo do what he does, messin' wit people, leadin' them astray and generally stirrin' up trouble all over the place?"

"The Supreme Being elects to impose Its will neither on mortals nor on the heavenly host. If they're going to come around, they've got to do it on their own. It takes a bit longer in some cases than others."

"You bet," Callie said. "How many eons has it been now?"

"Time has little meaning here," explained Thea, unruffled. "But your point is well taken."

"Somebody better step up and teach that rat bastard a lesson," said Callie emphatically. "Like pronto."

At this Thea laughed outright, a musical sound. "You just may be right about that, young lady," she said. "You just may be."

Chapter 64

Thea looked for a moment as if she were lost in thought. Then she said, "You will be in need of transportation where you are going. The Shipley station, isn't it?"

Everyone nodded, excitement growing at the prospect of going home.

"There's not much there," she continued, lapsing again into a kind of meditation.

"Wait. Yes. There is a tractor there by the side of the road. It hasn't been used in some time, but it should suffice to get you to the nearest town. From there, I am sure you will have no trouble finding your way back home."

"There's so much more I wanted to ask you about," said Callie in some dismay. "Now that we're here."

"I am afraid your questions will have to wait until you are back again for longer than just a brief visit," Thea said kindly. "I can promise you everything will be explained when we meet again."

With that, the luminous hallway and their radiant host disappeared, and they found themselves standing in the middle of a country road in central California.

"Whoa!" Callie said. The transition was so jarring that it was if she had stepped off a cliff. Eric had the presence of mind to grab her arm to keep her from falling over.

"It takes a little getting used to," he said sympathetically. "Ask Manfred here. He'll tell you."

"Wow," said Callie, when she had caught her breath. "That was amazing! What just happened?" Even now the memory of lightness and light was beginning to fade.

"I think we took the shortcut," said Eric, also obviously stunned by what had transpired. "Who could have guessed that little brown guy had a direct line to … headquarters."

"Thea practically said you two were angels," Callie said enthusiastically, "signed on to kick D'Angelo's heinie around the block."

"Angels? I doubt it," said Eric, scratching his belly with a chuckle, though it couldn't be said he was displeased at the notion either.

"Nobody has ever described me as an angel," Doc put in, "unless they were talking about the infamous motorcycle club."

In an overgrown field next to the roadway they spotted a faded red tractor with a wooden flatbed trailer attached to it.

"That must be our chariot," Eric said. "What do you think?"

"It appears to be the only vehicle in the immediate vicinity," Doc agreed, doing a full turn, taking in the scenery.

They left the road and slogged through the high grass toward the tractor. When they arrived Doc observed, "It has fallen victim to a certain neglect." A twinkle appeared in his eye. "But perhaps with a little TLC …?"

"And a miracle, maybe?" Callie couldn't help but add.

Eric held up his hands in an attitude of surrender. "I wouldn't know where to start to fix this thing."

Doc stepped in closer. "The principle is the same as with a car. Or a motorcycle, for that matter," he said. How hard could this be? he thought to himself.

"It just needs to get us to Prunedale," Eric reminded him. "A few miles at most."

Doc swung up onto the seat and was pleasantly surprised to find a rusted key dangling from the ignition. "Here's your miracle, Callie," he said with guarded optimism.

Once he had familiarized himself with the layout and with what the various switches and knobs did, he turned the key in the ignition, hardly daring to hope. From all indications this farm vehicle had been out in the elements for a long time, years, mostly likely. There was a prolonged buzzing sound. He tried again, and the engine began to crank over, slowly at first and then gathering momentum. "The battery still has some juice," Doc called above the noise. "I can scarcely believe it."

"I'll be damned," Eric muttered.

Doc tugged at what he identified as the choke, and the motor roared to life with a prodigious belch of black exhaust that immediately enveloped the trio.

"Krakatoa's got nothing on this baby," Eric managed between bouts of coughing. "It's running, though. Can't argue with that."

"Analog technology," said Doc happily.

The initial plume had dissipated as Callie and Eric climbed aboard the flatbed and seated themselves, backs to the front of the trailer.

"Let 'er buck!" Eric called over his shoulder.

Tractor and trailer lurched forward under Doc's guidance, and they bobbed and bounced their way toward the deserted roadway. The quality of travel over the rough ground was akin to bronco riding. Once they gained the asphalt, the ride smoothed out considerably. Doc glanced over his shoulder to make sure his passengers were still there. Satisfied, he gave the ancient rig some gas, and they soon achieved their maximum velocity of thirty miles an hour.

Within minutes they had entered and exited the sleepy hamlet of Shipley. A short time later the first houses appeared on the outskirts of Prunedale. In the middle of town, Doc pulled to the curb.

Eric and Callie jumped off the flatbed as Doc switched off the engine.

"I'm gonna be saddle sore for a week," Eric announced, rubbing the back of his cargo camos.

"I am frankly astounded that we were able to make it this far," Doc admitted.

"Ye of little faith," intoned Callie, her arms extended in front of her like a Halloween ghost.

They gathered on the sidewalk next to the tractor to consider their options. It felt good to see the central California sky again and to find everything from all indications back to normal. Nobody gave them or the tractor a second look.

Eric reached into his cargo pants and pulled out a cell phone. "Damn, it's dead," he said.

Callie tried her iPhone with similar results.

Fortunately they found that rarity in the 21st century, a functioning pay telephone, a half a block away. It was located next to the open entrance to a dive bar that exhaled beer fumes and stale fryer oil onto the sidewalk. Doc deposited some change and dialed.

"Chico?" he said after a moment. "It's me, Doc." He listened for a while and frowned. "My sincerest apologies," he said. "I did not mean to leave the band in the lurch. I was forced to leave town on short notice." He looked over at Callie. "A family emergency," he added with a wink. He listened a while longer "No, no," he said, "everything is fine. But listen, I need to ask a favor of you."

He spoke for a while longer and signed off.

"Chico, the organist in the band, lives nearby in Salinas. He said he would be here to collect us in about twenty minutes."

Little was said while they waited. Doc and Callie were mulling over the events of the last few days, contemplating how much of what they had seen and experienced they might conceivably impart to anyone else. Eric, on the other hand, was untroubled by such considerations. He had made the jump so often that he took the experience for granted. How much to tell others had never been an issue for him. He had always been ready to share with anyone who cared to listen the stories of his adventures in faraway places and times. That no one believed him was a matter of supreme indifference to him. As was being considered a derelict and a nutjob.

"You do not seem inordinately pleased to be back," Doc remarked, noticing his companion's demeanor.

"Just a feeling I have," he said, gazing down the road they had entered town on. "Call it a hunch, but I don't think we've seen the last of The Weasel."

Chapter 65

Angels' Keep had never looked better. It had only been a few days, but it felt like a lot longer. The town was bathed in the last light of the sunset as they approached on northbound Highway 1. Under these circumstances and in this light, it did indeed appear to be a heavenly apparition. After all that Doc had seen in the last few days, he was ready to believe just about anything.

"You know," said Eric from the back seat of Chico's lowered '62 Chevy Impala, "in other versions of the Keep there's a big Pacific Gas and Electric power plant right over there." He pointed to an open section of slough adjacent to the highway. "Can you imagine?"

"PG&E?" Callie said. "Really?"

"There are two big smoke stacks right there that you can see from Pacific Grove to Santa Cruz. Thing covers half the slough on the east side of the highway. In those versions the town is called Moss or Mossy something or other."

"You listening to this, man?" Chico said to Doc, who was riding shotgun. "What you doin' with this hombre loco, anyway?"

"You know I can hear you, right?" Eric said from the back seat.

"Just sayin'." It was hard to tell what intimidated Chico more, Eric's size or his rep as a crazy person. But the combination had the Latino looking in the rearview mirror every ten seconds.

"He is less crazy than you might think," Doc told his friend behind the wheel.

"You gotta know what you're doing," Chico shrugged. He pulled his car off the highway and into the small seaside town. "You, like, know we got a gig tonight, right?"

"Wednesday," said Doc. "Yes, of course. I intend to be there."

"Everything cool, man?" He shot Doc a worried glance.

"For the time being, yes."

Chico glanced over at Doc as he pulled to the curb across from Doc's dry-docked tug. "You'd tell me if you were in trouble, wouldn't you?"

Doc hesitated a moment. "I will explain what I can once the dust has settled a bit. OK?" he said.

"That bad, hunh?"

"It has been … educational."

Chico dropped his passengers off seconds before the sunset. The west-facing section of the hull was the color of amber honey.

Doc never thought it could feel so good to be home as they climbed out of the Impala. "You want to come in?" he asked Chico.

"Naw. I'm gonna go get some chow and then head over to the club. Jorge, my cousin, is bringing the B-3 and the Leslie. I need to be there to help him unload."

"You took the B-3 home?" It was always a job to transport the Hammond organ and its rotary speaker cabinet, so Chico usually kept them at the Fish Tank.

"I had a couple of solo gigs in Salinas while you were gone," Chico explained.

"Do I need to call to tell the others I'll be there tonight?"

"Already done, man. I called them the minute I heard from you. Catch you later, bra."

Chico couldn't resist laying a patch of rubber as he drove off down the street toward the bar. Callie took her leave and, armed with Doc's key, entered the tug through the workshop door. Doc and Eric stayed in the street.

"What about you?" said Doc to Eric. "Are you ready to take a break from the great outdoors? You are welcome to join us.?"

"No, no, that's OK," said Eric. "I've got to check up on my stuff."

Doc remembered Eric mentioning he owned an iPad. Then there had been the panel truck they been forced to abandon on Route 66 in 1963. And, more recently, the cell phone. He couldn't help but wonder what other gear Eric might have in his makeshift tent.

"It is unnecessary for you to remain outside," Doc insisted. After what they'd been through it was going to be difficult to go back to the way things were as if nothing had happened—Doc, the amp repair man and blues guitar player, and Eric the crazy homeless person in the field across the street. "I have ample room inside."

Eric smiled and shook his head. "It'll be good to be back under the sky again," he said, taking a deep breath to illustrated his point. "I'm looking forward to it."

"If you say so," said Doc skeptically.

"Who couldn't love it out here?" Eric said, straightening and looking around from his full 6' 7" in height. "Life couldn't be less complicated, and that's exactly how I like it."

He stopped and his Nordic features clouded. "Besides our buddy the Weasel's comin'. Count on it. If he tried to follow us through the portal back in Laguna—and I suspect he did before our friend, the medicine man, moved it on him--he's probably ready to come back here to look for us by now. He knows we'll end up here eventually, just like I knew he'd end up at his place in Laguna after he took the girl. Let's just say I can keep an eye on things better from out here."

Doc nodded solemnly. "I am indebted to you for your help in getting Callie back. It goes without saying I could not have done it without you. I would not have known where to start."

"Don't mention it," said Eric, obviously pleased. "This is what I do. Remember?"

"Are you planning on coming by the restaurant later?"

"Could be, could be" said Eric. "As long as everything stays quiet around here."

"You will be on the list at the door," Doc said. "It would be an honor if you came inside for a change."

Eric offered his thanks and departed for his makeshift tent.

Chapter 66

Back inside the tug exhaustion set in. The stresses and strains of the last several days made themselves known. Callie was already flopped on the couch, so Doc went downstairs to catch a couple of winks.

At 8:30 the phone rang.

"This is your friendly wake-up service," said Chico at the other end of the line. "Everything's ready down here. You've got a half an hour."

"I am on my way," said Doc.

He grabbed his guitar case, laid it on the bench and opened it. Everything looked just as he had left it. He closed the lid and climbed the stairs to the cabin. Callie was already up and about when he arrived. The Mr. Coffee was percolating. Doc shielded his eyes and looked out through the windows. It was pitch black outside. In the dim light from the street lamp he could barely make out the blue tarp that Eric called home.

"I think you had better come with me again tonight," said Doc. "But this time you stay inside the club. Is that understood?"

"Yes, sir!" Callie said, snapping to attention with salute.

"I mean it," said Doc, trying to sound as much like an authority figure as possible.

"Are you kidding? After what happened last time, I'm not going anywhere."

Doc had to endure the inevitable jabs about his prolonged absence before they settled into their set. Aside from that, the performance went off without a hitch. Many in the crowd insisted it was one of their finest shows. Callie was allowed to observe from the wings, standing in the hallway that led to the living quarters in a back. Even she was impressed.

Backstage at the break she said, "I could sorta understand what mom might have seen in you back then. James Brown, you ain't. But Albert Collins? Oh yeah."

Doc couldn't help but be pleased at the comparison. "The Ice Man," he said fondly.

"The Master of the Telecaster," Callie added.

"How do you know so much? Collins died years before you were born."

"Like I said. My mom was a fan. She always had something playing at home when I was growing up. Her tastes in music were all over the map. It would drive my stepdad crazy sometimes."

"Like what?"

"She could listen to Billie Holiday, Bartok and Captain Beefheart back to back."

"Yes, I see." Doc was starting to regret having let Callie's mom get away, if in fact their paths had ever actually crossed. The irony of the fact that had they become an item for the longer term Callie might never have been born was not lost on him.

"Do you have a picture of your mom somewhere?" he asked suddenly.

Without a word, Callie drew out her iPhone, now recharged. She paged through several photos until she came up with the one she wanted. It showed an attractive, nicely dressed woman standing easily next to a tall black man in a suit and tie. "This was a mixer my parents threw a few weeks ago," she said. "They like to entertain."

"This is your dad?" he asked.

"Stepdad. Yup."

"They make a nice-looking couple."

"He's alright, I guess. Pretty straight-laced. Workaholic. Definitely not a musician." It was obvious she thought it necessary to prop up Doc's ego a bit.

In fact, Doc did recognize the woman. A younger version of her had come to a number of his shows in and around Oakland in the mid-nineties. She would be hard not to notice. He doubted they'd ever actually slept together, however. He would have remembered.

"You having second thoughts?" asked Callie mischievously. "You regretting not having stuck it out with her?"

"Your mom is indeed an attractive woman," Doc allowed. "That cannot be disputed. She has certainly become rather upscale."

"Upscale, eh? She can let her hair down alright, believe me. I've seen it with my own eyes a time or two. She's got some killer dance moves."

"I can easily believe it," he said, his conscience tweaking him about not having pointed out to her yet that she could not be his biological daughter. To be fair, there hadn't been a lot of opportunity to do so in the past days. "I've got another set coming up," he said. "Please do me the favor of not venturing too close to the exits."

"No worries," she said dismissively.

Doc was somewhat surprised and quite pleased to see Eric sitting on a barstool just inside the front door of the club. Doc didn't normally do much talking from the stage, but on this occasion he stepped awkwardly to the microphone and, looking at the members of the band, said, "I would like to dedicate this song to a brother-in-arms, a fellow traveler and a man of honor." He glanced in Eric's direction but didn't want to embarrass him by mentioning him by name. Heads turned to see where he was looking, but no one could tell for sure who Doc was referring to. It was just as well. Eric would know, and that was the main thing. The band launched into an uptempo version of the Robert Johnson classic, "Crossroads."

Eric stayed for most of the set. But at the end of the show Doc looked toward the corner of the club where Eric had been sitting and saw that he was gone.

Chapter 67

After the evening's performance Doc met up with Lucy.

"OK, where guitar hero go? Have fun on side? Leave hot Chinese girlfriend slaving over hot wok!"

"It is not like that," Doc insisted, his face growing warm.

"Girlfriend not hot?"

Around her, embarrassment seemed to be his default setting. "No. I mean, yes, girlfriend hot." He realized that he was inadvertently sounding like her again. "I mean, it will take some time to explain."

"Asian girl got plenty time," said Lucy, fanning herself with her hand.

Doc couldn't help but smile. This was one of the many reasons he loved this woman, he thought. He could never take himself too seriously around her.

"I go for walk with American john." She grabbed his hand in delight.

"Wait, I must tell Callie."

"Chill, homeboy," Callie said, having heard the last part of the conversation. "I be hangin' with Chrissie til you get back. And no, I ain't goin' anywhere near the door this time."

Another thing Doc loved about Lucy was that she was patient. She wasn't quick to pass judgment. She said hardly a word while Doc described his highly improbable adventures since leaving The Fish Tank the week before.

When he had finished she held out her hand, palm up, and said, "Time traveler get special discount."

Doc looked down at her extended hand, not quite sure what to do.

Lucy pushed him and said, "German American boyfriend silly. No need cash. Credit accepted."

Doc didn't know what to say.

"Frankie and Annette. China girl like that part." She pronounced 'part' without the 't.'

After a moment's pause, she said, "Pint-size devil? He still after you?"

"Eric is convinced he is." Doc said.

"So round-eye not out of woods yet."

"That remains to be seen. But it seems prudent to be ready for the worst."

"Maybe you stay here at club." She smiled at him coquettishly. "Many perk."

"I am grateful for the offer," said Doc soberly. "But if he comes and is intent on causing mischief, the last thing I want is for you and Chrissie to be anywhere nearby. He does not strike me as someone who might be overly concerned about collateral damage. Eric is on the lookout for D'Angelo while I am here at the club."

"Maybe Callie could stay here, at least," Lucy said, switching back to American English. "He's looking for her too, I'm guessing."

"It is my intention to drive her back to her aunt's in Pacifica tomorrow. I will be taking her personally. I do not wish to have her out of my sight until I am certain she is safe."

"Father know best," Lucy said, unable to miss an opportunity to tease him.

"I am not the girl's father," said Doc, a mite defensively. "She has a perfectly fine family in Detroit. They have raised her admirably."

"Motown funky," Lucy said sagely. "But is not land of surf and sun."

Chapter 68

Callie had opted to tone down her look for the trip home the following day. Her mohawk was blue today, and she had on a pair of faded jeans, a white ruffled blouse under her faux leather jacket. Once again Doc marveled at the variety of clothing the girl had managed to fit into her duffel bag.

It was noon by the time they got underway. Showering, laundering, packing, and a light breakfast had taken up the morning. When they left the tug through the shop entrance, they were surprised to find Lucy and her daughter, Chrissie, there to greet them. Eric was there as well, having ambled over from his digs on the other side of the street.

"Don't look so glum," Eric said. "Things are going to be back to normal soon."

"That's the problem," said Callie.

"At least you won't have the Weasel to worry about."

"I ain't afraid of the Weasel," said Callie resolutely.

"The Weasel?" Chrissie said. "What's this 'weasel'? Does it have rabies?"

"A furry little animal, it ain't," said Callie. "It's a long story. I'd take rabies any day."

"I'll text you," Chrissie told Callie.

"And you've got to promise to keep me up to date on what's going on here. Deal?"

"Deal. I'm sorry you have to go back," Lucy's daughter said sincerely.

"Yeah," said Callie, already resigned to her fate. "Me too."

Callie went over and gave Eric a hug.

"You take care now, little lady," said Eric gruffly. "Keep those grades up. Stay away from drugs and stay out of trouble."

"How much trouble could I get into?" she said slyly. "Compared to here?"

Everyone laughed uneasily.

Callie hugged Lucy and Chrissie and swung onto the seat of the Harley behind Doc. Doc passed her a helmet and donned his own. He turned the key in the ignition, and the motorcycle came to life with a deep rumble. Callie grabbed a hold of Doc around the waist as Doc gave the bike some throttle, and they lurched forward across the hardscrabble and out toward the pavement. Doc raised his hand and, without looking back, gave a little wave as he gunned the Harley and rocketed down the street.

Lucy, Chrissie and Eric watched the duo until they were out of sight.

The pair drove north along Highway 1 to Santa Cruz. After a flurry of cross streets and congestion, the traffic thinned out and they found themselves rolling through the undeveloped open country north of town. They stopped at a gas station about fifteen minutes out of Santa Cruz and Doc tanked up. There was a small, unpretentious cafe next to the station, and the two travelers decided to break for lunch. Doc had a steak sandwich, and Callie had fish and chips.

"I can't believe all that's happened," said Callie, after a few silent mouthfuls,. "It's like it was all a dream. It just doesn't seem real."

"I am having difficulty believing it myself," Doc admitted. "I am forced to rethink much of what I once took for granted about the place I live in and what is possible in the world."

"I'll never be able to tell anyone, you do realize that," Callie said. "Unless I wanted to end up in a padded cell under heavy sedation."

"Best to keep it under your hair."

"My hat, you mean."

"Your hat."

"No kidding. And it all started with that poor guy next door getting killed."

"Willy Rasp."

"Only he wasn't really killed, was he? Because he had never actually been alive to begin with. At least not yet."

"That is the way I have come to understand it, with a little help from Eric."

"So everything the Weasel did after that was to keep word from getting out. Including kidnapping me. He couldn't have people scrutinizing what he had done and starting to ask awkward questions."

"In retrospect, the fate of Angels' Keep as it now exists hung in the balance," Doc said. "I cannot imagine what would happen if its true purpose became generally known."

"Its purpose as an entry point for souls returning from the sea."

"Precisely. Who knows what the consequences would have been for Angel's Keep and, by extension, for D'Angelo personally."

"It would have spoiled everything," Callie noted. "Could you see the tabloids getting a hold of the story? 'City of Spirits Discovered on Central Coast'. It would have been a zoo. And you can bet whoever had gotten D'Angelo the gig wouldn't have been too pleased. He woulda been in some deep sh … hot water."

"Seen with the wisdom of hindsight," Doc said, "I was as much to blame for the state of affairs as anyone. I should simply have kept out of it. You would never have been in danger, and life would have gone on as before in Angels' Keep, no one the wiser."

"But you didn't know. No one could blame you for wanting to solve Willy's murder. You were following your best instincts."

"That is what is unsettling about the whole matter. I acted in good faith, but I did not have all the facts. I simply did not know enough to make the correct choices. I never dreamed there could be legitimacy in Willy's removal from the Keep, some higher purpose served."

"I don't get why the Weasel would have agreed to take the job in the first place. You don't really think he was trying to turn the page, do you? Make a new start?"

Doc shook his head, a wry grin on his face. "Eric believes D'Angelo did it only because he thought it might benefit him personally somehow. Perhaps he hoped it would give him an edge over the competition. Increase his power and influence."

"Yup. That sounds more like the Weasel we know and love," quipped Callie.

They finished the last of their meal, and Doc signaled for the check. "There is something I must confess to you," he said solemnly.

"Oh yeah? What is it?"

Doc studied the table top before him. "It is not possible that I could be your biological father," he said. "You see, I have never been able to conceive. I've known this from an early age."

Silence greeted this admission.

"I would have told you sooner, but I did not want to hurt your feelings. You had come all this way. I am truly sorry."

Callie processed this new information for a long moment.

Finally, she just shrugged and said, "It doesn't really matter, I guess. It's something I wanted to believe. I guess I wanted a different life. I wanted to be a different person. And coming here was going to make all that happen. But I've come to realize that I'm lucky to have the family I have. And I'm pretty OK with the way I am. You've helped me see that."

Doc just nodded. They sat in silence for a long moment.

"Anyways," Callie said finally, "parents can come in lots of forms, can't they? Some biological. Some not. Now it feels like I've got family out here, too. You, Lucy, Chrissie. Even uncle Eric. It's a win for everybody as far as I can tell."

Chapter 69

A dozen or so Ducati motorcycles were parked outside the cafe. A bike club, no doubt, thought Doc as they exited the premises. The sleek motorcycles were painted in bold primary colors—yellows, reds and blues. The riders were dressed in skintight suits made of synthetic fabric ostensibly designed to minimize wind resistance.

As Callie and Doc approached the Harley, an especially tall, lanky character said, "Hey, it's Easy Rider!" Sniggers were heard among his bike mates. "Is that a hooker you've got back there? She seems a little on the scrawny side."

Doc stopped in his tracks.

"Leave it," Callie whispered. "They're not worth it."

"They are sorely lacking manners," Doc said calmly, ice in his voice.

"Don't even think about it, old man," said the tall one, who looked like an exotic species of tropical fish in his attire. "You wouldn't have a snowball's chance in hell against all of us."

Original, thought Doc.

"If you know what's good for you, you'd get on your antique there and just keep rolling down the highway. You ride on back into the Dark Ages where you came from." The other dozen or so riders drew up around the tall man, keyed up for any chance to demonstrate their manliness, especially in the safety of numbers.

The tall one, who appeared to be their leader, leered and said for the benefit of his companions, "You can leave the black chick here though. We'll take good care of her."

"I'm not going to get kidnapped again," Callie told Doc emphatically. "Once is enough, thank you very much."

Doc heaved a sigh and straightened, his back to his detractors.

"It's not worth it, Manfred," Callie warned. "There's thirteen of them. I counted. And two of us. And Eric's not here to watch our back."

"You will stay out of this," Doc said firmly. "And I will not need anyone else's assistance to deal with punks such as these. You think me an angel? This should dispel any such notions once and for all."

He turned to the fashion-conscious rogue's gallery behind him. "My companion and I require an apology from you for your rudeness," he said authoritatively.

"Oh yeah?" said the leader. "Or what?"

"Or a lesson in common courtesy will be in order," said Doc. He strolled over to the first in the line of shiny new bikes and propped his foot on the seat, tilting the bike towards the others, but not quite following through with the push.

"I have not heard an apology from you as yet," said Doc mildly.

The leader and his companions blanched visibly.

"Oh, we're going to kill you, alright," said the leader, the smile gone from his face. "We're going to tear you apart."

"Hey man, I just started making payments on my bike," one the beanpole's disciples whispered to him urgently. "I'm not ready to get it scuffed."

Urgent whispers ensued as the others crowded around, pressing the case for appeasing the man who controlled the fate of their new motorcycles.

With a smile as sincere as a politician's, the leader shrugged and told Doc, "OK, you win." He made a hands-off gesture. "We apologize."

Doc removed his foot from the bikes and returned to where Callie was standing.

That was when they struck.

Doc shrugged off the first two attackers as if he were taking off an overcoat. He turned, elbowing one and hitting the second in the solar plexus. Both went down, creating a natural barrier to those following. The next three failed to stop in time and fell over their fallen companions onto the asphalt, ripping the stretch suits they were wearing. The rest came to a full stop and took a step backward.

Seeing that a head-on assault was not proving as effective as hoped, they fanned out in a wide circle and began moving in for the kill.

They weren't fighters, not really. Like their Russian biker counterparts back in 1963, they were bullies relying on intimidation and superior numbers to cow their prospective victims. These were clean-cut upwardly mobile twenty and thirty-somethings from Silicon Valley, most likely, well-off enough to afford the sleek machines they rode. It was clear from their movements and postural displays that several had had some kind of marshal arts training and were itching for an excuse to use what they had learned on someone. Perhaps they all attended the same dojo. The group continued to close in around Doc, growing more confident with every step.

Whether or not they would have succeeded in besting Manfred St. Michel with this strategy would remain an open question. They were suddenly distracted by the clamor of their Ducati motorcycles crashing in domino fashion into one another other behind them. The sound of metal scraping metal and chrome denting chrome brought the company instantly to a halt. It was cartoon-like the way they froze and turned to see their expensive new bikes grinding into each other and then landing on the pavement in a protracted wave with the inevitability of Newtonian physics. The disaster took several seconds to run its course. When the last motorcycle lay rocking on its side, front wheel spinning, there was silence.

Callie, who had circled around the group while they were focused on Doc, was standing over the first bike, her Doc Martens resting on the rear tire. She was the picture of the conquering hero. It was obvious she had followed through on what Doc had threatened to do earlier. There could be little doubt it was she who had set the chain reaction in motion.

"Oops," she said, backing away and then breaking into a run past the fallen bikes northward along Highway 1.

Doc was summarily forgotten by all but those men still writhing and moaning on the ground before him as this much less intimidating target presented itself. Doc understood what needed to be done. He retreated quickly to his motorcycle, threw his leg over it, and brought it instantly to life in a smooth, practiced movement. He could see from where he sat that Callie had a good lead on her pursuers. She had the long legs of a distance runner, and they were serving her well under the circumstances. Plus, she had the adrenaline and the energy of youth on her side. Not so with the nine men who were huffing and puffing in her wake. But what they lacked in speed, they made up for in grim determination. They were going to run down their prey whatever it took.

Doc hit the throttle and gunned the Harley past the fallen group of four who were just picking themselves off the ground and inspecting the damage done to their outfits. He roared up the road toward where the unlikely marathon was in progress. He kicked the motorcycle up through the gears and was soon upon the men struggling to catch up to Callie. He brought a large, leather-booted foot up along the right side of the bike and planted it squarely in the middle of the last man's back, sending him plunging forward into the men directly in front of him. Three of them went sprawling on the pavement like fallen bowling pins, shredding their fancy outfits on the the gravel amidst yips of outrage and pain.

Doc continued to move up through the ranks, wreaking as much havoc as possible, cuffing one runner over the head with a gloved hand and elbowing another into the bushes adjacent to the highway. He cut the lead runners off with the weight of the big bike itself, sending them careening chaotically into one another. They finally landed in a heap in the dirt adjacent to the highway.

When Doc reached Callie pursuit had stalled. The men were slowly getting to their feet among loud and passionate curses, assessing their lumps and scratches and the damage done to their state-of-the-art riding uniforms.

Meanwhile, Callie slowed to a walk when she realized rescue was at hand. She wasn't even breathing hard when Doc drew alongside her. She took a moment to cast an approving look back at their disorganized and defeated adversaries before she climbed onto the seat behind him. Any urgency to escape had vanished. It was clear the fight had gone out of the group, and their anger was directed now mostly at themselves and their stupidity in trying to tangle with the tough-as-nails veteran biker.

Doc looked back over his shoulder to confirm they were not being followed. These were basically frustrated adults who had reverted to being snot-nosed kids on their day off work, thought Doc. Not a pretty sight. They would think twice about ganging up on some unsuspecting stranger in the future. They wouldn't soon forget that they had been trounced once upon a time by a middle-aged man on a dinosaur of a bike aided by a fleet-of-foot teenage girl. Score one for Easy Rider.

Chapter 70

When they had gone a few miles, Doc pulled onto the shoulder and cut the engine. He climbed off the bike and looked Callie over.

"Are you OK?" he asked.

"I'm just fine," she said. "What was with those guys? Having the kind of scratch to afford those bikes ain't enough?"

"My guess is they have lucrative, though emasculating, jobs over the hill and were in search of a means to vent their unresolved frustrations," Doc said. "Hence the attitude."

"Who are you? Sigmund Freud?"

Callie was less charitable in her assessment. "A bunch of spoiled, rich ass crackers, if you ask me, lookin' to be badass," she declared. "Turns out you proved to be a bigger badass than all of 'em put together. They were messin' wit' da wrooong relic." She laughed.

"I will take that as a compliment," Doc said with a smile. "It was cruel of you to topple their machines."

"If I hadn't done it, you'd still be back there mopping up the sidewalk with 'em. I was doin' them a favor."

"Very compassionate of you," Doc said wryly.

"You're welcome. Must be in the genes." She saw the look on Doc's face and laughed. "I'm just pullin' your chain. I'm not going to make you my dad if you don't wanna be."

Doc felt his face grow red the way it tended to when the women in his life teased him. "It's not that I ..." he began.

She held up a hand, indicating further explanation was unnecessary. "You really don't know when people are puttin' you on, do you?" she said.

Doc shrugged. After a moment he said, "I am certain your father is very proud of you. I know I would be."

They stood there on the shoulder, the traffic whizzing past, for a couple of minutes. Finally Doc said, "I think we had better get you to your aunt's."

Callie's aunt lived in a two-story row house in a densely populated, but well-maintained suburban subdivision in low-lying hills twenty minutes south of San Francisco. The expanse of the ocean glittered in the gaps between the houses on the west side of the street.

Doc pulled to the curb at the end of the block that Callie's aunt's house was located in the middle of.

"I guess this is as far as I go," said Doc.

"You sure you don't want to come in and say, hi?" Callie teased.

"You're going to have enough on your hands making up a story about scout camp without taking me into account," Doc said. "However, I am sure she is a very nice person."

"You're really sumpin', you know?"

She climbed off the back of the bike. "See you around," she said. "And in case you missed it. I don't care if you're not my real dad. I'll always think of you as family."

"I will miss you, too," Doc said.

Callie gave him an awkward hug. Then she turned and skipped off down the street toward her house like a five-year-old.

Doc pulled on his helmet and continued to stand watch as Callie climbed the stairs to her aunt's home. She opened the front door and, with a slight wave of her hand, disappeared within.

Only when convinced she was safely inside the house did he kick the starter pedal. He revved the engine and accelerated away from the curb, making a U-turn in the intersection. After that it was just a matter of letting his momentum carry him downhill toward the gleaming Pacific in the distance.

Chapter 71

The journey back to Angels' Keep was uneventful. Doc had plenty of time to contemplate what might lie ahead. With D'Angelo expected to arrive at any time, everyone in the Keep might be at risk, including Lucy and Chrissie. Now, at least, Callie was safely back her aunt's.

By the time he pulled off the road outside his domicile and parked his bike, he had come to a decision. Eric was standing outside his tent across the street, hands on his hips. Doc waved him over.

"Your girl alright?" asked Eric.

"Yes. I think she will be fine."

"Good. Better that she's far away. Things could get dicey around here anytime now."

"So, no sign of D'Angelo?"

"Not yet."

"I was thinking," Doc said.

"Yes," said Eric warily.

"What if we made the first move?"

"You mean confront him in Laguna, before he has a chance to leave there?"

"That way we would insure that no one in Angels' Keep will come to harm. They did not ask for a war on their doorstep. They do not deserve it. This is our fight."

Eric stroked his beard thoughtfully and nodded his head. "I like it," he said. "We take the fight to him. We fix it so he never comes back here again." He paused for a moment. "Any thoughts on what we do when we find him?"

Doc shrugged. "Whatever it takes. We play it by ear. Even if this turns out badly for us, he at least will have no further reason to come back to this place."

Eric was still nodding. "When do we leave?" he asked.

"Immediately," said Doc. "If we hope to get there before he gets here."

"What about wheels?"

"We can take the Harley. It is not ideal. But it will hold us both. And it is all we have right now."

"You still have the .38?"

"I do."

"Let me get my gear."

"It's perfect," Eric said, inspecting the bike closely. "It fits the period, unless you look real hard. And with all the Russian biker gangs at large in LA, we'll blend right in."

"I have no intention of abandoning my bike along the way, however," Doc said firmly. "Just so we are clear on that."

"You got it," said Eric. "We'll bring 'er back, come hell or high water. If we're still around."

Doc outfitted Eric with a heavy leather jacket he had been gifted by a 400 pound blues enthusiast from Salinas. It had always been too big for him, but it fit Eric perfectly. He then produced a helmet and goggles that looked like something out of World War I and gave them to Eric to wear. The bike rode low with the two men straddling it, supporting a combined passenger weight in the vicinity of 500 pounds. But the Fatboy seemed up to the task.

Soon they were speeding south on Highway 1 toward Castroville. They left the highway there and turned inland, crossing the 101 twenty minutes later. It was a sunny, late April morning with a few wispy high clouds overhead.

They rode through Prunedale and found themselves on the now-familiar stretch of road beyond Shipley. As on previously visits, there was no other vehicular traffic in sight. Again it felt as if they were in a pocket of terrain that was, whether by accident or design, lost to the world at large.

Eric pulled a little notebook out of his pants pocket and consulted the timetable scribbled therein as they sped onward. "We're right on schedule," he said.

The transition to the world circa 1963 was as smooth as it had been previously. They were back in the high desert north of San Bernardino as before, only this time in broad daylight. The desert here was as austere and beautiful as ever. But that soon began to change as they descended into the Los Angeles basin on Route 66.

The landscape, as they approached the City of Angels, was only slightly less sinister by day. The oil fires that burned constantly in the LA basin left a dense haze in the air that resulted in a kind of permanent twilight. As they continued on a southward course, it was like driving into an approaching storm front. Starting in San Bernardino the air thickened with smoke and oily sludge to the point where it quickly became unbreathable, just like last time.

They found respiratory relief, however, as they continued south at Eric's prompting, instead of turning westward. Their new course took them on an alternate route that swung wide of the Los Angeles basin. They passed through Riverside before angling west again toward the coast. A drive that normally took two hours on today's freeway system took most of the afternoon on the backroads and byways of Southern California, not least because they were constantly circumventing long lines of Soviet tanks and troop transports along the way.

It looked like a full-blown mobilization of the local Soviet forces was underway.

"Is it always like this during the day?" Doc inquired back over his shoulder.

"Just a training exercise, probably," Eric said.

What was inconvenient for them was that most of the military hardware seemed to be heading in the same general direction they were. Eventually, Doc quit trying to dodge the seemingly endless lines of trucks and tanks and simply joined the mass troop migration. He ducked in between two large covered transports like he was supposed to be there and maintained that position for most of the slow and steady trip south and west.

When they reached the Laguna Canyon turnoff, the were amazed to find that the convoy did not continue southward along the main thoroughfare as expected. Instead, the line of trucks and tanks also made the turn down Laguna Canyon Road toward the coast.

"Are you seeing this?" Doc called back to Eric.

"I am," said Eric hesitantly. "Maybe it's beach day for the Red Army."

"They do not appear to me to be on holiday," Doc remarked. The troops in the transports were clad in full combat gear and appeared to have their rifles at the ready. It was hard to shake the impression that a full-scale military invasion was underway. "Do you think it wise that we continue on our present course?"

"Nobody's bothered us so far," said Eric. "Let's hope our luck holds until we get to Frankie's. Someone there will probably be able to tell us what this is all about."

Chapter 72

The turnoff to Frankie's came up on the left. They peeled away from the convoy and bounced up the hill toward the house. No one followed them up the road. Apparently the Red Army's mission lay elsewhere.

All was quiet when they arrived. They dismounted, happy at the respite from riding. They approached the house cautiously, not quite knowing what to expect. Everything seemed in order.

Doc shaded his eyes and peered through the living room windows and saw nothing to indicate the house was occupied. Eric, meanwhile, tried the side door, the one that led toward the kitchen and dining area. It was unlocked.

"Over here," he called to Doc, entering the hallway. But his voice choked off. He found himself confronted by a dozen people dressed head to foot in black, all of them pointing handguns and rifles at their heads.

"Whoa," said Eric. He raised his hands slowly. "We come in peace."

Without a word being said, Doc and Eric were motioned onward into the kitchen by the gunmen closest to them.

"We're friends of Frankie's," said Eric. "We're not looking for trouble."

After a lengthy pause, one of the ninja-like soldiers before them nodded to a couple of other members of the group, not taking his eyes, or his gun, off the two visitors. Two of the black-clad gunmen broke away from the crowd and disappeared at the rear of the house.

The silence drew out. No one made a move to invite them to sit down or offer them a cup of coffee. About five tense minutes passed. Finally, there was a rustling in the hallway that led to the bedrooms in back. Frankie appeared. His head was bandaged and one arm was in a sling. He was walking with a limp.

"Hey guys!" effused Frankie, despite his apparent injuries. "Wasn't expecting you back again so soon."

"We missed it down here," deadpanned Eric. "Too quiet up north."

"Funny," said Frankie, smiling though it clearly pained him to do so. "You're a funny guy. So what's up?"

"That's pretty much what we wanted to ask you," said Eric. "It looks like the whole Soviet Army is parading past your front door."

The others had begun to relax a little during the exchange between Frankie and the strangers. Guns were now pointed toward the floor. A path opened up in the crowd through which Frankie walked to meet his guests.

"It's great to see you guys again," Frankie said. Since his right arm was in a sling, he had to use his left to shake hands. It was awkward but effective.

"Tell us what happened," Doc said, nodding at his injuries.

"It's nothing," said Frankie. "Just a nick."

There were appreciative sniggers around the room. This was a familiar and a well-worn joke—downplaying the severity of one's injuries.

"What happened really?" Eric put in.

"This? This is nothing. You haven't heard, I guess," Frankie said.

"Heard what?"

"The rebellion. It's in full swing. America has risen up as one to throw off the shackles of the commie invaders. The revolution against the Revolution of the Proletariat has begun. And it all started right here in little old Laguna Beach." He said this with unconcealed pride. "Can you dig it?"

"You're shitting me," said Eric in wonder.

"Gospel truth."

"Why here? Why Laguna. I don't get it. How did Laguna Beach become ground zero for the counterrevolution?"

"That's the crazy thing—and you're going to love this," said Frankie, warming to the topic. "Guess who's being credited for lighting the match that set it all off."

It took a long moment to sink in.

"No," said Eric with finality. "No way."

Frankie just nodded, a beatific look on his face. "When this is over his name is going into the history books right alongside Paul Revere and George Washington."

"No," said Eric. "Not Pete D'Angelo."

Chapter 73

"What the hell?" added Eric, uncomprehendingly. "The Weasel?"

"He's the man of the hour. A national hero."

Eric opened his mouth. But no sound came out. Finally he said, "The next thing you're going to tell me is that the Easter Bunny is a mass murderer."

Frankie just stood and smiled at the man's obvious distress.

Doc, meanwhile, was shaking his head. "Somehow I would not have taken Pete D'Angelo for a political activist," he said. "A cynic, certainly, interested only in personal gain. But an idealist? That is difficult to accept."

Frankie laughed. "Right on the money. It was a fluke, I'm pretty sure,--a byproduct of him looking out for his own interests, just like you said. Story goes the Reds had him backed into a corner and instead of caving like everyone has for the last decade, he fought back. You gotta give the guy one thing. He's got access to enough men and firepower to put up a decent fight. And psycho or not, he's not the type to be pushed around. Not even by the Russians. They picked the wrong cat to come down on. He gets his boys and their artillery in on the act and pretty soon you've got a shooting war goin' on. Word spreads. And practically overnight you've got a full-blown uprising in progress."

"That's how this happened?" said Eric, indicating the bandages.

Frankie grinned. "It was worth it. Look out there. This thing has exploded all across the country--north, south, east and west. It's happening everywhere at once. Used to be you risked getting shot at anytime you walked out the front door. Now at least you're getting shot at for a reason. And we're giving as good as we're getting, from all reports. People have been ready for this for a long time."

Doc and Eric fell silent, absorbing the news, trying to come to terms with the enormity of the transformation that had taken place literally overnight.

"Follow me," Frankie said, heading toward the hallway. He led Eric and Doc into a master bedroom at the back of the residence. "We've been extra careful to keep it cool up here. We don't want to raise any flags with that display of military might rollin' by outside."

Frankie told the men and women in black to stand back while he closed the door so that the three men could have a moment of privacy.

"So what do you make of that?" Frankie asked. "Pete D'Angelo, American hero?"

Doc looked over at Eric. "It seems surreal. To think that history would have selected someone like D'Angelo to galvanize America to rise up against the Soviets seems very odd."

Frankie shrugged and sat down on the bed. "Couldn't agree with you more there. But regardless how it started, there is now a real chance to get rid of the Russians for good. So nobody's complaining."

"So," Frankie said, taking a breath. "What brings you back to Laguna this time around?"

"We're here to find D'Angelo," Doc said. "We felt certain he would be coming after us, considering how we managed to outmaneuver him, take away his hostage and steal his beloved car."

"You took the Packard?" Frankie said incredulously. "I didn't know about that. Holy shit. Talk about stepping on the lion's tail!"

"Instead of waiting for him to show up in Angels' Keep," Eric put in, "we decided to confront him here."

"Sounds like a ballsy strategy," Frankie said. "But, as you can see, your pal Pete has been otherwise engaged."

"The circumstances have changed," said Doc thoughtfully. "But ultimately the threat he poses remains. Knowing him, he well doubtless still want to exact some form of revenge for his losses eventually."

"If you're lucky, the Russkies will take care of D'Angelo for you."

This gave Doc pause. "It is not my intention to do away with him," he said quietly. "Merely to find some way to discourage him from causing more trouble for us and our loved ones."

"Easier said than done," Frankie said, "from what I've heard."

Doc shrugged. "So tell us. What happened with …" He indicated the bandages with a nod of his head.

"I caught a couple of slugs when things blew up in town. I managed to get in a few licks but ended up getting hit for my trouble. I'll be alright. In a couple days I'll be good as new."

Doc considered Frankie's palor and obvious weakness with some skepticism. But the pop star was still young in this time and place. Plus, with the rebellion in full swing, he had more to live for than ever.

"So what's the status of the conflict?" Eric wanted to know. "What's going on?"

"The town is under siege," Frankie said. "But it's been hard for the Russians to lock things down. The mountains around here are a natural barrier to a full-on assault. So far, the Russians have had to funnel in from the three available entry points—Laguna Canyon, and north and south along Coast Highway. What's happening is that the Reds have been getting bogged down near the beach with their own traffic piling up behind them. Once they get to the city center, our side has them pined down from positions in the surrounding hills. They just haven't had enough breathing room to put together any kind of offensive."

"Why aren't the Russians sending in ground troops from inland, over the mountains? That's what I'd do," Eric said.

"They're still trying to get that together, as far as we can tell. They're massing around Mission Viejo, but it's taking time. They've never had to stage a major offensive down here since they took over. Right now we own the hills around Laguna. Nobody knows them better than we do. We know where all the booby traps are. And all the escape routes.

"They don't have time on their side, if I'm reading this right. The longer the stalemate lasts, the more people are getting involved, here and everywhere else. Pitch battles have broken out in all the major cities, from what we're hearing. Baltimore and Philadelphia have gone back to our side, and that's in an area where the Russians are thickest on the ground. The same thing's happening up and down the West Coast. Seattle, Portland and San Francisco are all back in American hands.

"It's a thing of beauty. It's like this explosion detonated in l'il old Laguna Beach and the shock waves have spread out across the country. Stress fractures are already showing up in the invincibility of the Soviets. It won't be long before the walls come tumbling down. It's pretty clear the Russkies don't even know where to begin to get a handle on the situation. It's been so long since they were challenged in any significant way. Any contingency plans they've made are taking a long time to materialize. It's just happening in too many places at once. They're getting pushed out of the heartland and they're under fire on both coasts. Pretty soon they'll have nowhere to go. They'll be facing their own rifles and tanks, manned by rebels like us."

"So where are you and your people in all this?"

"My group is monitoring the hills in case there's a major push across the mountains from the east. Like I said, it hasn't happened yet. My guess? Some of those soldiers out there are dragging their feet."

"You believe moral is running low?"

"Sure. They've been away from home for more than ten years, some of them. And what have they gotten out of it? The weather here's fine, better than Leningrad most likely. But the grunts never get to enjoy it. You've seen what Los Angeles looks like these days. It's a hellhole. The only thing the average soldier gets out of being here are ulcers. The commanding officers and party leaders siphon off all the spoils. For the glory of Mother Russia, of course. At least that's the party line. Everybody knows that the profits have been going to finance the Party bosses' estates on the Baltic and the Black Sea."

Frankie paused in his speech to catch his breath. After a moment, he said, "Those boys are tired of being cast as the bad guys in this occupying force scenario, I'd bet on it. And who could blame them? I'm thinking being this far from home for this long has lost its charm for a lot of 'em."

THE BATTLE OF
LAGUNA BEACH

Chapter 74

Frankie was talking to his people in the hallway. It sounded like the group was getting ready to break camp and head back into the war zone.

"What a difference a day makes," Eric observed drolly.

"What are you thinking?" Doc asked him.

"I'm thinking the Weasel isn't going to change his stripes. When whatever part he has in this is over, he's still going to be coming after us."

"If he is still alive."

"I have a lot of faith in the Weasel's ability to do what's necessary to save his own neck. He hasn't been around this long for nothing."

"How does that work? His living this long?"

"Rumor has it he reanimates corpses. When a body he inhabits has served it's purpose, he finds another, and another--on down the line. He's gone a long time without dying that way. From what I hear he hasn't actually kicked the bucket in centuries. They say this last time around he snagged the body of a con who died inside in '97."

"You know," said Doc, "a friend of mine with the police told me there was a Pete D'Angelo on file who had died in prison in the nineties."

"Sounds like he took over the jailbird's body and his identity."

"No wonder he looks as bad as he does," remarked Doc. "He is being held together with string and Scotch tape. At least that's how he looks."

"Yeah, somebody couldn't be that ugly naturally," Eric laughed.

"It cannot but effect one's outlook on the world."

"Being a walking corpse could put a crimp in your style. Be that as it may, I'm thinking we still need to find the guy. It's just going to be a little more complicated with all that's going on."

"Do you have any plan as to what we will do when we find him?"

"Nothing comes to mind. Whatever it is, we're going to need to keep our distance somehow. No physical contact. It'll be an interesting trick."

"What do you think? Thermal gloves? Heavy clothing …"

"If all else fails …" Eric patted the Desert Eagle in his pocket meaningfully.

Doc nodded. It was difficult to imagine that D'Angelo's would have changed much, even with his current celebrity. If past were prologue, he would find some way to use his newly found status to serve his own nefarious ends.

Frankie returned and eased himself back against the pillows on the bed, a look of fatigue on his face. It was obvious being up and about so soon after his injury was taking a toll on him. "I wish to God I could be a part of this," he said when he had caught his breath. "I didn't work hard for so long to be sidelined during the big game. But the shape I'm in, I'd only slow everybody down. I'd be more liability than help."

Doc and Eric were silent. It was clear Frankie would be ill-advised to do any fighting for the next several days at the very least.

"I noticed your friends are getting ready to move out," Eric said.

"They're doing a reconnaissance run into town."

"How are they getting there?"

"There's a deer path that runs along the ridge behind the house. If you follow it, you end up on the hill overlooking Laguna."

"Unless I'm way off, that's near where D'Angelo's place is," Eric added, glancing at Doc.

"What?" said Frankie. "You going after D'Angelo tonight? In what's out there?"

Eric cleared his throat. "Do you suppose your friends would mind us tagging along with them? You never know. We might be able to make ourselves useful along the way."

"You kiddin'? No one's going to complain about having Eric the Red on the team," Frankie said with a lopsided grin. He flinched, obviously still fighting off the pain from his wounds. "Bear!"

Doc and Eric jumped and glanced around before realizing he was summoning his lieutenant.

The big guy that Doc had first seen on the beach in Angels' Keep poked his head in the door. "Yeah, boss?"

"I told these guys they could come with you," said Frankie.

"Sure thing," said Bear immediately. He looked from Eric to Doc and back "We'd be stoked to have you guys with us." Looking at Doc again he added, "I remember you. Future Man, right? You warned us to be on the lookout for D'Angelo's Packard that day on the beach."

Doc shrugged modestly.

"How's the teenager?" said Bear. "The one with the hair?"

"Callie? Right now she is on her way back home, if she isn't there already. School is starting for her again soon," Doc said.

"School waits for no one," said Bear philosophically.

The ninja-like band moved swiftly up the hillside to the crest of the ridge behind Frankie's house. It was a practiced maneuver, one that had obviously been executed countless times before. Doc and Eric had to hustle to keep up. Everyone remained in a crouch until they were safely beyond the ridge. Here the path connected with another well-worn trail that led southward toward downtown and was shielded from view from the canyon road.

Smoke billowed up in the distance as the band of rebels approached the downtown area, muddying the sunset and merging with the rising tide of nightfall. The evening was punctuated with the thuds of mortar fire and the occasional detonation of heavier ordinance.

The battle of Laguna Beach was underway.

Chapter 75

Additional weapons had been handed around back at the house, and Doc and Eric found themselves cradling standard issue M-1s, circa WWII. They had to keep reminding themselves this was really happening. There was a better than fair chance they'd have to use the rifles against other human beings in the very near future.

Through the foliage on the ridge they could see an uninterrupted line of trucks, tanks and other military hardware at a standstill on Laguna Canyon Road below them. Several of the tanks were breaking ranks and attempting to roll up the steep hillside on the opposite side of the road. The maneuver proved too much for most and the personnel carriers and jeeps who attempted to follow. They fell back and were forced to rejoin the almost stationary procession on the canyon road.

The small band of counter-revolutionaries continued on unseen at a near run along the crest of the hill. Finally Bear, who was in the lead, held up a hand and everyone stopped. They were at a point just before the summit overlooking downtown. Small munitions fire and the pulse of army helicopter blades had been added to the mix of sounds that could be heard. A fierce firefight was raging somewhere before them, though any view of the battle was obstructed by the hilltop. Looking to the southeast across the wide inland valley behind them, they could see signs that a massive troop buildup was in progress. Tanks and trucks were lined up like an impenetrable wall for miles, ready to sweep into the greenbelt separating Laguna Beach from the rest of Orange County.

"Typical," Bear remarked. "They could be sending all this manpower north to LA where they've got some serious problems right now and instead they're here, obsessed with getting our little beachside burg back into the fold. It's like they figure if they can retake Laguna, everything will go back to the way it was. But it ain't gonna happen. They must be shellshocked or something. Not thinking straight. Probably never figured a ragtag army of artists and beach rats could ever give them a run for their money."

"What is the news?" asked Doc.

"The latest is that the occupation of LA is beginning to crack wide open. The Soviets would love nothing better than to bomb the whole place to hell and back, but they know they'd be killing as many of their own people as the enemy. There's no way to sort out who's who on the ground anymore at this point."

"And elsewhere?"

"Most of the eastern seaboard is back in our hands. And there's a huge battle being waged in and around New York City. Chicago, Cleveland and St. Louis are still a question mark. But I think it's just a matter of time. You know that Seattle, Portland, and San Francisco have been taken back."

Doc nodded. "Frankie informed us."

"That's where it stand right now. It's about fifty-fifty. But every hour gains are being made. If New York falls, the Russians will be cut off. It'll be a rout."

"Frankie believes the army rank and file are lacking in motivation," Doc said. "He believes they are tired of being here and want to go home, regardless what the leaders want."

"Frankie's a little modest," Bear said with a grin. "He's downplaying the role that Hollywood and people like him have had in bringing things to this point. Even B movies, like the one we just finished making. Scratch the surface and they're all about personal freedom. They're counter-revolutionary propaganda masquerading as kid's stuff. The anti-establishment message that's been going out has been heard loud and clear, even by the Russkies grunts. Especially the Russkies, 'cause they've been among the biggest consumers of what Hollywood's been cranking out since the invasion. They've been eating it up. And don't even get me started on the impact of rock 'n roll."

Doc was nodding. It made sense under the present extreme circumstances that something as seemingly innocuous as movies and pop music could have far-reaching consequences.

"And after we've sent the Reds home with their tails tucked between their legs, I'll bet it ain't going to stop there," Bear went on. "One day the whole Soviet empire is going to crumble under it's own weigh."

Doc had witnessed the Berlin wall coming down on television in the late eighties, but said nothing. He remembered hearing Putin interviewed on the occasion of a Paul McCartney concert held in Red Square, citing the importance of western rock 'n roll music, smuggled into Russia during the Cold War, as opening a window to freedom, as he put it, and even hastening the fall of the Soviet Empire.

Chapter 76

The line of a dozen men and women crept up to the ridge overlooking town. In their attire they were all but invisible against their surroundings. The sky was dark now, the sunset a fading line on the horizon. The munitions fire and the occasional blast of high explosives were deafening at this proximity. The crest of the hill was backlit by the stroboscopic flashes of automatic weapon's fire, flares and helicopter searchlights. It looked like they were coming upon the seventh circle of hell.

They slithered the remaining distance to the overlook on their stomachs. It was worse than they had imagined. Most of the downtown area had been devastated. The venerable Hotel Laguna was smoking rubble. Fires burned everywhere--structural fires, brush fires, vehicular fires. The Russians greatly outnumbered the resistance fighters and more were streaming in on foot along the main thoroughfares and being off-loaded on Main Beach from Sikorsky helicopters. Even so, the resistance ceded little ground. Mortar and machine gun fire from the hills surrounding the downtown area was withering and constant, while darkly clad figures moved among the ruins firing and then melting back into the shadows from ever-changing positions.

It was a bit like the Revolutionary war, Doc reflected, the enemy advancing more or less in formation, being picked off by a small, elusive bands of Americans who flanked them, sniped at them and disappeared again to reload and regroup. In this way, then and now, the rebels seemed improbably to be holding their own against the superior numbers and better equipped Soviet fighting force. The advancing Russian troops were turned back time and again by unrelenting cover fire from the hills. Even the tanks that were grinding through town were having a hard time locating targets to shoot at. Most of the structures had been leveled already, and the resistance fighters were proving elusive targets for the slow-to-respond heavy machinery. Even the Soviet steel was not impervious to grenades lobbed into air vents and into exhaust channels. The rebels seemed to be well-informed of their vulnerabilities and capable and courageous enough to exploit them to maximum effect.

"They must be outnumbered twenty to one," muttered Eric.

"Get ready to join the fray," said Bear. "We're going to be pretty exposed between here and the first line of houses down there, so we'll have to hustle. The trick is to keep moving no matter what. Don't give them a target to shoot at."

Doc just nodded. He still couldn't believe this was happening.

They had risen to their feet on the ridge and were about to plunge down the steep, barren hillside when Bear held up his hand. All forward movement ceased. It seemed to Doc, standing with his M-1 clutched in his hand, that the gunfire among the houses below their position had intensified. The Russians appeared to be chasing a band of Americans uphill through the suburban streets below them. The small cluster of fugitives broke into the open from among the houses and started up the incline toward them, dogged by machine-gun fire from behind them.

"We've got incoming," shouted Bear above the noise, bringing his rifle to his shoulder. The rest of the group did the same.

"Let's lay down some cover for these guys," he instructed the others, as they dropped to the ground behind the ridge to await further developments. "Start firing as soon as the Reds come into view."

The fugitives below them were struggling up the hill, losing traction in the soft soil. At the first sight of the armed pursuing force, Bear gave the signal and a massive barrage was unleashed from the hilltop. The pursuers took cover behind the houses, while their targets continued to weave their way precariously up the hill. Return fire from among the suburban dwellings kicked up dirt around the fleeing resistance fighters. One man fell and was still. But the rest, three in all, plodded onward, fatigue slowing their movements.

The pitched battle raged with the running men caught in the crossfire. Miraculously, they were able to make the top of the hill without further casualties and threw themselves down behind the line of fighters covering them.

Eric stopped shooting abruptly. He gave Doc a sharp elbow in the ribs, a tense expression on his face.

Doc had been so focused on returning fire that he hadn't had time to take stock of the survivors they had been protecting. He turned to look behind them and found himself face to face with Pete D'Angelo.

"You!" cried D'Angelo, his shock and outrage clear among wheezing gasps of breath. His eyes darted from Doc to Eric and back again from behind his signature aviators. "I'm gonna murder youse!"

"You're welcome, and nice to see you, too," quipped Eric.

Chapter 77

A blinding spotlight lit the group from above and heavy caliber machine gun rounds began to churn the ground around them. A Soviet helicopter gunship had risen above the houses before them and had them dead to rights.

"Retreat!" yelled Bear. "Into the draw!"

No further coaxing was necessary. Everyone, including an apoplectic D'Angelo, plunged down the backside of the hill into darkness, half-running, half-falling. Meanwhile, the helicopter swooped toward them. Geysers of earth erupted alongside them as they crashed headlong into the dense undergrowth below the crest of the hill. Even when they were hidden from view, the machine-gun fire continued to rake the foliage around them as if the gunners had x-ray vision. Tree branches and bushes exploded in a blizzard of twigs and leafy debris as the spotlight sought to penetrate the thick canopy.

Someone cried out, having been grazed by a high-caliber bullet. "Keep going!" the wounded man shouted. "I'll make it!"

Somewhere toward the front of the line someone else took a bullet with an anguished cry and went down heavily. It took a couple of seconds before Doc and Eric came upon the man, only to discover it was D'Angelo who had been hit. The man closest to him tried to roll him over in an attempt to assess the damage. But he was repelled as if by a live high-voltage wire.

"Jesus!" the would be rescuer cried, looking down at D'Angelo wide-eyed and shaking.

The strange force field surrounding him was still in effect, a threat to friend and foe alike. It seemed to be something D'Angelo had no control over.

As Eric and Doc stood over him, D'Angelo appeared somehow diminished, shriveled. Blood was seeping from his abdomen where the bullet had entered his back and exited through the front in a hideous bloom. He was gulping air, a wild look in his eyes. He couldn't believe he'd been hit. The prospect of his mortality seemed incredible to him even as the life blood continued to leech out of him.

"Stand back," ordered Doc.

"You're not going to try and help him, are you?" Eric said, under his breath. "We don't have time for this. Let nature take its course. This is the solution to our problem, right here. Don't you see? We walk away, and it's done."

But Doc wasn't having it. He stooped and touched D'Angelo's shirt sleeve tentatively. The shock of contact made Doc recoil reflexively, but he was able to hold his ground. The material did seem to act as somewhat of an insulator against the uncanny energy surrounding D'Angelo, but not enough to make lifting him possible or practical.

"I am not sure we can be of assistance," Doc said to no one in particular, trying to shake off the lingering affects of the malignant charge that surrounded the man.

"Your help is the last thing I need," D'Angelo spat, almost exultantly. A grimace of pain quickly replaced his defiance. "Leave me alone."

"Give me your vest," Doc said to Eric.

Eric removed Doc's leather jacket and the army surplus vest he had on underneath it, reluctantly handing the latter over to Doc. "This is a bad idea," he stated unequivocally.

Doc looped the vest's armhole over D'Angelo's right arm, taking care not to get closer than necessary. D'Angelo shrank back, unaccustomed to being handled in any way. But after a brief standoff, he seemed to lose the strength to resist. When Doc had secured the vest under D'Angelo's shoulder, he grabbed the dangling end of the vest, twisted it and drew it taut.

"This may be somewhat unpleasant," Doc told D'Angelo. "But this is the only way we will get you off this mountain. We are not going to leave you here."

Doc began dragging D'Angelo along the ground behind him. D'Angelo howled in pain and promptly lost consciousness. Doc did not pause, but maintained constant pressure on the vest, knowing that if they didn't get D'Angelo medical help soon he would bleed out.

The helicopter by this time had moved on ahead of them, the gunners firing indiscriminately into the bushes further down the hill where they estimated the group of rebels would now be. After a time the pulsing of the helicopter blades receded and was lost in the cacophony of explosions and gunfire from beyond the hilltop behind them. They appeared to be safe for the moment.

The spotlight having left them, the group proceeded in pitch darkness.

"We're almost even with the cutoff to Frankie's," said Bear. "If we can get up and over the hill without being seen, we'll be alright." He started up the steep incline next to them.

"Let me take him for a while," Eric volunteered with a loud exhalation to express his disapproval. He wasn't convinced saving Pete D'Angelo's life should be a priority for them. But neither could he completely disregard Doc's humanitarian intent and his own ingrained instinct to help the helpless. He grabbed the end of the vest away from Doc and gave it an extra twist. "We can trade off," he said.

Doc, who was starting to feel the effects of the exertion of dragging D'Angelo's body, stepped back and let Eric take over.

The group made good time weaving up the hillside, Eric dragging D'Angelo easily behind him as if he were nothing more than an assortment of rags. The remaining fifty feet or so to the ridge were the riskiest. They'd be exposed for a minute as they topped the rise and descended the far side. They stopped and searched the skies. But it appeared that most of the Russian air power was still focused on the downtown area to the south.

Bear motioned them on. They moved swiftly into the clearing, crested the hill, and plunged down the other side without being spotted.

Doc took over from Eric at this point. From here on gravity would be on their side.

Twenty minutes later they were at Frankie's house.

Chapter 78

Doc pulled D'Angelo, still unconscious, through the side entrance of the house, then down the hallway that led toward the rear. He found a vacant bedroom and, warning anyone who moved to help to stand back, dragged him inside. Still using the vest as a towline, he hoisted D'Angelo onto the bed, while the call went out for gauze and iodine. A linen closet across the hall provided what they needed for first aid purposes.

A young man with medical experience came forward. He was wearing leather work gloves as Doc had suggested. He gingerly peeled back the blood-soaked clothing covering D'Angelo's midriff without discernible negative consequences. Apparently D'Angelo's weakened state also extended to the repellent force around him. The wound looked ragged and swollen. He began to dress it as best he could with the materials at hand. It was clear from D'Angelo's pallor that he had lost a lot of blood. He seemed to be stirring occasionally at this point, sliding in and out of consciousness. He had never been a large man to begin with, but now he looked tiny, as dry as a husk. It was as if the wound had sapped what vitality he had possessed.

Frankie took Doc and Eric aside. "It ain't looking good," he said. "I don't think we're going to be able to do much for him at his point, except to try to take the edge off the pain. We can stanch the bleeding and inject him with some morphine. But that's about it."

Doc looked at Eric, who took this prognosis impassively. Suddenly he felt eyes on him. He looked up to find D'Angelo staring at him intently, fully awake.

Responding to the silent entreaty in those piercing eyes, Doc said, "Could you give us minute?"

"Suit yourself," said Eric with resignation. "But I wouldn't turn my back on him, if I were you."

Frankie relayed Doc's request to the others and the room was soundlessly vacated.

Doc took a seat on the bed near D'Angelo. "The prospects are not good, I am afraid," he said, embracing honesty as the best policy under the circumstances.

D'Angelo nodded as if expecting as much. "When you gotta go, you gotta go," he said dryly. "I don't know how long it's been since I actually died."

"You have managed to go from one body to the next, as I understand it," Doc said. "Why must it be any different now?"

"It ain't as easy as all that," said D'Angelo. "There's a lot 'a organizing needs to get done to make it happen. Money needs to change hands. Specialists need to be brought in. A suitable stiff needs to be found. There's no time for any of that now."

Doc was unable to offer much in the way of sympathy for the man's plight, so he said nothing.

Finally D'Angelo broke the protracted silence. "What happened to the car?" he asked in a raspy whisper.

Doc thought he hadn't heard correctly. "The car?"

"The Packard." It obviously pained him to talk.

"We had to leave it behind," Doc said. "After we made the jump. We had little choice, I am afraid."

D'Angelo just nodded, unsurprised. "You left it on the island, I'll bet," he said. "Nice place. I tried to follow you through the rabbit hole in time. But there was some kinda problem."

"The access point had shifted," Doc explained.

"That little brown bastard, I'll bet. I always suspected he had some serious pull. He never cared much for me showin' up on his turf. I don't think he liked me much, period."

Doc remained silent.

"So that's where the car ended up?"

Doc nodded in the affirmative.

"I guess there are worse places. Too bad that damn pygmy don't drive." His laugh devolved into hacking.

He grew more sober and licked his parched lips. "Alright," he said, after some deliberation. "I guess we can call it even. I took the girl and you took the car."

Doc didn't see how that was a fair trade, but he kept mum. "Why did you take Callie to begin with? What did you hope to accomplish?"

"She was … insurance. So's you'd stay out of it."

It began to dawn on Doc just how fearful D'Angelo had been of his becoming involved. "I do not understand. How could I have made trouble for you?"

D'Angelo looked at him for a long moment, a humorless grin spreading on his face. "Seems maybe I know more about you than you know about yourself," he said with a cackle.

Doc waited, but no other information was forthcoming. "I think you overestimate me," he said. "I am a blues guitar player, when I am generous with myself. And I have a certain facility with electronics. Nothing more."

"Sure, a guitar player," D'Angelo said sarcastically. "You should have been dead the first time we met. In the parking lot that night. That's what tipped me off."

"Tipped you off to what exactly?"

"I don't know why you were never told," said D'Angelo. "But I guess they wanted to keep you in the dark. It's frustrating as hell, is what it is. You never get to see all the cards, do you? 'Works in mysterious ways,' they call it. A load of bunk if you ask me. And they call me evasive!" He began to cough, violently at first, but less so as he lost strength.

When he finally stopped coughing, D'Angelo's eyes went wide as if he had just seen an apparition in the air between him and Doc. He began to perspire. The remaining color drained from his face, and his teeth began to chatter as if he were freezing cold. He clutched and wrung the bed sheets around him convulsively.

"What can I get you?" Doc inquired in alarm, rising from his end of the bed. "What is it you need? More medication?"

"Fuck a duck," D'Angelo said, ignoring him as some unspecified and horrific realization began to take root in his consciousness. "Shit, shit, shit."

"What is it? What is wrong?"

"I'm fucked is what's wrong."

"I am truly sorry about your injuries, the blood loss …"

"You really have no idea, do you?"

"What do you mean?"

"Why didn't you leave me out there tonight?" he wailed. "You shoulda left me. Why didn't you?"

"I could not in good conscience have left you to die," Doc stated. "It was not an option, as far as I was concerned."

"Why the hell not?" D'Angelo said, grinding his teeth in dismay. "It's what I woulda done if it had been you who got plugged 'stead a' me. I woulda just kept walkin'. I wouldna given it a second thought."

"I am not you," Doc said mildly.

"Shiiiit!" cried D'Angelo, flailing. "You risked your freakin' life to get me back here. Why? Why?"

"To be honest, I reacted," Doc said, no less perplexed. "I did not give it much thought. I would have done the same for anyone in your condition. It seemed the right thing to do."

"I'm wrecked," wailed D'Angleo pitifully. "Why couldn't you just have ditched me? Left me to croak? Better yet, why didn't you just put a gun to my head and pull the trigger? You hated my guts, right? I nearly killed you back there in Angel's bumfuck, or whatever they call it. I took the girl, for chrissakes. Nobody woulda blamed you. But no. You had to play the hero."

"I am afraid I am not following," said Doc. Clearly he was missing something here, but he couldn't for the life of him grasp what it was.

"It figures," D'Angelo said hopelessly, going lax on the pillow. "You wouldn't understand, would you? You're not even capable of comprehending what you've done to me, what a colossal shit storm you've unleashed. I was right about you all along. Right to worry. A lotta good it's done me." He hacked again, spitting blood onto the sheets.

Doc stood over the bed, rubbing his jaw, unable to fathom D'Angelo's ravings. He felt he had done nothing to incur such opprobrium.

"It's beautiful," D'Angelo went on sarcastically. "Just perfect. You don't have a clue, do you?"

Doc sighed, exasperated. "I understand that you are disappointed that I attempted to rescue you this evening, at some risk to my own well-being, I might add. I say 'attempted' because it appears my efforts have been in vain. I have not in fact succeeded in saving you, except perhaps to offer you a few more minutes in this world. What I do not understand is how things would have been better for you if I had left you behind in the brush, alone to die."

"Do I have to paint you a picture? We're not talkin' physical here. Forget physical. This is nothin'." He indicated his wasting, damaged body. "No different from a throwaway sack a' laundry headed for the dump. The mook's got no clue." He gazed woefully at the ceiling, a look of indescribable anguish on his face.

"I'm screwed," he said quietly. "Totally and eternally."

Then an unexpected thing happened. He began to cry.

Chapter 79

Doc could only stand by helplessly as the last vestiges of life drained out of Peter D'Angelo. He couldn't help but be reminded of Willy Rasp's demise in the back of his shop what seemed like eons ago. According to Eric, Rasp had made the transition to the physical world as a result of his dying in Angel's Keep. Where would someone like D'Angelo end up, he wondered.

Frankie stuck his head in the room.

"He is gone," Doc told him solemnly.

"Hey, I'm real sorry about that," Frankie said, more in response to Doc's mood than regret at D'Angelo's passing. "We've got a spot up the hill," he said. "It's where we take those of us who didn't make it fighting the Reds. I don't think anyone would mind it if we buried him up there."

Doc didn't say anything. He was still going over the conversation with D'Angelo in his mind. He was no closer to understanding what the man had been implying with his rant.

"If it's any consolation," Frankie said, mistaking Doc's taciturnity for remorse, "he died a bonafide national hero. They'll probably build him a monument when this over."

Doc couldn't help but marvel again at the irony. Literally overnight D'Angelo had gone from being a weaselly small-time crook to practically being canonized. Where was the justice in that? He doubted he'd ever know the answer.

Elsewhere in the house the mood was jubilant. Reports of new rebel victories were arriving by the minute via shortwave radio. The house was full of all-American kids who had grown up in the shadow of dictatorial communism now sensing the return of a freedom they barely remembered from childhood. Eric was easy to spot among them, taking part in the celebration, hoisting a tankard of homemade beer. He was talking to Annette, who had just arrived. In the back of the room Doc recognized the Beach Boys' Dennis Wilson. He'd been among the raiding party that evening, he realized, incognito under the black garb.

Doc pulled Eric aside with apologies to the young starlet.

"Hey," said Eric. "I was just starting to make some progress. Did you know she likes older guys?"

"Actually, yes," said Doc.

They stood looking sternly at each other. Then they simultaneously broke out in laughter.

"What's on your mind?" Eric asked. "You wanna head back?"

Doc nodded.

"You realize if we leave now we're gonna be missing one of the biggest parties in the history of the world, right? They're still gonna be dancin' in the streets six months from now. The liquor's gonna flow, the women are going to be grateful, and the light of democracy will once again shine on the lower forty-eight!"

"You could always come back," Doc pointed out.

"Nah," Eric said sobering. "We're done here. Seen one party, seen 'em all, as far I'm concerned. Let's go home."

In the kitchen where it was a bit quieter, they took Frankie aside and quietly informed him they were leaving.

"Man, the fun's just starting here," Frankie protested. "You sure you don't want to stick around? You guys are welcome to stay as long as you like. There's plenty of room. And now we can take the drapes off the front windows."

"Maybe another time," said Eric.

"Perhaps we will meet again in Angels' Keep," Doc said, extending his hand.

"Count on it," said Frankie. "Though I gotta say with the Russkies out of the picture I might not be making the jump as often as I used to. There's going to be lots to do around here to put things back together again."

Eric shook Frankie's hand. "I may have to download some of those beach movies when we get back," he said with a grin. "I think maybe I never gave 'em a fair shake."

"I wouldn't make any rash decisions," Frankie said amiably. "From what I've heard, they're an acquired taste, right?" He gave Doc an amused look. "I don't suppose they get any better after this one?"

"If I am being quite honest," Doc said. "*Beach Party* is the *Citizen Kane* of the genre, in my opinion."

"Kids go and see 'em though, right?"

"In droves."

"That's all I care about. I ain't in it to win any awards. But I can tell you one thing. I'm gonna have a helluva a good time making those movies, regardless. Especially with this nightmare over."

"That is just as it should be," Doc said.

He glanced over at Annette who was standing across the room and smiled wistfully to himself, knowing she would have departed from the future that he was going back to.

"Until we meet again," he told Frankie.

Chapter 80

It was 9 p.m. when they fired up the Harley once more. Out on the canyon road the line of military vehicles still trying to get into Laguna was at a standstill, both lanes blocked.

Doc accelerated down a hiking trail Frankie had pointed out to them which ran parallel to Laguna Canyon Road along the base of the hillside. From time to time they would catch glimpses of the mired Soviet convoy among the trees and bushes. The uneven terrain aside, the path ahead was clear of obstacles.

"They've lost the war and don't know it yet," Eric said in Doc's ear as they roared through the spindly trees.

"Defeated, in true Southern California-style, by a traffic jam," Doc noted with bemusement.

"Seems like poetic justice to me," Eric said.

It was well past midnight before the riders found themselves in familiar territory again in the high desert north of San Bernardino. They'd had a few near misses along the way, but the Russian patrols who tried to stop them were no match for the Harley and Doc's riding expertise.

"Say goodbye to the sixties," Eric said. "Next time we come back here—if we come back here—it'll be a different place."

"It can only be an improvement," Doc remarked.

The air changed, and the arid high desert landscape, ghostly in the light of a full moon, transformed into the lush hills near Shipley. Simultaneously, the temperature dropped several degrees. They inhaled the sweet air of central California farmland in the springtime and knew they were home.

Within thirty minutes they were back in Angels' Keep.

"Time traveler need hooch," Lucy declared before Doc could get started on his saga. She poured him a Jameson on the rocks. It was two o'clock in the morning at the Fish Tank, and everyone but a couple of bleary-eyed stragglers had cleared out. The couple was at one end of the long bar, talking in conspiratorial fashion. The Chicago blues being piped in over speakers hung throughout the room insured that their conversation remained private.

Doc recounted the events of his day in 1963.

"Fleedom coming to Amelica," noted Lucy. "Land of the Flee."

Doc couldn't tell if she believed any of what he was telling her or not.

"You say bad man Pete, he die?"

Doc nodded.

"First Wild Bill Willy. Now evil munchkin. Karma involved. No question. Man shoot man, then get self shot."

She saw the dejected look on Doc's face and tempered her tone. "Never OK have man, good or bad, ge' kill. Even if deserve it."

"He seemed convinced I was part of some plot to undermine him by saving his life. He behaved as if that were the worst thing that could conceivably have happened." Doc shook his head. "I do not get it."

"Maybe that true," Lucy said in accented English, "from his perspective. Maybe by rescuing bad man, you also save bad man. He expect hate. Ge' compassion. You remind him of who he was--long ago, before dirty deals and shady business. Light bulb go on. Even munchkin mannequin see light."

"It seemed like it was the last thing he wanted."

"Life of crime addictive," observed Lucy. "He hooked like fish. No want change no matter wha'."

"Yes, that I can see, I guess."

"You put him in your debt," Lucy continued. "Must change. Have no choice. Must be better person now. You awaken conscience. Cannot think only of self anymore. He caught like rat in trap. He go to heben kicking and screaming." The image she had evoked caused her to laugh out loud.

Her laughter was infectious, it turned out. Doc imagined D'Angelo a petulant child being dragged away from an ice cream shop of evil. He started to grin. Soon he was laughing outright alongside Lucy.

When the guffaws had finally tapered off and ceased, Doc looked at Lucy, drying his eyes. "But he died two minutes later. He didn't have much opportunity to mend his ways."

"Not this time," Lucy said sagely. "But maybe next time. When he come through Angels' Keep again like everyone else. To become innocent child."

"Callie said she thought Eric and I were angels," Doc said, still trying to control resurgent bursts of mirth.

"That funny," Lucy deadpanned.

They started laughing again full-force.

"You and Eric. Big, hairy Caucasian angels. How can round-eye be foreign devil and angel at same time? Is lidiculous. Best forge'."

"You are right, of course. It is a silly notion."

Lucy pulled him down so she could whisper in his ear. "China girl tell secre'."

"Oh?"

"Sometimes see wings. You. Out of corner of eye."

"You are pulling my leg now. You cannot be serious."

"Swear to Confucius!" hissed Lucy.

"I do not believe you."

"Best that way," said Lucy, contently.

"Wha'?" Lucy said, noticing that Doc had become pensive.

"It is something the woman Thea said, in the white room I told you about. She said that D'Angelo was himself an angel once upon a time. Very high up in the hierarchy."

"Then he fallen angel. Big time."

"But since I do not believe in any of this, I suppose it hardly matters."

"Thing not have to be believed to be true," said Lucy enigmatically.

Doc looked at her in amazement and wondered again what she really did believe.

"Tell you wha'," Lucy said. "I make deal. If boyfriend angel, then China girl incarnation of Quan Yin, all-seeing, all-knowing goddess." She was referring to the female Bodhisattva revered by Chinese Buddhists.

"And why not?" Doc said. "It would be far easier for me to imagine you as Quan Yin than to think of myself as an angel of any variety."

"Many time package deceiving," Lucy intoned, Charlie Chan-style. "Must not judge book by covah."

THE ARTIST

Chapter 81

The landlocked tugboat Doc called home seemed especially empty without Callie. From the window Doc could see the distinctive blue tarp across the street, fluttering in the gentle sea breeze, and beyond, the vast expanse of the Pacific, mottled with gray clouds. It might have been a storm coming in. Or just a fog bank beginning to form, a harbinger of the overcast days of late spring and early summer on the California coast.

Downstairs in the repair shop work was piled high. The long workbench was loaded with more miscellaneous electronics, wires, switches, knobs, pick guards, guitar pickups and gutted solid-body guitars than usual. The corners of the room were heaped with newly arrived tube amps of every make and model, many of them vintage, some of them rare,—all new orders which had accumulated during his absence from the Keep. But truth be told, Doc had no inclination to be indoors today. He needed time to let the events of the last several days settle.

He fixed his coffee, made a breakfast of bacon, eggs and toast and scanned the local newspaper. It was the usual. During the night, a gas station in Seaside had been robbed. There was a report of shots fired during a drive-by in Watsonville. No injuries reported. Meanwhile desalinization alternatives were being proposed before the city council in Monterey.

He put the paper down. He grabbed a cable-knit fisherman's sweater, drew it over his head, donned a black watchman's cap, and emerged on the boat's deck. He patiently took the elevator down to ground level—he was in no rush today--and ambled off down the street in the direction of the Fish Tank. He passed Bunny Raft's gift shop and Larry Conner's Photography on the way. Through the plate glass window, he caught sight of Larry studying a large print at his desk inside his tiny gallery. He was too absorbed in what he was doing to notice Doc walking by.

Ten minutes later he was in front of Alice Stillwater's place at the end of the cul de sac. No one was about. The garage door was open, and he was immediately drawn to the paintings on display within. He stood transfixed at the diversity of the artwork on exhibit. There were idyllic pastoral scenes that radiated peace and serenity, some including people who seemed vaguely familiar, locals perhaps. There were watercolors and thickly-layered oil and acrylic canvases, some photorealistic in nature, while others were ominous abstracts, aggressive, almost violent, in the chaotic movement they contained.

Doc's eyes came to rest on one such piece in particular. It was a study in stark contrasts--a nighttime scene, it appeared. The center portion of the work was taken up by a wedge of white suggesting a spotlight with an implacable darkness looming all around. The longer Doc looked at the painting, the oil still glossy from recent application, the more a feeling of deja vu took hold of him. He couldn't shake a sense of familiarity as he gazed at the painting.

As he continued to stare at the canvas, his focus began to shift. It seemed suddenly that he was able to identify distinct shapes silhouetted against a blinding light. With a jolt of recognition he discovered he was looking at a depiction of the Laguna Beach hilltop he had been on the previous night, backlit by the glaring searchlights of the Soviet helicopter as it rose menacingly above the crest of the hill. Tiny points at the bottom of the painting resolved themselves into Frankie's ninjas, including him and Eric, getting ready to scramble for cover below the lip of the hill. Doc blinked. The impression did not go away. His eyes moved to a small typed caption under the painting which read: The Battle of Laguna Beach, 1963.

His vision blurred. For a moment he felt he might lose consciousness. But he steadied himself, repeating to himself that this just wasn't possible. It had to be some kind of bizarre coincidence, nothing more. But while the painting itself was subject to interpretation--it was after all highly stylized--the message on the caption was not. It implied that Alice Stillwater had somehow witnessed the scene. But try as he might, he couldn't picture the elderly woman chasing him and Eric through the portal, across the war-torn Los Angeles basin, and then hiding in the bushes while they were being ambushed, scratching away all the while on her sketch pad. A feeling of unreality overtook him as he stared at the painting.

He managed to tear his eyes away from the canvas and glanced anxiously around the garage, unnerved at the prospect of what else he might discover there. Another stark meditation in black and white caught his eye. This one featured a Russian tank of World War II vintage, the distinctive white star on its side, negotiating a blackened urban landscape against a backdrop of burning hills. It immediately called to mind the night Doc and Eric had first entered Los Angeles from the desert. More amazingly still, tucked in behind the oil canvas and partially hidden by it, was a watercolor of an idyllic subtropical island exactly like the one he, Callie and Eric had visited after fleeing D'Angelo. This painting showed the diminutive figure of an old aboriginal man, captured in profile, staring outward toward the horizon from the side of a mountain, staff in hand.

It could not be. Doc felt as if he were caught in the grip of a treacherous riptide of unreality which threatened to drag him under. He needed to get away from here.

He stumbled backward into the street, almost tripping himself in his haste to escape, and made for the beach beyond the end of the cul-de-sac. Once there, he set out southward as quickly as he could, sometimes breaking into a run. When he had settle down a bit, he slowed and trudged onward with a determined pace in the direction of Monterey, his thoughts still in an uproar, all but oblivious to his surroundings.

Finally he stopped, realizing how far he'd come, and sat down heavily on the sand. An onshore wind, carrying the last chill of winter, rustled the resilient flowers and grasses that sprouted around him as Doc gazed out to sea. Doc hugged himself to keep the cold at bay.

He kept thinking of Alice Stillwater, town elder and artist.

Chapter 82

The sound of feet padding on wet sand caught his attention and drew him out of his ruminations. He glanced over his right shoulder to find Alice Stillwater coming down the beach toward him. His first reflex was to scuttle away and hide. But his European upbringing forced him to stand firm against this impulse. It would have been impractical anyway, he saw. He was fully exposed on flat ground.

The old woman had on denim dungarees over a plaid shirt today. She wore the same shiny new moccasins she had worn the day Doc had first met her what seemed like ages ago. She spat a stream of tobacco juice onto the sand as she approached. It kicked up a puff of silt, the way a bullet might.

"Whatcha doin' out here all by yer lonesome, sonny?" Alice Stillwater said genially, by way of greeting. "Not mopin' are we?"

"No, ma'am," said Doc. "I was only thinking."

When the old woman arrived, she sank cross-legged onto the sand a few feet from Doc.

"Purty nice view from here," she remarked cheerfully.

"It is indeed," Doc agreed. "And unless I am much mistaken, the credit is entirely yours."

"What are you sayin', sonny?" she said, amusement dancing in her eyes. "Could it be ya maybe done ferreted out ma secret? What gave it away?"

"I mean no disrespect, but I had the sense since our first meeting that you knew more about Willy Rasp and what happened to him than you were willing to say."

"Go on."

"And then there are the paintings. I am afraid I could not help but notice …"

"No need to worry none 'bout that. The paintings are for everybody to see. And if they're able, ta appreciate. Proceed."

"Someone else may have missed the references. But having experienced what they depicted firsthand, I could not but understand them in a different way. In addition to being a superlative artist, you would have to be an extremely talented seer to have painted those scenes. But that would surely be an insult to your capabilities, would it not? Your artwork implies mastery of a much higher order. I suspect you are far more than a talented seer. Indeed that designation can barely scratch the surface of who you are and what capabilities you possess."

"Oh?" Alice Stillwater cocked her head to the side. "And what capabilities might you be referrin' to?"

He took a deep breath before plunging ahead. "The feat you have accomplished in bringing those scenes to life on canvas indicates to me that you may well be omniscient. And, perhaps, all-powerful as well."

There was the smallest pause before Alice Stillwater continued. "You know, you ain't half bad as a deeetective, Manfred St. Michel," the old woman said, chewing her tobacco avidly. "But before you get a swelled head, let me just say for the record that ya wouldna found out if ah wasn't OK with you findin' out."

"That goes without saying. You are not concerned I will tell others?"

"Ah know you ain't no blabbermouth, Manfred. And if you tell Quan Yin, ah wouldn't mind. Ah could hardly e'spect you not to. Ah love that gal."

How could she know about Lucy proclaiming herself an iteration of Quan Yin the previous night? But of course. She knew everything, he had to remind himself.

"So," said Doc. "What happened to Willy would have to have been, in some measure, your doing. The movement of the stars. The passing of the seasons. You are behind them all."

"Well. If you wanna get technical about it, ah suppose," Alice said a mite testily. "But do you see me pullin' strings here? No. See, there's always free will involved. People'll do what they'll do. They make their own decisions. Ah don't interfere, as a rule. Tell you the truth, ah stepped back from the day to day workin's a long time ago. The operation purt near runs itself now. But ah still sign the checks, so ta speak." She couldn't help but chuckle at her own metaphor.

"Ah gotta say, you done good, sonny boy," she went on. "You done reeeal good. You brought me back my golden boy. Weren't sure he'd ever come 'round. His shennanigans was gettin' pretty tiresome, even ah gotta admit that. And don't think ah wasn't aware of the rumblin' and grumblin' 'round headquarters 'bout his behavior. What you did was remind him of the sweet l'il tyke he used ta be, chasin' 'round the rafters with the rest a' the cherubim and seraphim. He didn't exactly thank you for it, ah know, but after the years a' dissolution 'n bad habits, you couldn't expect too much a' him right off. But he's comin' around, sure as shootin'. All them hardened layers is fallin' away, now that he's home where he belongs. He's gettin' more angelic by the minute.

"See, ah needed you to straighten him out, and straighten him out you did. You came through with flyin' colors. But then again you and that lunkhead, Gunnerson, have been favorites of mine since the beginnin' a' time, too. You must know that. Y'all are brothers in my eyes. And you did just what any good brother 'ould do. You helped the Weasel, ah mean Peter, in his hour a' need, even if he didn't think he needed it."

Doc considered this, still not entirely reconciled to Pete D'Angelo's miraculous transformation. But then again, equally remarkable things had happened of late, he had to admit.

"Eric says Angels' Keep is a kind of stopover for disembodied spirits on their way to manifestation in the physical world," Doc said to change the subject. "They assume their adult form for a brief time and then move on to their chosen place in the scheme of things to start life anew."

"Sounds 'bout right. The air's lousy with ghosts 'round here, especially down on the dock. But they ain't the ghosts of the recently departed, ya see. They're the spirits of the as-yet-to-be born. There's a difference. There's a sense a' anticipation here you don't find anywhere else. This here's a place a' new beginnin's--an Ellis Island for souls, ya might say. They come through here on the way to their next adventure, their next spin on the ole merry-go-round."

"And Willy Rasp was one of these souls."

"Yuh," said Alice Stillwater, still chewing a mile a minute. "He settled in, which weren't exactly on the program. Hung around long enough to sign a lease on that place a' his and take out a loan for inventory, if you can believe it. Most don't stay for but a few hours, days at the most. But he'd been around here for months. Started hemmin' and hawin' when the time came. He was a born procrastinator, that un. Well, not-quite-yet-born, to be exact. Ah thought ah'd give Pete a shot at lightin' a fire under 'im, offer 'im the chance to apply hisself to something useful fer a change. And well, you know how that turned out."

Doc was thinking Eric had been right about everything.

"That boy's got a lot on the ball," Alice said, reading his thoughts. "Don't know what ah'd do without 'im. Sometimes you need someone around who ain't shy 'bout crackin' heads when the occasion calls for it. You know what ah mean? Why, ah can see the two a' you hittin' it off real good. Got a lot in common, you and him. And sometimes even Gunnerson needs a little help, though I doubt he'd come right out 'n say it.

"Ah wouldn wanna be puttin' ideas in your head, but you two 'ould make a formidable crime fightin' team, if you were so inclined. On the other hand, this town will always be in need of a fine blues guitar player and amp repairman. Maybe you could moonlight a little on the side?--Fightin' agin the forces a' ignorance and injustice in the world? No spandex necessary." She waited expectantly for a beat, and when no response was immediately forthcoming, said, "Don't mind the ramblin's of an old woman. It's just a thought."

Doc continued to stare out to sea. "What of Callie?" he said. "Will she be alright?"

"She's gonna be just fine. Got a feelin' you ain't seen the last a' her. Ah wouldn't be surprised if she showed up at that highfalutin university just up the coast when the time comes. It's practically within spittin' distance." She unleashed another stream of tobacco juice onto the sand for emphasis.

"UCSC?"

"That's the one. She's a bright kid. And gutsy. Ah like that. Girl's got a fine future ahead a' her."

They sat silently watching the cloud bank that hovered offshore. Doc felt the weight of her incongruous blue eyes on him, studying him from that wrinkled brown face. They contained the colors of sky and sea, as well as a hint of thunder and the sparkle of sunlit waters on distant shores.

"What?" she said. "You ain't gonna ask me for no miracle, now's you know who ah am and what ah can do? Most folks in yer position 'ould have a whole passel a' things lined up--stuff they'd be wantin' me ta conjure for 'em. But seein' it's you, and 'cause of what you done for me by bringin' Pete back into the fold, there's a better'n middlin' chance ah'd grant it, whatever it might be."

"Thank you for the kind offer, ma'am," Doc said. "I am most appreciative of it, believe me. But perhaps another time. I have seen enough of the miraculous of late to last me a long while yet. To be honest, I would like nothing better than to sleep for a week."

"Suit yourself, kid," said the old woman. "A rain check it is, then. Ah may be older than the hills, but ah do not forget."

"Old lady one chopstick short of set," Lucy proclaimed, rolling her eyes after she had heard the details of Doc's disorienting encounter with Alice Stillwater.

"She called you Quan Yin," Doc said. "I thought it an interesting coincidence."

"She vely smar' lady," Lucy amended smoothly. "Must not argue with Supreme Being of Universe, if know what good for you."

Printed in the United States
By Bookmasters